2001 *was just the beginning*

"We think that science fiction can be not only entertaining and amusing but also profoundly stimulating and illuminating, capable of examining timeless human problems with unique intensity . . . science fiction has for some time now been struggling back toward the heights it reached in the hands of such masters as Wells, Huxley, Orwell, and Stapledon: we hope to extend and continue the present movement. . . ."

—Robert Silverberg, from his Introduction

Avon Books edited by
Robert Silverberg

NEW DIMENSIONS 2
EDITED BY ROBERT SILVERBERG

AVON
PUBLISHERS OF BARD, CAMELOT, DISCUS, EQUINOX AND FLARE BOOKS

AVON BOOKS
A division of
The Hearst Corporation
959 Eighth Avenue
New York, New York 10019

First Avon Printing, December, 1974.

AVON TRADEMARK REG. U.S. PAT. OFF. AND
FOREIGN COUNTRIES, REGISTERED TRADEMARK—
MARCA REGISTRADA, HECHO EN CHICAGO, U.S.A.

Printed in the U.S.A.

CONTENTS

INTRODUCTION

This is our second annual sampler of contemporary science fiction; as in the case of *New Dimensions I*, all the stories are published here for the first time and represent the yield of a yearlong search for the best work currently being done in what is now one of literature's most exciting branches. The policy of NEW DIMENSIONS is a straightforward one. We believe that science fiction's special themes and images and concepts offer a valid mode for serious writers, and we intend to provide a sympathetic haven for such writers. We think that science fiction can be not only entertaining and amusing but also profoundly stimulating and illuminating, capable of examining timeless human problems with unique intensity and vividness. Too long self-ghettoized as a simple-minded species of juvenile adventure fiction, science fiction has for some time now been struggling back toward the heights it reached in the hands of such masters as Wells, Huxley, Orwell, and Stapledon: we hope to extend and continue the present movement away from clichés and clumsiness, toward deeper insight, vision, and craftsmanship.

This is not to say that NEW DIMENSIONS repudiates the achievements of the era when science-fiction stories appeared only in gaudy pulp-paper magazines. Some distinguished writers—Ray Bradbury, Arthur C. Clarke, Theodore Sturgeon, Fritz Leiber, Walter M. Miller, Robert A. Heinlein, and others—emerged from those flamboyant and unsophisticated journals. One of the most capable writers of the magazine-fiction era is present in this very volume: Isaac Asimov. But the best work of that group of writers is now twenty and thirty years behind them, in the main; and gifted newcomers have appeared, building on the foundations provided by their elders but often working with new and more complex tools. While seeking to sever the links between themselves and the trashier forms of crude pulp science fiction, these new writers make no attempt to deny the sense of kinship they feel with the finest science-fictionists of the previous generation. They wish to extend and to expand, not to destroy, the accomplishments of that generation. So do we. NEW DIMENSIONS' emphasis is on evolution, not revolution.

Of the ten contributors to this second volume, only two—Isaac Asimov and Miriam Allen deFord—were writing for publication in the pre-1960 era that now seems so remote. R. A. Lafferty and Joanna Russ first appeared in print in the early 1960s, Barry N. Malzberg and James Tiptree, Jr., toward the close of that decade; but not until very recently have these four begun to attain any real frequency of publication or any strong public following. And the remaining four—Edward Bryant, Gardner R. Dozois, Gordon Eklund, and Geo. Alec Effinger—are very much writers of the 1970s. The book thus is weighted heavily in favor of newer voices, those who will be dominating the science fiction of the years to come. Which is, I think, as it should be in a volume that promises a peep into new dimensions.

ROBERT SILVERBERG

NOBODY'S HOME

JOANNA RUSH

After she had finished her work at the North Pole, Jannina came down to the Red Sea refineries, where she had family business, jumped to New Delhi for dinner, took a nap in a public hotel in Queensland, walked from the hotel to the station, bypassed the Leeward Islands (where she thought she might go, but all the stations were busy), and met Charley to watch the dawn over the Carolinas.

"Where've you been, dear C?"

"Tanzania. And you're married."

"No."

"I heard you were married," he said. "The Lees told the Smiths who told the Kerguelens who told the Utsumbés and we get around, we Utsumbés. A new wife, they said. I didn't know you were especially fond of women."

"I'm not. She's my husbands' wife. And we're not married yet, Charley. She's had hard luck: first family started in '35, two husbands burned out by an overload while arranging transportation for a concert—of all things, pushing papers, you know!—and the second divorced her, I think, and she drifted away from the third (a big one), and there was some awful quarrel with the fourth, people chasing people around tables, I don't know."

"Poor woman."

In the manner of people joking and talking lightly they had drawn together, back to back, sitting on the ground and rubbing together their shoulders and the backs of their heads. Jannina said sorrowfully, "What lovely hair you have, Charley Utsumbé, like metal mesh."

"All we Utsumbés are exceedingly handsome." They linked arms. The sun, which anyone could chase around the world now, see it rise or set twenty times a day, fifty times a day—if you wanted to spend your life like that—rose dripping out of the cypress swamp. There was nobody around for miles. Mist drifted up from the pools and low places.

"My God," he said, "it's summer! I have to be at Tanga now."

"What?" said Jannina.

"One loses track," he said apologetically. "I'm sorry, love, but I have unavoidable business at home. Tax labor."

"But why summer, why did its being summer—"

"Train of thought! Too complicated" (and already they were out of key, already the mild affair was over, there having come between them the one obligation that can't be put off to the time you like, or the place you like; off he'd go to plug himself into a road-mender or a doctor, though it's of some advantage to mend all the roads of a continent at one time).

She sat cross-legged on the station platform, watching him enter the booth and set the dial. He stuck his head out the glass door.

"Come with me to Africa, lovely lady!"

She thumbed her nose at him. "You're only a passing

fancy, Charley U!" He blew a kiss, enclosed himself in the booth, and disappeared. (The transmatter field is larger than the booth, for obvious reasons; the booth flicks on and off several million times a second and so does not get transported itself, but it protects the machinery from the weather and it keeps people from losing elbows or knees or slicing the ends off a package or a child. The booths at the cryogenics center at the North Pole have exchanged air so often with those of warmer regions that each has its own microclimate; leaves and seeds, plants and earth are piled about them. Don't Step on the Grass!—say the notes pinned to the door—Wish to Trade Pawlownia Sapling for Sub-artic Canadian Moss; Watch Your Goddamn Bare Six-Toed Feet!; Wish Amateur Cellist for Quartet, Six Months' Rehearsal Late Uhl with Reciter; I Lost a Squirrel Here Yesterday, Can You Find It Before It Dies? Eight Children Will be Heartbroken—Cecilia Ching, Buenos Aires.)

Jannina sighed and slipped on her glass woolly; nasty to get back into clothes, but home was cold. You never knew where you might go, so you carried them. Years ago (she thought) I came here with someone in the dead of winter, either an unmatched man or someone's starting spouse—only two of us, at any rate—and we waded through the freezing water and danced as hard as we could and then proved we could sing and drink beer in a swamp at the same time, Good Lord! And then went to the public resort on the Ile de la Cité to watch professional plays, opera, games—you have to be good to get in there!—and got into some clothes because it was chilly after sundown in September—no, wait, it was Venezuela —and watched the lights come out and smoked like mad at a café table and tickled the robot waiter and pretended we were old, really old, perhaps a hundred and fifty. . . . Years ago!

But was it the same place? she thought, and dismissing the incident forever, she stepped into the booth, shut the door, and dialed home: the Himalayas. The trunk line was clear. The branch stop was clear. The family's transceiver (located in the anteroom behind two doors, to keep the task of heating the house within reasonable limits) had damn well better be clear, or somebody would be blown right into the vestibule. Momentum- and heat-compensators kept Jannina from arriving home at seventy degrees Fahrenheit internal temperature (seven degrees lost for every mile you teleport upward) or too many feet above herself (rise to the east, drop going west, to the north or south you are apt to be thrown right through the wall of the booth). Someday (thought Jannina) everybody will decide to let everybody live in decent climates. But not yet. Not this everybody.

She arrived home singing "The World's My Back Yard, Yes, the World Is My Oyster," a song that had been popular in her first youth, some seventy years before.

The Komarovs' house was hardened foam with an automatic inside line to the school near Naples. It was good to be brought up on your own feet. Jannina passed through; the seven-year-olds lay with their heads together and their bodies radiating in a six-personed asterisk. In this position (which was supposed to promote mystical thought) they played Barufaldi, guessing the identity of famous dead personages through anagrammatic sentences, the first letters of the words of which (unscrambled into aphorisms or proverbs) simultaneously spelled out a moral and a series of Goedel numbers (in a previously agreed-upon code) which—

"Oh, my darling, how felicitous is the advent of your appearance!" cried a boy (hard to take the polysyllabic stage). "Embrace me, dearest maternal parent! Unite your valuable upper limbs about my eager person!"

"Vulgar!" said Jannina, laughing.

"Non sum filius tuus?" said the child.

"No, you're not my body-child; you're my godchild. Your mother bequeathed me to you when she died. What are you learning?"

"The eternal parental question," he said, frowning. "How to run a helicopter. How to prepare food from its actual, revolting, raw constituents. Can I go now?"

"Can you?" she said. "Nasty imp!"

"Good," he said. "I've made you feel guilty. Don't do that," and as she tried to embrace him, he ticklishly slid away. "The robin walks quietly up the branch of the tree," he said breathlessly, flopping back on the floor.

"That's not an aphorism." (Another Barufaldi player.)

"It is."

"It isn't."

"It is."

"Its isn't."

"It is."

"It—"

The school vanished; the antechamber appeared. In the kitchen Chi Komarov was rubbing the naked back of his sixteen-year-old son. Parents always kissed each other; children always kissed each other. She touched foreheads with the two men and hung her woolly on the hook by the ham radio rig. Someone was always around. Jannina flipped the cover off her wrist chronometer: standard regional time, date, latitude-longitude, family computer hookup clear. "At my age I ought to remember these things," she said. She pressed the computer hookup: Ann at tax labor in the schools, bit-a-month plan, regular Ann; Lee with three months to go, five years off, heroic Lee; Phuong in Paris, still rehearsing; C.E. gone, won't say where, spontaneous C.E.; Ilse making some repairs in the basement, not a true basement, really, but the room farthest down the hillside. She went up the stairs and then came down and put her head round at the living-and-swimming room. Through the glass wall one could see the mountains. Old Al, who had joined them late in life, did a bit of gardening in the brief summers, and generally stuck around the place. Jannina beamed. "Hullo, Old Al!" Big and shaggy, a rare delight, his white body hair. She sat on his lap. "Has she come?"

"The new one? No," he said.

"Shall we go swimming?"

He made an expressive face. "No, dear," he said. "I'd rather go to Naples and watch the children fly helicopters. I'd rather go to Nevada and fly them myself. I've been in the water all day, watching a very dull person restructure coral reefs and experiment with polyploid polyps."

"You mean you were doing it."

"One gets into the habit of working."

"But you didn't have to!"

"It was a private project. Most interesting things are."

She whispered in his ear.

With happily flushed faces, they went into Old Al's inner garden and locked the door.

Jannina, temporary family representative, threw the computer helmet over her head and, thus plugged in, she cleaned house, checked food supplies, did a little of the legal business entailed by a family of eighteen adults (two triplet marriages, a quad, and a group of eight). She felt very smug. She put herself through by radio to Himalayan HQ (above two thousand meters) and hooking computer to computer—a very odd feeling, like an urge to sneeze that never comes off—extended a formal invitation to one Leslie Smith ("Come stay, why don't you?"), notifying every free Komarov to hop it back and fast. Six hikers might come for the night—back-packers. More food. First thunderstorm of the year in Albany, New York (North America). Need an extra two rooms by Thursday. Hear the Palnatoki are moving. Can't use a room. Can't use a kitten. Need the geraniums back, Mrs. Adam, Chile. The best maker of hand-blown glass in the world has killed in a duel the second-best maker of hand-blown glass for joining the movement toward ceramics. A bitter struggle is foreseen in the global economy. Need a lighting designer. Need fifteen singers and electric pansensicon. Standby tax labor xxxxxpj through xxxyq to Cambaluc, great tecto-genic—

With the guilty feeling that one always gets gossiping with a computer, for it's really not reciprocal, Jannina flipped off the helmet. She went to get Ilse. Climbing back through the white foam room, the purple foam room, the green foam room, everything littered with plots and projects of the clever Komarovs or the even cleverer Komarov children, stopping at the baby room for Ilse to nurse her baby. Jannina danced staidly around studious Ilse. They turned on the nursery robot and the television screen. Ilse drank beer in the swimming room, for her milk. She worried her way through the day's record of events—faults in the foundation, some people who came from Chichester and couldn't find C.E. so one of them burst into tears, a new experiment in genetics coming round the gossip circuit, an execrable set of equations from some imposter in Bucharest.

"A duel!" said Jannina.

They both agreed it was shocking. And what fun. A new fashion. You had to be a little mad to do it. Awful.

The light went on over the door to the tunnel that linked the house to the antechamber, and very quickly, one after another, as if the branch line had just come free, eight Komarovs came into the room. The light flashed again; one could see three people debouch one after the other, persons in boots, with coats, packs, and face masks over their woollies. They were covered with snow, either from the mountain terraces above the house or from some other place, Jannina didn't know. They stamped the snow off in the antechamber and hung their clothes outside; "Good heavens, you're not circumcised!" cried someone. There was as much handshaking and embracing all around as at a wedding party. Velet Komarov (the short, dark one) recognized Fung Pao-yu and swung her off her feet. People began to joke, tentatively stroking one another's arms. "Did you have a good hike? Are you a good hiker, Pao-yu?" said Velet. The light over the antechamber went on again, though nobody could see a thing since the glass was steamed over from the collision of hot with cold air. Old Al stopped, halfway into the kitchen. The baggage receipt chimed, recognized only by family ears—upstairs a bundle of somebody's things, ornaments, probably, for the missing Komarovs were still young and the young are interested in clothing, were appearing in the baggage receptacle. "Ann or Phuong?" said Jannina. "Five to three, anybody? Match me!" but someone strange opened the door of the booth and peered out. Oh, a dizzying sensation. She was painted in a few places, which was awfully odd because really it was old-fashioned; and why do it for a family evening? It was a stocky young woman. It was an awful mistake (thought Jannina). Then the visitor made her second mistake. She said:

"I'm Leslie Smith." But it was more through clumsiness than being rude. Chi Komarov (the tall, blond one) saw this instantly and, snatching off his old-fashioned spectacles, he ran to her side and patted her, saying teasingly:

"Now, haven't we met? Now, aren't you married to someone I know?"

"No, no," said Leslie Smith, flushing with pleasure.

He touched her neck. "Ah, you're a tightrope dancer!"

"Oh, no!" exclaimed Leslie Smith.

"I'm a tightrope dancer," said Chi. "Would you believe it?"

"But you're too—too spiritual," said Leslie Smith hesitantly.

"Spiritual, how do you like that, family, spiritual?" he cried, delighted (a little more delighted, thought Jannina, than the situation really called for) and he began to stroke her neck.

"What a lovely neck you have," he said.

This steadied Leslie Smith. She said, "I like tall men," and allowed herself to look at the rest of the family. "Who are these people?" she said, though one was afraid she might really mean it.

Fung Pao-yu to the rescue: "Who are these people? Who are they, indeed! I doubt if they are anybody. One might say, 'I have met these people,' but has one? What existential meaning would such a statement convey? I myself, now, I have met them. I have been introduced to them. But they are like the Sahara; it is all wrapped in mystery; I doubt if they even have names," etc. etc. Then lanky Chi Komarov disputed possession of Leslie Smith with Fung Pao-yu, and Fung Pao-yu grabbed one arm and Chi the other; and she jumped up and down fiercely; so that by the time the lights dimmed and the food came, people were feeling better—or so Jannina judged. So embarrassing and delightful to be eating fifteen to a room! "We Komarovs are famous for eating whatever we can get whenever we can get it," said Velet proudly. Various Komarovs in various places, with the three hikers on cushions and Ilse at full length on the rug. Jannina pushed a button with her toe and the fairy lights came on all over the ceiling. "The children did that," said Old Al. He had somehow settled at Leslie Smith's side and was feeding her so-chi from his own bowl. She smiled up at him. "We once," said a hiking companion of Fung Pao-yu's, "arranged a dinner in an amphitheater where half of us played servants to the other half, with forfeits for those who didn't show. It was the result of a bet. Like the bad old days. Did you know there were once five billion people in this world?"

"The gulls," said Ilse, "are mating on the Isle of Skye." There were murmurs of appreciative interest. Chi began to develop an erection and everyone laughed. Old Al wanted music and Velet didn't; what might have been a quarrel was ended by Ilse's furiously boxing their ears. She stalked off to the nursery.

"Leslie Smith and I are both old-fashioned," said Old Al, "because neither of us believes in gabbing. Chi—your theater?"

"We're turning people away." He leaned forward, earnestly, tapping his fingers on his crossed knees. "I swear, some of them are threatening to commit suicide."

"It's a choice," said Velet reasonably.

Leslie Smith had dropped her bowl. They retrieved it for her.

"Aiy, I remember—" said Pao-yu. "What I remember! We've been eating dried mush for three days, tax-issue. Did you know one of my dads killed himself?"

"No!" said Velet, surprised.

"Years ago," said Pao-yu. "He said he refused to live to see the time when chairs were reintroduced. He also wanted further genetic engineering, I believe, for even more intelligence. He did it out of spite, I'm sure. I think he wrestled a shark. Jannina, is this tax-issue food? Is it this year's style tax-issue sauce?"

"No, next year's," said Jannina snappishly. Really, some people! She slipped into Finnish, to show up Pao-yu's pronunciation. "Isn't that so?" she asked Leslie Smith.

Leslie Smith stared at her.

More charitably Jannina informed them all, in Finnish, that the Komarovs had withdrawn their membership in a food group, except for Ann, who had taken out an individual, because what the dickens, who had the time? And tax-issue won't kill you. As they finished, they dropped their dishes into the garbage field and Velet stripped a layer off the rug. In that went, too. Indulgently Old Al began a round:

"Red."

"Sun," said Pao-yu.

"The Red Sun Is," said one of the triplet Komarovs.

"The Red Sun Is—High," said Chi.

"The Red Sun Is High, The," Velet said.

"The Red Sun Is High, The Blue—" Jannina finished. They had come to Leslie Smith, who could either complete it or keep it going. She chose to declare for complete, not shyly (as before) but simply by pointing to Old Al.

"The red sun is high, the blue," he said. "Subtle! Another: Ching."

"Nü."

Ching nü ch'i."

Ching nü ch'i ch'u."

"Ssu."

"Wo."

"Ssu wo yü." It had got back to Leslie Smith again. She said, "I can't do that." Jannina got up and began to dance—I'm nice in my nasty way, she thought. The others wandered toward the pool and Ilse reappeared on the nursery monitor screen, saying, "I'm coming down." Somebody said, "What time is it in the Argentine?"

"Five A.M."

"I think I want to go."

"Go then."

"I go."

"Go well."

The red light over the antechamber door flashed and went out.

"Say, why'd you leave your other family?" said Ilse, settling near Old Al where the wall curved out. Ann, for whom it was evening, would be home soon; Chi, who had just got up a few hours back in western America, would stay somewhat longer; nobody ever knew Old Al's schedule and Jannina herself had lost track of the time. She would stay up until she felt sleepy. She followed a rough twenty-eight-hour day, Phuong (what a nuisance that must be at rehearsals!) a twenty-two-hour one, Ilse six hours up, six hours dozing. Jannina nodded, heard the question, and shook herself awake.

"I didn't leave them. They left me."

There was a murmur of sympathy around the pool.

"They left me because I was stupid," said Leslie Smith. Her hands were clasped passively in her lap. She looked very genteel in her blue body paint, a stocky young woman with small breasts. One of the triplet Komarovs, flirting in the pool with the other two, choked. The non-aquatic members of the family crowded around Leslie Smith, touching her with little, soft touches; they kissed her and exposed to her all their unguarded surfaces, their bellies, their soft skins. Old Al kissed her hands. She sat there, oddly unmoved. "But I *am* stupid," she said. "You'll find out." Jannina put her hands over her ears: "A masochist!" Leslie Smith looked at Jannina with a curious, stolid look. Then she looked down and absently began to rub one blue-painted knee. "Luggage!" shouted Chi, clapping his hands together, and the triplets dashed for the stairs. "No, I'm going to bed," said Leslie Smith; "I'm tired," and quite simply, she got up and let Old Al lead her through the pink room, the blue room, the turtle-and-pet room (temporarily empty), the trash room, and all the other rooms, to the guest room with the view that looked out over the cold hillside to the terraced plantings below.

"The best maker of hand-blown glass in the world," said Chi, "has killed in a duel the second-best maker of hand-blown glass in the world."

"For joining the movement to ceramics," said Ilse, awed. Jannina felt a thrill: this was the bitter stuff under the surface of life, the fury that boiled up. A bitter struggle is foreseen in the global economy. Good old tax-issue stuff goes toddling along, year after year. She was, thought Jannina, extraordinarily grateful to be living now, to be in such an extraordinary world, to have so long to go before her death. So much to do!

Old Al came back into the living room. "She's in bed."

"Well, which of us—?" said the triplet-who-had-choked, looking mischievously round from one to the other. Chi was about to volunteer, out of his usual conscientiousness, thought Jannina, but then she found herself suddenly standing up, and then just as suddenly sitting down again. "I just don't have the nerve," she said. Velet Komarov walked on his hands toward the stairs, then somersaulted, and vanished, climbing. Old Al got off the hand-carved chest he had been sitting on and fetched a can of ale from it. He levered off the top and drank.

Then he said, "She really is stupid, you know." Jannina's skin crawled.

"Oooh," said Pao-yu. Chi betook himself to the kitchen and returned with a paper folder. It was coated with frost. He shook it, then impatiently dropped it in the pool. The redheaded triplet swam over and took it. "Smith, Leslie," he said. "Adam Two, Leslie. Yee, Leslie. Schwarzen, Leslie."

"What on earth does the woman do with herself besides get married?" exclaimed Pao-yu.

"She drove a hovercraft," said Chi, "in some out-of-the-way places around the Pacific until the last underground stations were completed. Says when she was a child she wanted to drive a truck."

"Well, you can," said the redheaded triplet, "can't you? Go to Arizona or the Rockies and drive on the roads. The sixty-mile-an-hour road. The thirty-mile-an-hour road. Great artistic recreation."

"That's not work," said Old Al.

"Couldn't she take care of children?" said the redheaded triplet. Ilse sniffed.

"Stupidity's not much of a recommendation for that," Chi said. "Let's see—no children. No, of course not. Overfulfilled her tax work on quite a few routine matters here. Kim, Leslie. Went to Moscow and contracted a double with some fellow, didn't last. Registered as a singleton, but that didn't last, either. She said she was lonely and they were exploiting her."

Old Al nodded.

"Came back and lived informally with a theater group. Left them. Went into psychotherapy. Volunteered for several experimental, intelligence-enhancing programs, was turned down—hm!—sixty-five come the winter solstice, muscular coordination average, muscular development above average, no overt mental pathology, empathy average, prognosis: poor. No, wait a minute, it says, 'More of the same.' Well, that's the same thing.

"What I want to know," added Chi, raising his head, "is who met Miss Smith and decided we needed the lady in this Palace of ours?"

Nobody answered. Jannina was about to say, "Ann, perhaps?" but as she felt the urge to do so—surely it wasn't

right to turn somebody off like that, *just for that!*—Chi
(who had been flipping through the dossier) came to the
last page, with the tax-issue stamp absolutely unmistaka-
ble, woven right into the paper.

"The computer did," said Pao-yu and she giggled idioti-
cally.

"Well," said Jannina, jumping to her feet, "tear it up,
my dear, or give it to me and I'll tear it up for you. I
think Miss Leslie Smith deserves from us the same as
we'd give to anybody else, and I—for one—intend to go
right up there—"

"After Velet," said Old Al dryly.

"*With* Velet, if I must," said Jannina, raising her eyebrows, "and if you don't know what's due a guest, Old
Daddy, I do, and I intend to provide it. Lucky I'm keeping house this month, or you'd probably feed the poor
woman nothing but seaweed."

"You won't like her, Jannina," said Old Al.

"I'll find that out for myself," said Jannina, with some
asperity, "and I'd advise you to do the same. Let her garden with you, Daddy. Let her squirt the foam for the new
rooms. And now"—she glared round at them—"I'm going
to clean *this* room, so you'd better hop it, the lot of you,"
and dashing into the kitchen, she had the computer helmet on her head and the hoses going before they had
even quite cleared the area of the pool. Then she took the
helmet off and hung it on the wall. She flipped the cover
off her wrist chronometer and satisfied herself as to the
date. By the time she got back to the living room there
was nobody there, only Leslie Smith's dossier lying on the
carved chest. There was Leslie Smith; there was all of
Leslie Smith. Jannina knocked on the wall cupboard and
it revolved, presenting its openable side; she took out
chewing gum. She started chewing and read about Leslie
Smith.

Q: What have you seen in the last twenty years that
you particularly liked?

A: I don't ... the museum, I guess. At Oslo. I mean
the ... the mermaid and the children's museum, I don't
care if it's a children's museum.

Q: Do you like children?

A: Oh no.

(No disgrace in *that*, certainly, thought Jannina.)

Q: But you liked the children's museum.

A: Yes, sir. . . . Yes . . . I liked those little animals, the fake ones, in the—the—

A: The crèche?

A: Yes. And I liked the old things from the past, the murals with the flowers on them, they looked so real.

(Dear God!)

Q: You said you were associated with a theater group in Tokyo. Did you like it?

A: No . . . yes. I don't know.

Q: Were they nice people?

A: Oh yes. They were awfully nice. But they got mad at me, I suppose. . . . You see . . . well, I don't seem to get things quite right, I suppose. It's not so much the work, because I do that all right, but the other . . . the little things. It's always like that.

Q: What do you think is the matter?

A: You . . . I think you know.

Jannina flipped through the rest of it: normal, normal, normal. Miss Smith was as normal as could be. Miss Smith was stupid. Not even very stupid. It was too damned bad. They'd probably have enough of Leslie Smith in a week, the Komarovs; yes, we'll have enough of her (Jannina thought), never able to catch a joke or a tone of voice, always clumsy, however willing, but never happy, never at ease. You can get a job for her, but what else can you get for her? Jannina glanced down at the dossier, already bored.

Q: You say you would have liked to live in the old days. Why is that? Do you think it would have been more adventurous or would you like to have had lots of children?

A: I . . . you have no right . . . You're condescending.

Q: I'm sorry. I suppose you mean to say that then you would have been of above-average intelligence. You would, you know.

A: I know. I looked it up. Don't condescend to me.

Well, it was too damned bad! Jannina felt tears rise in her eyes. What had the poor woman done? It was just an accident, that was the horror of it, not even a tragedy, as if everyone's forehead had been stamped with the word

"Choose" except for Leslie Smith's. She needs money, thought Jannina, thinking of the bad old days when people did things for money. Nobody could take to Leslie Smith. She wasn't insane enough to stand for being hurt or exploited. She wasn't clever enough to interest anybody. She certainly wasn't feebled-minded; they couldn't very well put her into a hospital for the feeble-minded or the brain-injured; in fact (Jannina was looking at the dossier again) they had tried to get her to work there and she had taken a good, fast swing at the supervisor. She had said the people there were "hideous" and "revolting." She had no particular mechanical aptitudes. She had no particular interests. There was not even anything for her to read or watch; how could there be? She seemed (back at the dossier) to spend most of her time either working or going on public tours of exotic places, coral reefs and places like that. She enjoyed aqualung diving, but didn't do it often because that got boring. And that was that. There was, all in all, very little one could do for Leslie Smith. You might even say that in her own person she represented all the defects of the bad old days. Just imagine a world made up of such creatures! Jannina yawned. She slung the folder away and padded into the kitchen. Pity Miss Smith wasn't good-looking, also a pity that she was too well balanced (the folder said) to think that cosmetic surgery would make that much difference. Good for you, Leslie, you've got some sense, anyhow. Jannina, half asleep, met Ann in the kitchen, beautiful, slender Ann reclining on a cushion with her so-chi and melon. Dear old Ann. Jannina nuzzled her brown shoulder. Ann poked her.

"Look," said Ann, and she pulled from the purse she wore at her waist a tiny fragment of cloth, stained rusty brown.

"What's that?"

"The second-best maker of hand-blown glass—oh, you know about it—well, this is his blood. When the best maker of hand-blown glass in the world had stabbed to the heart the second-best maker of hand-blown glass in the world, and cut his throat, too, some small children steeped handkerchiefs in his blood and they're sending pieces all over the world."

"Good God!" cried Jannina.

"Don't worry, my dear," said lovely Ann; "it happens every decade or so. The children say they want to bring back cruelty, dirt, disease, glory, and hell. Then they forget about it. Every teacher knows that." She sounded amused. "I'm afraid I lost my temper today, though, and walloped your godchild. It's in the family, after all."

Jannina remembered when she herself had been much younger and Annie, barely a girl, had come to live with them. Ann had played at being a child and had put her head on Jannina's shoulder, saying, "Jannie, tell me a story." So Jannina now laid her head on Ann's breast and said, "Annie, tell me a story."

Ann said: "I told my children a story today, a creation myth. Every creation myth has to explain how death and suffering came into the world, so that's what this one is about. In the beginning, the first man and the first woman lived very contentedly on an island until one day they began to feel hungry. So they called to the turtle who holds up the world to send them something to eat. The turtle sent them a mango and they ate it and were satisfied, but the next day they were hungry again.

" 'Turtle,' they said, 'send us something to eat.' So the turtle sent them a coffee berry. They thought it was pretty small, but they ate it anyway and were satisfied. The third day they called on the turtle again and this time the turtle sent them two things: a banana and a stone. The man and woman did not know which to choose, so they asked the turtle which thing it was they should eat. 'Choose,' said the turtle. So they chose the banana and ate that, but they used the stone for a game of catch. Then the turtle said, 'You should have chosen the stone. If you had chosen the stone, you would have lived forever, but now that you have chosen the banana, Death and Pain have entered the world, and it is not I that can stop them.' "

Jannina was crying. Lying in the arms of her old friend, she wept bitterly, with a burning sensation in her chest and the taste of death and ashes in her mouth. It was awful. It was horrible. She remembered the embryo shark she had seen when she was three, in the Auckland Cetacean Research Center, and how she had cried then. She didn't know what she was crying about. "Don't, don't!" she sobbed.

"Don't what?" said Ann affectionately. "Silly Jannina!"

"Don't, don't," cried Jannina, "don't, it's true, it's true!" and she went on in this way for several more minutes. Death had entered the world. Nobody could stop it. It was ghastly. She did not mind for herself but for others, for her godchild, for instance. He was going to die. He was going to suffer. Nothing could help him. Duel, suicide, or old age, it was all the same. "This life!" gasped Jannina. "This awful life!" The thought of death became entwined somehow with Leslie Smith, in bed upstairs, and Jannina began to cry afresh, but eventually the thought of Leslie Smith calmed her. It brought her back to herself. She wiped her eyes with her hand. She sat up. "Do you want a smoke?" said beautiful Ann, but Jannina shook her head. She began to laugh. Really, the whole thing was quite ridiculous.

"There's this Leslie Smith," she said, dry-eyed. "We'll have to find a tactful way to get rid of her. It's idiotic, in this day and age."

And she told lovely Annie all about it.

FILOMENA & GREG & RIKKI-TIKKI & BARLOW & THE ALIEN

JAMES TIPTREE, JR.

The first of James Tiptree's science-fiction stories to
see print appeared early in 1968—a long time back, by
the reckoning of some, but just an eyeblink ago to
those of us who have Cosmic Perspective. It attracted
no particular attention, nor did his next two or three;
but by 1970 he was finding his way into anthologies and
getting nominated for awards, and now it is apparent
that a major new short-story writer is in our midst:
deft, original, vigorous. What he can do in the longer
forms is still something of a mystery as of this writing,
but the odds favor him. Tiptree the man likewise remains something of a mystery at present. He lives
south of Mason-Dixon, though not very far, seems to
travel a good deal, and describes himself as "a Mid-
westerner who batted around jungly parts of the globe
when young and worse jungles with desks when old."
Perhaps he's the Secret Master of the CIA; perhaps
he's Ho Chi Minh in a clever plastic disguise. One
thing is sure: he's a writer.

The first alien to land on Earth stayed seventy-two
seconds; he was a televolpt. He did three back-volpts and
collected himself from the region of Lyra. "Good grief,"
he said later. "What a mess. Everybody sending, nobody
receiving. I shall insist that a warning be placed in the
Ephemeris."

Earth was next seen by a flock of xenologists from Highfeather, who can stand anything. "Intelligence simply simply hasn't evolved there," they reported. "Social structure is at the level of crude incubation ritual with some migratory clanning. Frankly, it looks unnestworthy. A pesky lot of mammals have clobbered up the place with broken shells. Of interest only to students of pseudo-evolution."

Some time later an obscure mimestrel happened by and stayed long enough to compose a toccata for hydraulion known as "The Sportsday Mass Flushing Rites." For a while thereafter Earth enjoyed a minor vogue as a source of trendy audio seizures.

At the time of our story the only aliens in permanent residence were a small evangelical mission near Strangled Otter, Wis., and four crazy firemice from the planet Dirty who were speculating in New York real estate on the premise that the air would soon be oxygen-free. There was also a rumor of something or somebody holed out in the central Australian plateau.

No regular transmission lines ran near the system. Thus our hero, in a manner of speaking—our hero when he arrived did so by chartered slambang, incidentally indicating that he was very rich or very desperate. As a matter of fact he was both.

His name would be rendered as an energy configuration followed by several gestures and is of no importance here.

He had ordered his tailor to culture him a soma of the dominant mammalian type, using the specs from the old Highfeather report. In consequence he materialized in the New State Department parking lot on a May morning rush hour in the form of a bare baboon-bottomed youth eighteen feet tall with very peculiar arms.

Luckily his biotech had included some optional adjustments. After a short stroll down E Street which greatly enriched the Washington psychiatric industry, he ducked into the lobby of the International Ladies' Garment Workers Union for a quick retouch. He came out looking like a young, idealized David Dubinsky and when he had extinguished the halo he blended right into the fleeing crowd.

The first thing he discovered was that the females of Earth had a mysterious appeal.

"So that's what that thing is for," he said to himself. "Imagine!"

A supple young female was clinging to his neck and sending tremors through Dubinsky's 1935 single-breasted.

"Will you nest, madame?" he inquired as the crowd carried them through a police line. Fortunately he inquired it in Urdu, in which it sounds remarkably like "Help, help!"

She left off biting his shirt button and looked up. His enthusiasm mounted.

"Hey, you're just as shook as I am," she gasped. "I can hear your heart."

Her gentle wild song thrilled him, her lower lip was a perfect tractrix. "Let us hasten to the shade of the roble tree!" he exulted in Quechuan. What an environment! He beamed, waving his free arm at the riot wagons and fire trucks howling by. "How flashing the lights, how mellow the siren song!"

"Oh, my," said the girl, her visual organs radiant around 430 millimicrons. She made a delicious blowing sound with her lower lip, dislodging soft strands of hair. "Look, you absolutely cannot trip out on the street. Not here." She pushed back and examined him. "Do you have a car?"

He was achieving contact telepathy. "No," he smiled.

A loudhailer began barking behind them. "Holy Toledo," she muttered.

Flight! Fear! He reached in tenderly.

"Sweet spring is your time," he pleaded. "Is my time is our time, for springtime is lovetime and viva sweet love. E-e-cummings. I am Filomena."

"Oh-h-h ... ?" she breathed. Was it recognition? She had stopped going away. "I'm Filomena. You're going to get busted." To his joy she took his arm and began pulling him toward Twenty-first Street.

"I'm still confused in this form," he told her, stroking a fire jeep. "My luggage lacks."

Filomena steered him away from the jeep. "Who isn't? What's your name?"

"Such a sky and such a sun I never knew!" he agreed.

"Your name. I can't remember you."

"Name." He turned slowly around, admiring the wilderness of Pennsylvania Avenue. "Rex?" he said. "Rexall-Liggett? Humble Oil!" It was all so perfect. The female was tugging him across a torrent of free vehicles saying, "Move, hurry," whenever he stopped to savor it all. Presently they reached an open clearing with an artifact in the middle. She seemed to be looking for something. He teetered on the curb gaping at the Washington Circle traffic grinding around them. "Fantastic! Oh, how primal. How unspoiled. Such peace!" He inhaled deeply as a D.C. Transit bus belched by.

"Oh mother." She pulled him away from the curb; a gentle girl.

"I reluct—no, I am reluctant to find mine Handkoffer. It will recall me. I sigh." He sighed expansively, peering into her point four three micron eyes. "Are you typical? Is my nose right?" He changed Dubinsky's nose a little to make the most of the monoxide.

Filomena's lovely lips now opened as wide as her eyes but she did not let go his hand.

"Hey!" somebody heyed at them.

RT bustled up, too excited to remember to look like Ralph Nader. He was called RT, short for Rikki-Tikki, although some people in White Plains thought of him as Schuyler Rotrot, Jr. "Did you hear it? There's a nekkid thirty-foot monster marching on the White House. The whole city's freaking out!"

Filomena didn't say anything. RT went over and prodded a large yellow-haired person whose large sandaled feet were propped up on a bench nearby. "Wake up, Barlow."

When Barlow remained unstirring the alien came over too with Filomena. He put his free hand on Barlow's toes.

"How dear to me is sleep," he said. *"For while evil and shame endure, not to see, not to feel is my good fortune. Michelangelo."*

Barlow's eyes snapped open.

"Did I do that right? Your song?" The alien felt wonderful; confused but wonderful. He turned and rested his hand on RT's head. *"Every emancipation is a restoration of the human world and of human relationships to man himself. Marx, 1818–1883.* Great grooblie grock in the morning!"

"Great grooblie grock in the morning," said RT faintly,

backing. Barlow got up. The alien let his hand go with RT a ways and then recollected himself. He stretched both arms over his head, stood on tiptoe, inhaled, exhaled, farted, spun around and snapped his fingers. Sparks came out of his fingers and shot into his hair, which turned red.

"Oh, oh, oh."

"NO FIAHWORKS INNA PAHK!" A squad car was in the curb lane. They hustled the alien over behind the drinking fountain.

"Was it wrong?" he asked them anxiously. "The bird-watcher is unseen, unheard. Let me hear you," he pleaded, reaching for hands.

"You're It!" RT howled softly. "Aren't you? Aren't you? What, who, Project Ozma? You picked up the atomics, you've come to save us, right? Omigod. Look, let me fill you in—"

"I think we should go elsewhere," Barlow said. He was very tall and plump; the alien stretched up to look in his face and then stretched down again.

"Don't do that," yelped RT. "Quick, a forcefield, an invisibility screen. Listen, the military-industrial feed-forward in this country alone—"

"Woman, find a place," said Barlow.

All this time Filomena hadn't said anything but just watched the alien carefully, holding his hand.

"You said, about your luggage," she reminded him now.

The alien's smile faded. He waved largely toward Arlington. "No hurry." He patted Barlow, RT, smiled again. "Why do we not nest? *Everybody never breathed quite so many kinds of yes.*"

"Oh great, oh groovy," said RT. "Listen, if your approach is basically sociotechnological, you still have to factor in the psychological-ecological scene."

"Woman," said Barlow.

Filomena nodded and started leading the alien down New Hampshire Avenue with the others on both sides. There was a lot of noise over toward the Ellipse.

"It's hard to realize I'm really here," said the alien, squinting around luxuriously. "Utterly untouched. Nature."

"Runaway forward oscillation," RT was saying. "Locked into entropic slide."

"I feel like that after a trip," said Filomena. She led them around a drop pole into the George Washington University parking lot. "I know where Greg keeps her car keys." They followed her into an unpaved alley and found Greg's Toyota four-door, which came a little above Barlow's knees. Filomena crooched down and started groping under the back floor mat. Just as she found the keys a hand came in from the other side and took them.

"Oh, hi, Greg," they all said.

"Last time I had to get it out of Carter Barron amphitheater," Greg said. "I am brilliantly shitted." She put her books in the Toyota; a small, clean, thrumming girl in a majority suit.

"We have to help him get his gear," RT told her. He pushed the alien around to Greg. "Go on, show her. Do the psi thing."

The alien took hold of Greg's hand.

"The-crystalline-style-is-a-gelatinous-rodlike-affair-with-a-head-that-goes-around-clockwise-at-a-rate-of-sixty-to-seventy-rpm-in-a-certain-area-of-the-bivalve-stomach," he exclaimed delightedly. "*It is perhaps the only rotating part of any animal, the nearest approach to the wheel found in nature.* Huxley calls it one of the most remarkable structures in the animal kingdom. I don't believe it."

"It's come," howled RT. "They're really, truly here!"

There was some more of that until Greg said, "All right, but I'll drive," and they all got in the Toyota with the alien in the front seat between Greg and Barlow. "Make yourself thin," said RT, so he did until they told him not so thin. They started down Twenty-first Street to Memorial Bridge. RT was into pollution.

On the bridge approach lane they saw policemen stopping everybody. Filomena took off her tam and put it on Barlow's blond head and started pulling out his shirt. "Spread it over your knees," she told him. Somebody suggested the alien should make his hair gray. When the park policeman put his head in the Toyota Greg told him she was taking her folks out to see President Kennedy's grave. Barlow smiled shyly around his hair. "That's where it's at," the gray-haired alien said rather loudly. The policeman's head swiveled, withdrew.

"That's where it's at," the alien repeated as they drove onto the bridge.

"What's at?"

"Mes equipajes. Valise. Portmanteaux," he explained. "It just called me."

"At Kennedy's grave?"

"That figures," Greg snorted.

The alien touched her cheek to see what the joke was. "Breakfast in *Betelgeuse*, dinner in *Denebola*, baggage in *Arlington*," he chanted, laughing. Barlow was sticking the antenna of Greg's radio out the window. WAVA's teletype went *Rattle-rattle police cordon rattle White House*. They drove into the Arlington Cemetery Public Parking and got out to walk up to President Kennedy's grave.

When they got up to the marble place they found a dozen people standing by the ropes, looking at the gas flame. Flowers, some of them real, were leaning on the big white box.

"Excuse me," said the alien. He reached in his mouth and took out a sort of micronode which he held out toward the catafalque. A bunch of daffodils fell over and something small and shiny whizzed out and snapped into the alien's hand where it began making a yattering noise.

"I saw that," said a woman in a pink slacks suit.

"Quick," hissed RT. "The shield, the hypnotic distorter!"

"I can't," the alien hissed back. "There's an overtime stasis charge."

"Stealing souvenirs," said the woman, louder. "I saw him!"

"Pay it, pay it," RT bayed.

The alien stuck his little finger into the yammering thing, which quieted. When he pulled his finger out it was shorter; he put it in his mouth.

"I'm going to report you," said the woman, working up. Her face was shaped like the inside of a sneaker. "Vandalism. *The President's* grave." She started toward them.

Barlow stepped in front of her, taking off the tam.

"You'll have to excuse him, lady. He is the Muscular Dystrophy Father of the Year. We'll put it right back." He took the thing out of the alien's hand and tossed it back among the flowers.

"Your claim check!" said RT. It was gone too.

Barlow was herding them all away from the Kennedys' place across the grassy hillside filled with ordinary dead people. Greg tried her radio again. *Buses bumper-to-bumper, rattled WAVA, moving into position rattle-rattle reserves blah-blah Pentagon.*

"What's a pentagon?" the alien asked.

"That's what I'm trying to *tell* you," said RT. "The professional military syndrome inevitably evolves—"

"Incredible," said the alien. They were standing on six ex-corporals, looking across the river at a platter of smog with white bits sticking out into the sunlight.

"The Indians are sending fresh-air signals," said Greg.

The alien sighed deeply. "The wild millions in their primordial might," he exclaimed reverently. "The dust of their passing darkens the sun." A 727 burst up from National over them, trailing kerosene, and two police choppers crossed below it going *woodchuck-woodchuck.* "The thunder, the wild majesty," said the alien. He inhaled the kerosene.

Barlow had sat down restfully on the corporals with his eyes closed.

"Terrible, terrible," said RT. "Do you think we can possibly qualify for Galactic membership?" He tore a little at his short hair and went back to see if the people had left the Kennedys.

Filomena was standing quietly holding onto the alien. They turned around so that he was holding her, and she put her other arm up around his neck and they slowly kissed. His hair was now a beautiful dark red.

"Hey, everybody's gone," cried RT, running up. "We can go back." He poked the alien. "Hey."

"Guard at ten o'clock," said Barlow, getting up. Greg put hands questioningly on the alien's other arm and he wrapped it around her too. They walked back to the grave like that.

"How'll you get it?" asked RT. The flowers were a couple of yards beyond the rope where the guard could see them.

The alien tightened his arms around Filomena and Greg. "I don't really desire . . ." he mumbled.

"You should," said Filomena. "All your things."

"I packed in a hurry," the alien said apologetically.

"Get it, get it!" urged RT.

The alien reluctantly unhooked one arm. It was a delicate moment. "Don't watch me."

When they looked back the thing was in his hand. A trapezact lattice; it twinkled.

"Open it," panted RT. "Aren't you going to open it?"

"It's so small," Greg said.

"It's only partly in this dimension," RT explained. "Time-independent spin waves. Magnon phasing." The alien looked at him admiringly.

"Open it!"

But the alien continued to hold it in a tentative way; it seemed to disturb him. "I don't really need anything now," he said. "Later. There is time." He put the thing in his pocket and laughed and hugged the girls. "I feel so, so yes! Let us do more native things."

"We could eat," said Barlow.

So they got back in the Toyota and went to the riverside Howard Johnson. The Howard Johnson Muzak was saying *Unexplained electromagnetic blackout blah-blah Fort Myer.* The alien ate three subs and a paper napkin and kissed Greg. He wasn't a vegetarian. The Muzak voice said *National Guard* and warned everybody not to park on emergency snow routes. Greg tried to show the alien at least the Beatles on the Music Menu but it came out *Man of La Mancha* in white noise. RT went into minorities. Filomena explained to the alien that he had to katabolize with Barlow and RT instead of with her and Greg. He went with them happily and after he had adjusted the hydraulic pressure they compared everything; it was empty hour at the Howard Johnson.

"A totally sick society," RT said, back at the table. "It's hard to know where to start. What's the baddest, the very worst? What's your impression?" he asked the alien. "Our area of maximum entropy?"

"What's your name, really?" asked Filomena.

The alien considered this, making a tch-tch-tch noise. Until he opened his luggage he really couldn't know.

"Binary groups," RT interpreted for them. "Naturally everybody carries index numbers. We couldn't pronounce it." The alien admired him some more, hugging Filomena and Greg. RT began telling him about behavioral sinks. Barlow's eyes were closed.

When they decided it was time to go the alien made a wailing sound and sat back down.

"The soma," he told them. "I seem to be inflated."

"Well, deflate," said RT. "You can change things."

They watched his nose shrink and swell and then his ears.

"It doesn't seem to work," he reported. "My tailor said there could be problems."

"Think of square roots," RT directed. "Cube roots. Intragalactic coordinates. Higher prime numbers."

The alien wrinkled his forehead, trying. Then he shook his head. "Isn't there a better way?"

Filomena made a soft noise.

Barlow opened his eyes. "There you are," he said.

And there they were.

"This. Is. A. Cosmic. Moment," announced RT. "Oh. Omigod. You female persons have a stupefying responsibility. Are you truly, existentially aware?"

Filomena was leaning on the alien with her nose in his ear.

"Out," said Barlow. "Out."

When they achieved the Toyota Greg's radio said Georgetown hippie hangouts rattle-rattle strictly enforced. M Street was closed off.

"My aunt is in Costa Rica at a WHO conference," Greg said. "I water her violets. She lives in Bethesda."

The Toyota scuttled north and around and over Chain Bridge and rushed up Seven Locks Road.

"Oh, oh," RT groaned. "Hard-core kitsch. African violets. Split-level breezeways. Metal script house numbers. Desecration." He pawed the alien's shoulders. "We're not really like this. Don't look."

When they trooped into Greg's aunt's cellar rumpus room they found the blinds were closed. It was dim and mild.

"There's some incense somewhere," said Greg. She showed them her aunt's violets in the Plant-a-window. Some of them were three feet tall with feathery gray leaves.

"No," said Barlow. But he let her put Pink Floyd on the stereo deck. Then he took off his shirt and sat down on Greg's aunt's wall-to-wall and took off his sandals. Then he took off his jeans. In the dimness he was huge and plump and gleaming. From the stereo *Ummagumma* made all right sounds. "Omigod." RT was getting out of his Trevira double-knit. "Are you aware?" Filomena unlaced her skirt and they were unzipping and peeling and stepping out of their clothes, and the alien dissolved Dubinsky's suit, all except the buttons, which fell on the carpet. He had no underwear and his soma was amazing. They sat down in a circle with Barlow and the alien put his arms around both Filomena and Greg and clasped them to him. There was a complicated interval until he put his face out. "Two at once is not possible, I think?"

"Not really," said Barlow.

The alien looked from Filomena to Greg to Filomena and then his body flowed along the simple strong imperative of Filomena's welcoming legs.

Over his shoulder they could see one of her eyes looking very surprised and then it rolled up and closed; she was feeling herself entered, enveloped, in total empathy and augmentation. RT drew his breath in hard as the two bodies rocked and plunged in the dim Bethesda afternoon. Then Filomena arched and came twice with finality. The alien feeling her change around him raised his head and backed out bewildered, his soma incandescent, prodding air.

It was obvious what was going to happen. But Greg scrambled onto his lap and he went off into her, *into the heart of the sun.*

"Yes, oh, yes," he panted, and then before he could cool down her feelings caught his nerve nets and his body began to build with hers until Greg mewed and rolled him over completely clutched to him tight—and then she was finished and he was stuck again, kneeling over her homeless.

So RT put his hand on the alien's back and they

turned facing each other for a moment and then the alien put his hand on RT and RT did the same for him and they took care of everything that way.

Barlow was sitting relaxed against Greg's aunt's modular sofa with Filomena's hair over his ankles.

"Touch him," Filomena told the alien.

The alien reached out his hand a little shyly and Barlow took it and they clasped hands awhile, looking in each other's eyes.

"To sleep," the alien said.

"Perchance to dream," agreed Barlow quietly and that was it for them. Greg went over and put on Brahms's Quintet for clarinet in B minor with Reginald Kell, which was just right.

Presently they all got up and showed the alien Greg's aunt's shower and had some root beer, and RT winced and flinched over Greg's aunt's kitchen mottoes but you could see he was deeply happy too.

"Virgin wilderness," said the alien, drinking root beer and listening to the diesels on the Beltway rattling Greg's aunt's windows. "The unspoiled grandeur of the wild."

"You sound like we're bison." Greg laughed. "Passenger pigeons."

"Some people don't listen enough," said Barlow.

"Aren't you going to open your gear?" RT fussed. "Oh, Gandalf. Earth's greatest day. I'm living it. The first alien contact. Me. You too," he added. "Us. The first."

"The purity of the moment." The alien sighed happily.

"Come on," said RT. He pushed them all back downstairs and rooted in the pile of buttons. "All the great things."

"I don't really," said the alien. "I was in a hurry."

RT put the lattice thing in the alien's hand. As soon as it touched him it gave a musical tweep and Greg's aunt's phone jumped in sympathy.

"Does that mean more overtime?" asked Filomena.

"No, somebody is calling me." The alien shook his head and pressed a facet of the trapezact. A circuit chip thing popped out.

"Galactic Central," breathed RT. "Now you report, right? Wait—"

"Actually it's local." The alien peered. "Forty-two north, uh, seventy-five west."

"Isn't that New York City?" asked Greg, who always knew where things were.

"You mean you—you mean you've landed in New York too?" RT protested. "But you're the first, aren't you? Aren't you?—Oh!" He broke off as the chip spun, threw up a flaw in space which bloomed into a round vertical lens like a 1910 Stutz Bearcat windscreen.

"Oooh, aaah," they all said.

"The *hardware*," sighed RT, hanging over the alien's shoulder. "The real thing."

The alien tiddled things at the base of the screen, Greg's aunt's phone jingling empathically. The screen opaqued, flowed into black and white and became Julia Childs punishing some food on WNET.

"Wrong number."

"The New York phone system is in crumbs." RT leaned over further to watch the alien's fingers. This time the screen irised into a close-up; something large and pale and sluglike.

"Oh, my," gasped Filomena.

"Where's its head?" Greg asked.

The thing on the screen effortfully hoisted up one limb and began snapping an instrument at itself. Over one of its mounds they could see a mat lettered "Peanut butter for God."

"That's no alien!" RT yelped. "That's my father in White Plains cutting his toenails. Oh, tune it out, cut cut!"

"You better lean off him, it's picking up your vibes," said Filomena.

On the next try the screen formed in living color: a persimmon-red executive scene with a devilishly mod older man clasping his knee in a lucite pedestal chair. He glanced around and his face lit up with sincere david frost-type joy.

"Frempl'vaxt? Asimplaxco?" he beamed.

"Vlngh. Excuse me," their alien said hesitantly. "I don't think so."

"Oh, forgive me, I thought you were my clients coming in. Look, by the by—are you an anaerobe?"

"Well, I haven't unpacked yet."

"Yes, yes, always a problem." The cordial person wreathed his arms around his chair back. "I do hope you turn out to be, I'd love to show you around. Would you believe less than twenty years to a climax ecology in this area?" He laced his fingers and cocked his head on one side merrily. "If I didn't force myself to be conservative I'd say ten, some days we hardly need filters at all. I've picked myself the most marvy site right on the estimated high slime line. Hi." He cocked his head the other way, peering at them. "You haven't been peeking about by yourself, I hope?"

"Well, no," said their alien.

"You have gone native," he giggled, waggling one finger at them. They could see his mouth was down in his neck where his chin should be. "Tut-tut-tut. A friendly word, we have a firm option on everything on this side above twenty. The, ah"—he glanced at his console—"North American. The cream. Unless you're aquatic of course." He tapped his buck teeth, grinning like mad. "And you haven't any silly planet-forming schemes, no, no, no." One of his legs stamped nervously, gerbil-wise. "It's been a joy, a real joy. I have to break now, I hear my clients." He twiddled his fingers ta-ta and the screen went blank.

There was a silence in Greg's aunt's rumpus room.

"Anaerobic means not needing oxygen," Greg said slowly. "In twenty years?"

"They're the bad guys, right?" RT demanded. "You're here to help us, to block the—aren't you?"

"What did he mean about buying North America?" Filomena asked. "I mean, nobody could sell it to him."

"Nobody here," said Barlow. The alien looked at him and looked down again, not touching anybody.

"You help us buy it back." RT frowned. "Galactic credits. What do we use? Universal unit of wealth. Rare life-prolonging spices. Time Planetary time-energy—"

The lattice tweeped again. The alien sighed and tip-tapped the base of the screen, which lit up to show a repellent greenish armored head with honeycomb eyes. "Oh god, more," muttered RT.

"Greetings in grexhood," rasped the monster. "We, ah, happened to overhear your communication. I grasp your present condition and trust that we do not offend your life values?"

"Not so far as I know," said their alien.

"I wish merely to observe that we too would deplore any rearrangements here. We being a chartered evangelical mission." His eye grids swiveled. "By the same token, we feel concern over the rush of prospective development by this anaerobe group. We're thinking of filing on behalf of the dominant species. It's been making the most gratifying progress, really an evolutionary threshold—Oh, thank you, Olaf." He interrupted himself to accept a light green drop of something from a jointed black arm. Olaf loomed briefly into view; bulbous black and shiny.

"Well, that's all I wished to impart. That will do, Olaf." He patted Olaf's mandible. "We'll be in touch when you get your identity together."

The screen blanked.

"Does that mean he'll help us?" burst out RT. "Where are they? What else is going on here, what else?"

"What was that black thing?" asked Filomena.

"I think that was an ant," Greg replied quietly. "*Comonotus herculeanus*, maybe. Like one centimeter high. He's converting bugs."

"No ally is trivial," said RT bravely, but he sounded hollow. The purity of the situation, the beautiful thing. . . .

Barlow got up and picked up his jeans.

"It's time," he told the alien. "Let's find out who you really are."

They all stood up. The alien folded up the screen and it snicked back into the lattice. He looked very unhappy.

Filomena touched his arm. "Is that thing going to change you?"

"Just my memory. At first," he sighed.

Filomena reached up and kissed him gravely. Greg stepped up and kissed him too, and RT shook his hand. "We should stand back, there may be an energy vortex." They went and stood with Barlow on the other side of the conversation pit.

The alien stood alone, looking at them. Then he raised the trapezact and stuck out his tongue and held the thing to it. Nothing happened. After they'd been holding their breaths about a minute the alien took the thing away from his mouth, still staring at them.

At first they thought he hadn't changed at all. Then they saw his posture was subtly different. His shoulders sagged. His mouth sagged too, and his eyes puckered up, still staring at them. He groaned.

"What is it? What is it?"

The alien groaned again and stumbled toward them, holding out his hands. "I . . . I *ochquopl*—the word, help, let me touch you—"

He grabbed hold of Barlow.

"I'm pregnant," he said and put his face on Barlow's chest.

"Oh, you poor thing." Filomena and Greg began patting his back.

"Of. All. The. Stupid. Bourgeois. Irrelevancies," RT said furiously. "Great flying dog do."

The alien groaned again and they heard Greg's aunt's front door opening upstairs in the hall.

"Hi, kids! I'm back."

"Hi, Aunt Dorothy," Greg yelled. She took a breath. "Your violets are fine, I hope we didn't mess up the bathroom. We're just on our way from the, the park. How was Costa Rica?"

"I'm bushed," her aunt yelled back. "Don't try to go downtown, there's some kind of riot."

After a little more yelling they were all back in the Toyota. Greg had the alien's buttons in a Baggie and he was wearing RT's shorts under Filomena's poncho and shaking his head as if it hurt him.

"Are you really a woman, I mean a female?" Filomena asked.

"Cruddy epiphenomenon," RT was muttering. "Mod Squad. Fleeing from social censure. Looking for its father, maybe? You didn't even intend to come here, to Earth."

"Oh, I *did*." Tears welled into the alien's eyes. He rubbed at them distractedly.

"How can you be so heartless?" Filomena hugged the alien from the back seat and he grabbed her hands gratefully and groaned again.

"Where to?" said Barlow as Greg inserted the Toyota into the afternoon Beltway stampede.

"I think they're supposed to take the chain off Turkey Run Park last week."

"We should get something to eat, you must be hungry, dear," Filomena said.

The alien nodded miserably. He kept looking at Barlow and then looking out at the General Motors demolition derby on both sides and sighing.

"Refugees from interplanetary war?" RT grumbled. "Unborn heir to a lost empire. Oh, what a ripoff."

The Toyota shot out of the Dolly Madison exit and ran into the McLean McDonald's. "I'll get the Hi-Prot," Greg said. "And milk," Filomena called. The alien took the parcel on his lap with the lattice thing on top and they doubled back onto the parkway and into the Turkey Run cutoff. Sure enough, the chain was down. There was a Volkswagen camper in Parking Area A.

"Let's go down to the view."

"It's getting cold," said Filomena as they straggled down to the scruffy place above the remains of the Potomac. The alien's muscular calves were all goose-pimply.

"As an unwed mother your image is pretty sad," RT said venomously. "Can't you do something to keep warm?"

"If I only remembered to pack it." The alien fiddled with the lattice. "Oh yes, here." A gentle wave of warmth spread over them. The alien fiddled some more and they were kneedeep in invisible foam padding. "Hey!" Even RT cheered up. It felt fine sitting on the unseen foam.

"Now tell us all about it," said Greg, dealing out the food. "Why are you so sad? Is pregnancy a crime where you come from? Are you exiled from your planet?"

"Planets," said the alien a trifle sharply with his mouth full. He was looking less and less like Dubinsky. "Well, no, as a matter of fact it's an honor. I was"—he touched RT's arm—"elected. I w-won." He put his Hi-Prot down and gazed at them distressfully.

"I can't adjust to your being a female." Filomena gave him a hug.

"I—it's not—oh, it's all so complicated." The alien leaned toward Barlow and his features seemed to melt a little. "I had no idea it was so beautiful—the two kinds and all the—all you—" He choked up, patting blindly at them all.

"Why, dear? Why? Tell us."

The alien pulled himself together. "I was desperate, I mean, after I got elected. There wasn't much time. And I'd made up my mind I was going to give my—my off-spring the best possible start. Even where I grew up—and we're very vrangh, you know—even there was all so nothing. So used. I want to give them a good start. Meaningful."

They understood. "Of course."

"Some place fresh and wild, I thought. Free. So I went all through the directory—Look." He squeezed the lattice thing and it extruded a fan of helices. "Oh, I forgot, you can't. I found your place here. Of interest only to students, it says."

"We're listed in that?" RT poked at it. "Hey, it tingles. Telepathic engrams," he murmured. "A K-object."

"Actually you're not in a very good volume, you know. Funeral homes, is that your word? They were planning to use the system out beyond as a place for, well, garbage."

"A dump," said RT. "Neat."

"What kind of garbage?" Greg asked.

"Oh, space kipple. Boil-offs. I don't know. But I stopped it. I'm really very high vrangh." He nodded at them, wide-eyed. "Clout, glue. I recall now, I used a snaggler."

"A what?"

"Never mind," said Barlow. "Go on."

The alien gazed back at Barlow and melted some more. They saw he was coming to resumble Barbra Streisand.

"So I came here and it was so great." He choked up again. "So beautiful. All the yes." He hiccuped and a kind of shimmer came over him. "I began thinking of you as pnong. People. We had so much together. Oh, I just hate to do it here." He pawed at his eyes.

"Why not do it here?" said Filomena gently. "We'd love to have your baby."

"Wait," said Barlow.

"It's not just one," the alien told her.

"How many?"

"Thirty," the alien sniffed. "I mean, thirty thousand. Approximately."

"At one go?" RT whistled.

The alien nodded, gripping Filomena's hand, his bosom swelling, turning creamy.

"Well, that's kind of a lot," Greg admitted, "but couldn't we manage to care for them, maybe the UN—"

"Especially if you're rich," said RT. "There's really no problem. H'mmm. Thirty thousand high-status infant aliens, wow. Trade treaties? Cultural exchange. Conquest of space."

"No!" cried the alien. "I can't, I can't! Not after sharing your— Oh, what have I done?" He hid his face in Filomena's shoulder.

"These kids," said Barlow slowly. "What about them?"

The alien lifted his or her head and met Barlow's stare. The shimmer was quite strong now. He or she drew a deep breath.

"It's not like with you. I mean, the first phase is like almost crude energy. They just f-fight and eat, you can't even see them and they're dreadfully fast. They trash everything. That's why we use special planets now. And we send in like soldiers to collect the survivors. After the third molt, that is. When they start to be pnongl. There wouldn't be anything l-left."

The alien's eyes were streaming and the shimmer was brightening fast.

"When?" demanded Barlow.

The alien put her beautiful face in her hands.

"In a f-few minutes. As soon as the s-soma goes."

They gasped, trying to realize.

"Does the trashing start right away?" RT stuttered. "What, how—"

Barlow had got up. The alien was still looking up at him in a peculiar intense way. Suddenly they all understood that something unreally real was going on between them.

"Don't, don't," the alien whispered, holding the lattice thing. "You can't."

"I can try," said Barlow.

"It's too late anyway," the alien told him. "It's almost time."

Barlow flexed his large hands. "Can't you go someplace else?"

"I looked, I looked. The whole galaxy," the alien cried softly, not looking very human any more. "Oh, you're so real to me, it's dreadful, you think a place is just wild and then they're people with all their—"

"Yeah," said Barlow.

"Did you look in the Magellanic Clouds?" demanded Greg.

"Where?" The alien touched Greg to understand. "That's a different directory. Did I? It's so hard to think in this condition." She or it squeezed another helix out of the lattice thing and riffled it with shimmering fingers.

"Nothing. Nothing. Wait—how does this sound? Under *kveeth*-type: EMG profile sum unity. Postglacial, scenic, unaffiliated. Et cetera. But *scenic*, that's nice."

"What about the peo—" Filomena began.

"Can you get there in time?" Barlow cut her off.

"Da. Sí, sí. Il s'âgit seulement de"—the alien clutched one of Barlow's hands and was able to continue—"pay for clearing the coordinates and *frinx* the *drevath*. Oh, my soma is going."

"Good-by," said Barlow.

Still holding on to Barlow, the alien nodded solemnly. Then it clicked something very fast in the lattice thing and tossed it down.

"Matter transmitter, end-point simultaneity," RT muttered automatically.

"I'll never forget your song," the alien said wistfully. Filomena stroked its beautiful mane. "We'll miss you, dear." The lattice suddenly sparked and disappeared, leaving a microchip. RT handed it to the alien to put in its mouth. Its teeth seemed to be very active.

"Are you going to be all right?" Greg asked. "Don't you need a doctor or anything?"

"No." The alien's form had begun to waver and break up like a watery reflection; they felt the sliding under their hands and pulled back but still. . . .

"It was so *threengl*, so *plegth*," it told them.

"Tell us again the name of your planet," said Greg.

"Come back afterwards," Filomena cried.

"I *vred*, my official—"

"Hey," exclaimed RT, "about that garbage—"

The alien strobed into discontinuous spectra and the empty air whomped in, rocking them.

"KNOCK OFF THE FAHWUHKS," someone yelled faintly from the parking area above.

They sat down in silence in the warmth, looking at where the alien had been. Across the river the mercury lamps were flaring along Canal Road and the sky above D.C. was the color of melted tigers. A jet crawled down it, whirling lights.

"Would you really have tried to kill him, Barlow?" Greg asked.

Barlow lifted his hands a little and let them fall.

"I wonder how long this lasts." RT prodded the invisible softness. "I should show somebody. National Science Council. CIA." He didn't get up.

"I have a B-baggie full of buttons," said Greg.

"How could he, I mean her children be so awful?" Filomena was crying quietly. "What about the people where he's g-going?"

Barlow sighed. "Call me Calley," he said.

"I think he left us some of his t-telepathy," Filomena told them. "Touch me and see if you know what I'm thinking."

Greg touched her and after a minute RT touched them both.

"Will it ever be like that again?"

They blew their noses. Barlow settled back and gazed up at the high glowing contrails. "Evil and shame endure." He closed his eyes. "I think I'll go back to Australia."

OUT FROM GANYMEDE

BARRY N. MALZBERG

The themes of science fiction are made to order for surrealism; but in the days when s-f writers directed all their creative energies toward producing as realistic and literal-minded a picture of the future as they could, the notion of heightening the focus until the vision was nudged into the surreal never occurred. In the early 1950s Philip K. Dick showed the way out of the trap of realism, and today Barry Malzberg is one of the most successful exponents of the technique of using a distorting lens to gain greater clarity. A recent escapee from Manhattan, Malzberg now occupies himself studying the folkways of Suburbia, a territory hardly less alien to him than the Ganymede of this eerie tale.

I

Settling into orbit around what he has decided to call the Mad Satellite (nothing personal but the mission itself is insane, so tough on Ganymede), Walker finds himself thinking of his estranged wife: unquestionably she was a terrific fuck. Often after he had emptied himself into her as the culmination of simply hours and hours of heaving, bucking, moaning perversity, she had fluttered her eyes underneath and invited him with a coy yank of her head, letting him know that, for everything he had done, the essential part of her lay untouched. How it had infuriated him! He thought that she had been subtly insulting his adequacy when all the time he failed to see the plea beneath the insouciance. The woman had been insatiable. He never should have left her. Still there were other things, other reasons; nothing is as simple as it seems and sexuality is only a metaphor. He comforts himself with this as he works on controls, does computations, juggles the ship into a tight circuit. Deprivation and tension turn the mind in strange ways; he has never really regretted leaving her. He concentrates on Ganymede, which hangs below him darkly, aspects of rock filtering through the cloud formation, the gas of Jupiter high behind him in the anterior port. It is really a great little moon, very Earthlike in its gravity and appearance, to say nothing of being the gateway to Jupiter.

Base, which has talked him into the orbit, asks Walker how he is coming along. Walker says that everything is fine, fine; he had merely been preoccupied for a few moments setting up the orbit on the computer and had dropped out of contact. "That's nonsense, kid," Base says, "everything is plotted right here, you know that. Don't let all that space get to you now. Keep organized."

"It isn't easy, you know," Walker points out. He does not have to address a microphone, the whole craft being wired for sound in such a way that even the sounds of his evacuation can be evaluated by medical personnel at Base. "I mean, it's difficult to carry on as if this was strictly routine. You could try a little understanding."

Base points out that it has cost billions of dollars to put Walker in orbit around Ganymede, that the security and importance of the project cannot be risked because of personal quirks and that nothing must get in the way of the successful completion of the mission. It advises Walker to shape up and reminds him that there is a broadcast due in some twenty minutes, audio and video. Therefore, Base adds rather petulantly, it would make sense to get the cabin in order and put all debris out of visual range. The question of the apogee can be left to the computer.

"The hell with that," Walker says but he says this subvocally and with his face turned toward the floor. Not that the floor does not have pickups also.

II

Walker has been selected for the Ganymede project since he is the fittest of the twenty astronauts left in the program. This says little for his competence—fifty years ago there were several hundred and Walker would have barely qualified for steward's duty—but the agency has been in decline for a long time and, relative to the present situation, Walker is about the best that they can get. He reminded them of this during the examinations, at the physical and at the final briefing but it hardly seems to have done him much good. There is a certain failure of respect. "You are but a piece in the machinery," they had warned him but he had been in no mood to accept that until he was on his way. Now the situation has changed; recently he has been feeling very much like an engine with a certain pistonlike creaking or hammering beneath the joints. Also his voice seems to have become somewhat metallic and his mind moves with the convulsions of slow gears. He does not want to be a machine, not particularly, but then again he understands the agency very well and is willing to agree that the alternatives might have been worse.

Walker has not had sex for several months and then in an inept performance with his estranged wife, who told him that she would do it once for the memories and then, limbs spread, regarded him with cold ferocity as he worked against her. Several times he has considered covert masturbation within the ship but even during the sleep periods they surely have ultraviolet light and would be able to detect everything that he was doing. Besides, there seems to be something ridiculous in the idea of a man carried past Mars twirling his genitals. Something mystical should happen to a man past the moon to drive him past need. Masturbation had never been part of the briefing process for reasons he now thinks he understands.

III

After he superficially cleans the cabin there is a five- or ten-minute dead space before the broadcast during which he has little to occupy him and he sits, looking at the walls of the cabin, admiring certain notations the agency has put up in bulletin forms, with absolutely no interest in turning rearward and looking at Ganymede. This way is much better; he can believe that he is only on another simulation. During this period, the aliens come to him. There are two of them, strange yellow bipeds with glowing eyes who wear archaic clothing. On their chests is stenciled *Ganymede Police* and they carry weapons in their appendages which look rather menacing. "Stay calm," one of them says to him, "we just want to talk."

"I'm perfectly calm," Walker says. They are the first living beings he has seen for twelve days and fourteen hours and, despite their dangerous appearance, he is rather glad to see them. Excellent training has long since made him matter-of-fact in relation to all challenge. "As you can see, I'm not too busy at the minute. I am due for a transmission soon, though, and I'm afraid that I'll have to make it."

"That's fine," the spokesman says. He shrugs and replaces his weapon inside his clothing. "I'll do the talking, the other one is just along verifying. The next time he'll do the talking. We work in shifts that way, it's much easier."

"I can understand that," Walker says. "But how did you get into the cabin?"

The alien shrugs again, this time with a rather coy tilt of his appendages which marks him instantly to Walker (who has been well trained) as a cunning article. "Dematerialization," he says. "Don't think about it too much. We want to take up with you this issue of invading our planet. Ganymede is sovereign territory, you know, and you just can't settle into orbit that way. Furthermore, you've got enough armament on this ship to sink a planet. Exactly what do you have in mind?"

"Oh," Walker says, "I knew that there would be trouble about that. The armament is just for show. There's no intention of using it." He blushes faintly. "I wouldn't even know how to make it work," he says. "I'm not sure that it *does* work. They don't bother me with things like that from the ground."

"Nevertheless," the alien says, "nevertheless, I'm afraid that you people simply didn't consider the situation.

You're dealing with free territory here. You have absolutely no right in orbit and you must agree that if the situation were reversed you'd find it pretty frightening. You're going to have to leave."

"Well, how the hell did we know Ganymede was inhabited?" Walker says, trying to be reasonable. "There wasn't any sign at all. It's just a dead moon. How do I know that you people even are from Ganymede?"

"We're not people," the alien says, "nevertheless I understand your terminology. I'm afraid that you're not being very reasonable about the matter. We're giving you two hours, your time, to turn around and go back to your planet, otherwise we will have to take retaliatory action. I don't want to be more specific than that."

"You don't understand," Walker says. "I can't make any decisions like that. I can't even make promises. I'm just an engineer sent along for the ride. I have no authority."

"That," the alien says, "is your problem." He nods at his companion, his companion gives a brusque strained nod at Walker, they huddle together and at some prearranged signal vanish. Walker is left in the cabin sniffing a faint aroma of ozone which they seem to have left behind them. Base comes on and says that it is time for the transmission to begin. Walker asks them if they heard what just went on and Base says that they have had no time to monitor, they are very busy down there, does Walker really think the first transmission from Ganymede is routine business and they will replay the tapes at their leisure sometime when they get around to it. Everything going on inside the cabin is part of the perfectly preserved public record.

IV

Walker delivers a speech to the assembled people of Earth. He reads it slowly, precisely, off the prompter they have installed out of range of the camera, the words unreeling rather majestically. Someone in the higher echelons of the information division has a dash of eloquence although perhaps he is merely thinking of the top levels of the government; it is impossible to tell precisely who is guiding the mission. Walker reminds the people of Earth that in a time of torment and trouble mankind has historically looked toward the heavens from which heavens judgment and a sense of purpose have always come and that it is the spirit of the stars no less than that of the Earth which makes mankind human. By going to Ganymede as we have, by this rare act of disciplined courage on the part of thousands of dedicated people of whom he is only the most visible, Earth has been given a beacon, an instrument of its purpose. "We did not, after all, travel all this vast distance in the ether only to repeat the small banalities of our mistakes, we are refreshed and renewed by our glimpse of the void," Walker says, thinking vaguely about the machinery of the agency compound and how, at the checkpoints on the few occasions when he had had to leave the Base, he had seen thousands of people behind the barricades staring at him and mumbling. What the hell were they saying? Exactly what brought them there? Walker wonders as he goes on to recite some technical data; Ganymede is the largest satellite of the planet Jupiter, it was discovered by an Italian scientist in the seventeeth century; of all the satellites of the planets it is the most Earthlike in appearance and atmosphere, more habitable than Venus, and may eventually be the only place in the solar system where men will be able to maintain a colony independent of the home planet. He turns the camera so that the audience, with him, can see the terrain five hundred miles beyond, swimming in gases, and then turns it back to the cabin, advising them that he will be transmitting three more times during his orbits of Ganymede and hopes that all men of faith and will can join him in the mission. The speech runs out but the transmission, judging from clicks and winks, apparently does not; he fills an embarrassed ten seconds with greetings to his wife and parents and then the light goes out and Base tells them that he has done very well, that everything is in excellent shape, that he should rest for the next cycle in preparation for his next broadcast.

"Yes," he says, "but are they listening?"

"We have a full hookup, right through the satellites," Base says. "I would think that four billion heard you just now."

"Ah yes," Walker says, "but did they *attend*?" He feels lightheaded, slightly disconnected. "And about those aliens; I want to tell you about the aliens."

"No time," Base says. "Rest cycle must begin now and you're slipping out of range."

"But look," Walker says, "you're not following me. Just before the transmission I was visited by these two aliens from Ganymede and they said—"

"No time," Base says, "we'll pick it all up on the monitors."

"But there's *life*—"

"No time, no time," Base says and slips out of contact; it is like the bodies sliding apart after intercourse, all evasion, all collapse to some central, detached part and, clenching his fists, Walker finds himself alone in the cabin and nothing to do but sleep. Well, sleep then. He can deal with the situation later.

V

In his sleep Walker dreams and in the dream his wife is in the cabin talking to him. "It's all your fault," she says, "every bit of it is your fault, you never understood, you never cared, you never for one moment considered the implications of what you were doing." "Now wait a minute," Walker says to her (he seems to be in some kind of nightdress and his wife, wearing an opaque gown which he used to despise, is sitting cross-legged on his bunk, her chin in her hands, a complacent hostility severing her from him forever), "don't get started on that tack again, I'm just an employee. A functionary of the agency. In fact I'm only a technician so don't start pinning me with that guilt and culpability stuff again. It was only a job and I was in it long before you knew me and you took me on those terms so it's too late now."

She says nothing for a moment, this being one of her most infuriating habits, and then, quite horridly, winks at him. "That won't go any more," she says. "You're forty years old. You know exactly what's going on and you've known for a long time now. You're a man. You're one of the oldest people in the project."

"But in very good physical condition. I'm in such good physical condition—"

"Three hundred years of death and dreams to put you on Ganymede," she says. "Three hundred years. Isn't the price a little too high?" And he leans forward to tell her for the first time what he truly thinks of her and what he has wanted to do to her on so many unspeakable nights but the bitch flicks out, just wanders out of there the way the Ganymedian police have, and there is nothing to confront.

"You bitch," he says, "you dirty bitch," but this is not too satisfactory either and so he only drifts into another dream, much vaguer and more sordid this time, having something to do with campaigning for national office after his triumphant return from Ganymede and finding himself at a party with fifty blondes and a fat national committeeman who fondles all of the women obscenely as he asks Walker to tell him, in twenty words or less, exactly why he thinks he is entitled to public office and what he will do for the national committeeman if he is granted the nomination.

VI

He is awakened by the aliens. They perch at the foot of his bed, shimmering in a kind of haze, and the spokesman reminds him that Walker has exceeded the two hours granted him to reverse the mission and return home. "You're leaving us little choice," the alien says. "We're going to have to take very serious action."

"I don't know what to tell you," Walker says. "I tried to talk to them about you but they cut me off. I really wanted to discuss this, I mean I wasn't sitting on it or anything like that."

"I'm afraid that's no excuse."

"And in the second place," Walker says, tearing himself from the bunk and starting to move around the cabin, trying to force some jauntiness into his bearing, no reason to let a couple of aliens get you down, "in the second place, I couldn't turn the mission around even if I wanted to. It's all remote control. It's all computer. All that I do is come along for the ride. Everything is triggered from the Base."

"That's very interesting," the alien says, "but I'm afraid has nothing to do with the situation. You really have to get out of here, you know; you're pushing us beyond our limits."

"Why don't both of you talk?" Walker says, slapping a bulkhead, dodging an overhang, reeling to his knees to reach the medicine cabinet and some simulated caffeine. "Wouldn't it be easier that way?"

"Policy and procedure," the spokesman says. The aliens exchange nods. "He's only assisting me on this tour."

"I'd really like to leave," Walker says. "I mean, don't get me wrong. The fact that Ganymede has life on it and so on makes your case a very strong one. I'm not a lawyer but I think that you have some very good arguments. But what can I do?" He shows them the palms of his hands. "I have no essential control."

The silent alien looks at him and says, "You have enough armament on this thing to destroy a planet."

"Yes," Walker says, "that's quite true, quite true. I told that to you before and I admit that that happens to be the case. But we didn't intend to use it. It's just that the agency is essentially military in nature and we have to carry along war technology in order to make the financing. If you understand what I'm saying, it's very complicated the way they do things. Also, the armament is just for show so if we run into any aliens in space we can protect ourselves. Of course we've never met any aliens up until now and I wouldn't do anything at all to you. I mean, you can see that my position is hardly aggressive."

"Can you operate the armament?" the silent alien says. He seems to be genuinely engaged; unlike the other, once talking, he has a real interest in his work. Perhaps on Ganymede he is an ordnance expert.

"I don't know," Walker says. "I've received a little instruction, just the basics and so on, but actually it's pretty sophisticated stuff and I don't think that anyone directly in the agency knows exactly how to operate it. I mean, I know a few things about it, yes."

"I mean, is it voluntary?"

"Oh. Is it voluntary? You mean, unlike the operation

of the craft, could I actually use the weapons myself? Well, that's an interesting point," Walker says, "now that you bring it up. The answer is that I probably could, come to think of it. It isn't connected to the Base computer like everything else. Actually, it's kind of antiquated and hand-controlled, I believe."

"Well then," the chief alien says, "you certainly could destroy us if you elected to, now couldn't you?"

"But I wouldn't think of it," Walker says hastily. "I'm non-aggressive. Utterly. Really, I'm embarrassed about the whole thing, and I want to take it up with Base just as soon as possible. I'm sure that when they learn that Ganymede has inhabitants they'll be just as upset as I and cancel the mission. I'm sure they'll cancel the mission."

"I don't know," the alien says. "The whole situation is very dangerous. Should we eliminate him?"

"Let's give him a little while longer," the other alien says. "After all, he's being honest with us. He has no authority."

"But I have good faith," Walker says. "I can show good faith." He feels the shaping of an idea. "I really could show you that I mean what I'm saying and that—"

"How about another two hours?" an alien says. "Two hours so that he can explain the situation."

"Give him three."

"Yes," Walker says, "I'll clear the thing up in three hours. That would be fine. And if I don't—"

"If you don't," the ordnance expert says, rubbing his appendage through the P on Ganymede Police, bringing it to something of a shine, "if you don't, we'll take measures."

"I will," Walker says, "I really will," and leans forward to tell them a lot more about the good faith he will show but they vanish; so much for their interest, and certain beeps from the transmitter indicate that Base thinks it is about time that he came out of rest period and did some useful tasks. "You dirty sons of bitches," Walker says to the receiver and then shudders with a thin sense of shock; he had never realized until this instant that he felt that way about them.

VII

He tries to bring up the matter of the aliens with Base but they are not hearing any of it at the moment; for reasons which are not made quite clear, he is to give another speech almost instantly. "Come on, come on," Base nags him as he moves around the cabin setting up the equipment once again, "don't you understand there's no time to waste? It seems to have something to do with riots and protests or perhaps Walker is merely working on a chain of inference. At any rate, the speech when he delivers it is full of soothing phrases and rather frantic reassurances which, because he has had no time to discuss it beforehand, make his delivery rather strained and awkward. "The project was rebuilt from the ground up for the sake of mankind," he finds himself saying and "Certain insignificant but noisy fractions of the populace are participating in a poison campaign" and "Ganymede, the jewel of the heavens, hangs before me now as a token forever of the ingenuity of mankind, his courage, his mission," and "The purpose of this expedition goes far beyond advantage to one party or persons" and when he has finished the speech the transmitters go into a glittering series of explosions, wires and circuits jetting a pure horrifying flame which he can only witness until they turn to smoke and ash. Base informs him that there is some minor problem, sabotaged circuits on the conveyors or whatever, and asks him to hold firm; they will be back to him in due course. "Another speech," Base says, "you'll have to do another speech."

"Listen," Walker says, "about those aliens—"

"No time," Base says. "Certain adjustments have to be made here."

"But there are aliens—"

"I'm sorry," Base says. The tone is regretful, contained, the sound of disconnection a crisp pop in the empty spaces of the cabin. Walker squeezes himself through a hatchway or two and, blowing some dust off the armaments, looks it over. It seems comprehensible enough. He recalls vaguely reading an instruction booklet once.

VIII

"Children?" his wife had said. "Do you think I'm crazy?" and had looked at him with a mad, bleak expression; confronting her that way, in the jammed spaces of the bed, he had understood for the first time how far it had all gone and the depths of her estrangement. "Do you really think that I'd bring children into this situation? You don't understand me, do you?" she said, turning, her back fitting smoothly, coldly, against the palpitations of his chest, "you don't understand a single thing that ever went on; I can see that now. I can see everything."

"It isn't that bad," he said, mumbling, futile, holding himself below in an instinctive gesture of loss, feeling the sag of his scrotal sac through spread fingers. (Could such devastation come from something that minute, that vulnerable?) "Things aren't what they should be but we're still going on; there's been a real leveling off of international tension and the race problems, well, we'll always have a race problem but some of the space pressure is easing and—"

"Oh, you damned fool," she said against him, her voice mingling into laughter, "you damned *fool*, do you think I'm talking about the world? The hell with the world! Do you really think I'd bring children to *us*?" And broke into laughter then, full harsh laughter, and Walker turned from her, back to back; like some sea beast, they had jammed against one another in the night, his mumbles and sighs against her whimpers, the conjoinment of their buttocks hard and yet somehow perfect under the cold damp of the sheets. And in the morning had fucked, simply and unspeakingly, he rising above her to such heights that he felt he could confront the walls.

Well, that had been a long time ago. No point in getting into any of that so late in the game.

He finds himself thinking that in many ways, in certain aspects, she had looked like the aliens.

IX

Base tells him that the mission must be aborted. They

have no specific explanation but say that it has something to do with certain strains and stresses surrounding the project and also a vague issue of public safety. It has nothing to do with his conduct, which was exemplary but failed, somehow, to work. Perhaps later on they will be able to explain things to him in detail although there cannot be any guarantees; matters are somewhat confusing. Walker asks if there are any more transmissions for him to deliver and Base says no, thank you, not at this time, there is no point to it and in any event there is certain difficulty with the communications. They will wheel him out of the next orbit and take him home. He asks them if they want him to do the planned probe and the leaving of the artifacts and Base says no, there really is no time for this and they can do it, perhaps, next time around. Walker gathers that the situation is somewhat obscure and perhaps they are withholding certain information from him. "Trust us," Base says. "It's going to be a very difficult re-entry because of certain problems here but we'll talk you through without the automatics and everything will work out well. Trust us," Base says and leaves him alone for the time being. Walker busies himself dismantling the equipment for transmission and then lies on his bunk, arms behind his head, whistling absently through his teeth and trying to think of nothing at all. There really is little enough on his mind; the ship will be yanked out of orbit through remote control. The aliens return, looking dour. Walker raises a hand.

"I'm leaving," he says. "Don't worry about a thing. I'm leaving after the next orbit."

"Ah," the spokesman says, "that's fine. Nevertheless, you did not obey our instructions. More than three hours have elapsed since our final warning."

"I'm leaving anyway. What's the difference?"

"You defied us."

"Listen," Walker says, "you understand that there was no intent to intrude. We had no hostile intent. It was all a mistake."

"Nevertheless you were warned."

"I did what I could. Still, I'm leaving."

"Not sufficient," the alien says. He turns to the other. "Not sufficient," the other says. "It's a serious infraction."

"Listen to me," Walker says, sitting and coming over to crouch near the aliens (they are really quite short and at this height he can regard them level; see what truly attractive creatures they are). "I'll show good faith. I understand your position and I'm willing to show good faith. Just to point out to you that this was all a mistake."

"How can you? We can take very severe retaliatory action, you understand."

"Don't worry about it," Walker says. He leans forward, throws out an explicatory palm. Everything is very simple as long as you take it step by step. He explains.

The aliens listen quietly, look at one another, finally nod. They agree that what Walker offers seems sufficient. Under the circumstances it is a fair and equitable offer.

Walker smiles and relaxes. For the last ten minutes of his stay in the orbit of Ganymede, he and the aliens talk intimately to one another, exchanging reminiscences, observations and, in Walker's case, some very frank details about sexual preferences of his wife which, unjustified as they were, simply drove him mad.

X

Crouching over the armaments, suspended heavily against the wall, Walker finally sinks into a tension-induced doze, a sleep supported by sedatives and loss which carries him through five million miles of space. In this sleep he dreams that he is once again fifteen years old and present at the End of the World; staring through the window of the home in which he was born, he sees the sky turn into fire, the fire into streaks which encircle and enflame everything which he has always known. There goes the tree in the back yard, there goes the boot factory up on the hill, there goes the home of the girl whom he will, in some years, marry. She appears in the center of the flames, mournful, stricken, yearning, her mouth slowly opening to passion or torment at the center of the fire, and as the flames take her to agony she breaks into an expression more yielding than any he has ever known and, pressed as he is against his window, watching her through binoculars, he feels that he could reach and touch her, hold her in his arm, protect her against the devastation . . . but this is impossible, she is dead beyond recovery, and he wakes screaming, screaming, against the cold web of the armaments which seem to snatch at him with gears come alive and he hangs on for all he is worth, waiting, waiting, only a few million miles more to Earth and he can bring upon them, upon her, a judgment more truthful than any they have ever known. "Because you deserve it, you sons of bitches," he says.

Behind him, the two aliens, along for the ride, chuckle wisely and make circles of approval at one another with their strange webbed appendages.

NO. 2 PLAIN TANK

Auxiliary Fill
Structural Limit 17,605 lbs.
Fuel—PWA Spec. 522 Revised

EDWARD BRYANT

Ed Bryant, whose crisply executed short stories have been appearing in many s-f collections in the past few years, here draws together half a dozen strands of contemporary paranoia in a sharp-edged little item that goes straight to its target with the impact of a rocket-propelled spear.

"The sub-underground Henry Bliss Society was apparently organized in July 1976, in a root-cellar somewhere near Wichita, Kansas. The group was named in memory of the first recorded automobile statistic. On September 13, 1899, Henry H. Bliss was knocked down and run over by an automobile as he was alighting from a southbound streetcar at Central Park West and 74th Street, New York City."

—RADICAL ECOLOGY GROUPS:
AN INQUIRY AND EVALUATION

So the stewardess appears at the front of the compartment in her redwhiteandblue jumper, bright and cornfed, looking a bit constipated. Her smile has been permanently glazed in place at the airlines school. I doubt she sleeps with anyone; who would want to roll over and kiss her *rictus sardonicus?*

"Good afternoon, ladies and gentlemen, and welcome aboard United Flight 880, Concorde service to New York. May I direct your attention to the oxygen mask directly above your seat? It is unlikely that the cabin should lose pressure, but in the event that—"

A strange thing has happened to me this morning in the Denver Drumstick Restaurant on East Colfax. I get in just before the 11:00 A.M. deadline after which you can no longer order the two eggs, toast, and hash browns special for 69¢, and take a Naugahyde lap at the counter.

"Okay," I say to the waitress, who bears an uncanny resemblance now that I think about it (genetic? environmental?) to the nice girl at the front of the compartment who is explaining why we can't smoke in our masks in the event of explosive decompression. Anyhow, to the girl in the Denver Drumstick I say, "Give me the breakfast special," and she automatically asks if I want coffee and I, of course, answer yes. She brings the coffee and I find the cream's curdled. I drink the little white speckles anyway since I don't want to cause trouble and draw attention to myself.

Then into the Drumstick walks a dude with a big burlap sack (like barley or oats come in) over his shoulder. He sits down beside me and flops the bag down on the counter. I shield my coffee cup with my palm so that oat chaff doesn't blow in—curdled cream's bad enough. On the other side of the bag a guy's chicken-fried steak gets pushed off the counter and makes a gravy Rorschach. But it's only a short Ceylonese in a turban on a Discover America tour and who cares anyway?

The dude upends the sack and out roll three little kids. "My sons," he says. "Set 'em up Cokes, all three." The kids look around vacantly and autistic drool runs down three chins.

I don't wait for my eggs and hash browns, but get up and leave. I realize outside the restaurant and halfway down the block that I left fingerprints on my spoon and the handle of the cup. Hell, I'll take the chance, so I don't go back.

"May I also point out the emergency escape doors located on either side of the plane, over the wings and in the rear."

I look out the window of the emergency door on my side above the wing and wonder what would happen if they pumped in seventeen thousand, six hundred and six pounds. Never know.

There's a line waiting to take off and we roll to a rest on the runway approach. I get the old clipping out of my wallet. It's faded and brittle along the fold-lines. From the *Rocky Mountain News*, years ago:

> Former CSU student Cameron Davis, 27, is sought in connection with the dynamiting in January of 1969 of three Public Service Co. power transmission towers in the Denver area.
>
> Davis, who has been placed on the FBI's "10 Most Wanted" list, has been the object of an extensive search by the FBI.
>
> He is believed to be out of the country.
>
> The dynamiting charge against Davis was filed under the Sabotage Act of 1918, which makes it a federal crime for any person to disrupt any communications or installations classified as "necessary for the defense of the nation."
>
> The FBI said due to outage of a Public Service Co. tower at 10th and Ulysses streets in Golden, the production of war materials at the Coors Porcelain Plant was disrupted.

I have time to reread the clipping a few hundred times during the forty minutes we wait at the head of the runway.

Metal detectors are easy to fool.

The man who blew the power towers! Cameron Davis, you are a goddamn genuine folk hero. And someday you'll be a myth. To hell with Emmett Grogan. Cameron Davis, you live.

I wish I understood fully that sign stenciled on the wing below my window.

My partner has bought it last night at the Crazy Horse Revolving Bar in Denver. Krista Puffin (billed as the girl with the German 88s) is on the turntable flashing around at about 150 rpm doing her thing with centrifugal force. Arthur screams something about "Borden defense contracts" and leaps at her. Just inside the advertised Radius of Ecstasy there is a KA-PLAFF! of flesh against skull and Arthur flips sideways, landing on his head. Concussion, I guess. I cut out before the ambulance gets here. A deliberate strike—CIA? FBI? OSS? Maybe just an accident; I don't know. Maybe it all has something to do with strontium 90. Arthur was a physics grad at Berkeley before he went underground.

(Whoof! Heavy kick in the butt, these engines on the SST. And already I see Stapleton Field dwindling to port as we bank and head for Fun City.)

Plastique and fluoric acid fuses. You can do it with your Gilbert Chemistry Set.

Another stewardess lurches out of her cubby saying, "There is a short in the electrical system, disregard the sign, do not remove your safety belts yet."

This one's nicer-looking, with green eyes and oriental features. I fantasize us together naked in a telephone booth. She squeezes Gleem toothpaste all over my body and then brushes me down. Makes the skin all tingly.

"Would you like something to drink, sir?"

"Seven-up," I say. At least give my tongue a tingle.

Clouds down below, and we gain more altitude. I think about all the supersonic crap spewing out into the greenhouse effect and I feel like having a rash. ECOLOGY IS REVOLUTION, says the Day-Glow sticker on the bumper of my VW back in Colorado. Or is it REVOLUTION IS ECOLOGY? One or the other.

Agnew wristwatch says (loudly) maybe another minute. Fuse time is approximate.

Read my clipping again.

Where's the Seven-Up?

And why not use the clipping as a bookmark—a direction to the future? In it goes. My book, so carefully disemboweled, was just the right size.

Some reviewer in 1969 called Ehrlich's ecology book *The Population Bomb* "an explosive text."

Oh, he should see it now.

EUREMA'S DAM

R. A. LAFFERTY

This is a story about a schlemiel, to use a word probably not too often heard in Raphael Aloysius Lafferty's home town of Tulsa, Oklahoma. The schlemiel story is a genre I always thought I'd avoid if I were an editor, for it has seemed to me that stories about losers, twerps, dullards, and schnooks would be of interest only to an audience of losers, twerps, dullards, and schnooks, at best, and no such people would be reading anything I edited. Well, never mind all that. R. A. Lafferty is a cunning and tricky writer, and—as can quickly be seen—the schlemiel he creates for us here is of an extraordinary sort.

He was about the last of them.

What? The last of the great individualists? The last of the true creative geniuses of the century? The last of the sheer precursors?

No. No. He was the last of the dolts.

Kids were being born smarter all the time when he came along, and they would be so forever more. He was about the last dumb kid ever born.

Even his mother had to admit that Albert was a slow child. What else can you call a boy who doesn't begin to talk till he is four years old, who won't learn to handle a spoon till he is six, who can't operate a doorknob till he is eight? What else can you say about one who put his shoes on the wrong feet and walked in pain? And who had to be told to close his mouth after yawning?

Some things would always be beyond him—like whether it was the big hand or the little hand of the clock that told the hours. But this wasn't something serious. He never did care what time it was.

When, about the middle of his ninth year, Albert made a breakthrough at telling his right hand from his left he did it by the most ridiculous set of mnemonics ever put together. It had to do with the way dogs turn around before lying down, the direction of whirlpools and whirlwinds, the side a cow is milked from and a horse is mounted from, the direction of twist of oak and sycamore leaves, the maze patterns of rock moss and tree moss, the cleavage of limestone, the direction of a hawk's wheeling, a shrike's hunting, and a snake's coiling (remembering that the Mountain Boomer is an exception), the lay of cedar fronds and balsam fronds, the twist of a hole dug by a skunk and by a badger (remembering pungently that skunks sometimes use old badger holes). Well, Albert finally learned to remember which was right and which was left, but an observant boy would have learned his right hand from his left without all that nonsense.

Albert never learned to write a readable hand. To get by in school he cheated. From a bicycle speedometer, a midget motor, tiny eccentric cams, and batteries stolen from his grandfather's hearing aid Albert made a machine to write for him. It was small as a doodlebug and fitted onto pen or pencil so that Albert could conceal it with his fingers. It formed the letters beautifully as Albert had set the cams to follow a copybook model. He triggered the different letters with keys no bigger than whiskers. Sure it was crooked, but what else can you do when you're too dumb to learn how to write passably?

Albert couldn't figure at all. He had to make another machine to figure for him. It was a palm-of-the-hand thing that would add and subtract and multiply and divide. The next year when he was in the ninth grade they gave him algebra, and he had to devise a flipper to go on the end of his gadget to work quadratic and simultaneous equations. If it weren't for such cheating Albert wouldn't have gotten any marks at all in school.

He had another difficulty when he came to his fifteenth year. People, that is an understatement. There should be a stronger word than "difficulty" for it. He was afraid of girls.

What to do?

"I will build me a machine that is not afraid of girls," Albert said. He set to work on it. He had it nearly finished when a thought came to him: "But no machine is afraid of girls. How will this help me?"

His logic was at fault and analogy broke down. He did what he always did. He cheated.

He took the programming rollers from an old player piano in the attic, found a gear case that would serve, used magnetized sheets instead of perforated music rolls, fed a copy of Wormwood's *Logic* into the matrix, and he had a logic machine that would answer questions.

"What's the matter with me that I'm afraid of girls?" Albert asked his logic machine.

"Nothing the matter with you," the logic machine told him. "It's logical to be afraid of girls. They seem pretty spooky to me too."

"But what can I do about it?"

"Wait for time and circumstances. They sure are slow. Unless you want to cheat—"

"Yes, yes, what then?"

"Build a machine that looks just like you, Albert, and talks just like you. Only make it smarter than you are, and not bashful. And, ah, Albert, there's a special thing you'd better put into it in case things go wrong. I'll whisper it to you. It's dangerous."

So Albert made Little Danny, a dummy who looked like him and talked like him, only he was smarter and not bashful. He filled Little Danny with quips from *Mad* magazine and from *Quip*, and then they were set.

Albert and Little Danny went to call on Alice.

"Why, he's wonderful!" Alice said. "Why can't you be like that, Albert? Aren't you wonderful, Little Danny? Why do you have to be so stupid, Albert, when Little Danny is so wonderful?"

"I, uh, uh, I don't know," Albert said, "uh, uh, uh."

"He sounds like a fish with the hiccups," Little Danny said.

"You do, Albert, really you do!" Alice screamed. "Why can't you say smart things like Little Danny does, Albert? Why are you so stupid?"

This wasn't working out very well, but Albert kept with it. He programmed Little Danny to play the ukulele and to sing. He wished that he could program himself to do it. Alice loved everything about Little Danny, but she paid no attention to Albert. And one day Albert had had enough.

"Wha- wha- what do we need with this dummy?" Albert asked. "I just made him to am- to amu- to make you laugh. Let's go off and leave him."

"Go off with you, Albert?" Alice asked. "But you're so stupid. I tell you what. Let's you and me go off and leave Albert, Little Danny. We can have more fun without him."

"Who needs him?" Little Danny asked. "Get lost, Buster."

Albert walked away from them. He was glad that he'd taken his logic machine's advice as to the special thing to be built into Little Danny. He walked fifty steps. A hundred. "Far enough," Albert said, and he pushed a button in his pocket.

Nobody but Albert and his logic machine ever did know what that explosion was. Tiny wheels out of Little Danny and small pieces of Alice rained down a little later, but there weren't enough fragments for anyone to identify.

Albert had learned one lesson from his logic machine: never make anything that you can't unmake.

Well, Albert finally grew to be a man, in years at least. He would always have something about him of a very awkward teen-ager. And yet he fought his own war against those who were teen-agers in years, and defeated them completely. There was enmity between them forever. He hadn't been a very well-adjusted adolescent, and he hated the memory of it. And nobody ever mistook him for an adjusted man.

Albert was too awkward to earn a living at an honest

trade. He was reduced to peddling his little tricks and contrivances to shysters and promoters. But he did back into a sort of fame, and he did become burdened with wealth.

He was too stupid to handle his own monetary affairs, but he built an actuary machine to do his investing and became rich by accident; he built the damned thing too good and he regretted it.

Albert became one of that furtive group that has saddled us with all the mean things in our history. There was that Punic who couldn't learn the rich variety of hieroglyphic characters and who devised the crippled short alphabet for wan-wits. There was the nameless Arab who couldn't count beyond ten and who set up the ten-number system for babies and idiots. There was the double-Dutchman with his movable type who drove fine copy out of the world. Albert was of their miserable company.

Albert himself wasn't much good at anything. But he had in himself a low knack for making machines that were good at everything.

His machines did a few things. You remember that anciently there was smog in the cities. Oh, it could be drawn out of the air easily enough. All it took was a tickler. Albert made a tickler machine. He would set it fresh every morning. It would clear the air in a circle three hundred yards around his hovel and gather a little over a ton of residue every twenty-four hours. This residue was rich in large polysyllabic molecules which one of his chemical machines could use.

"Why can't you clear all the air?" the people asked him.

"This is as much of the stuff as Clarence Deoxyribonucleiconibus needs every day," Albert said. That was the name of this particular chemical machine.

"But we die from the smog," the people told him. "Have mercy on us."

"Oh, all right," Albert said. He turned it over to one of his reduplicating machines to make as many copies as were necessary.

You remember that once there was a teen-ager problem? You remember when those little buggers used to be mean? Albert got enough of them. There was something ungainly about them that reminded him too much of himself. He made a teen-ager of his own. It was rough. To the others it looked like one of themselves, the ring in the left ear, the dangling side-locks, the brass knucks and the long knife, the guitar pluck to jab in the eye. But it was incomparably rougher than the human teen-agers. It terrorized all in the neighborhood and made them behave, and dress like real people. There was one thing about the teen-age machine that Albert made. It was made of such polarized metal and glass that it was invisible except to teen-ager eyes.

"Why is your neighborhood different?" the people asked him. "Why are there such good and polite teen-agers in your neighborhood and such mean ones everywhere else? It's as though something had spooked all those right around here."

"Oh, I thought I was the only one who didn't like the regular kind," Albert said.

"Oh no, no," the people said. "If there is anything at all you can do about it—"

So Albert turned his mostly invisible teen-ager machine over to one of his reduplicating machines to make as many copies as were necessary, and set up one in every neighborhood. From that day to this the teen-agers have all been good and polite and a little bit frightened. But there is no evidence of what keeps them that way except an occasional eye dangling from the jab of an invisible guitar pluck.

So the two most pressing problems of the latter part of the twentieth century were solved, but accidentally and to the credit of no one.

As the years went by, Albert felt his inferiority most when in the presence of his own machines, particularly those in the form of men. Albert just hadn't their urbanity or sparkle or wit. He was a clod beside them, and they made him feel it.

Why not? One of Albert's devices sat in the President's Cabinet. One of them was on the High Council of World-Watchers that kept the peace everywhere. One of them presided at Riches Unlimited, that private-public-in-

ternational instrument that guaranteed reasonable riches
to everyone in the world. One of them was the guiding
hand in the Health and Longevity Foundation that provided those things to everyone. Why should not such
splendid and successful machines look down on their
shabby uncle who had made them?

"I'm rich by a curious twist," Albert said to himself
one day, "and honored through a mistake of circumstance.
But there isn't a man or a machine in the world who is really my friend. A book here tells how to make friends, but
I can't do it that way. I'll make one my own way."

So Albert set out to make a friend.

He made Poor Charles, a machine as stupid and awkward and inept as himself. "Now I will have a companion," Albert said, but it didn't work. Add two zeros together and you still have zero. Poor Charles was too much
like Albert to be good for anything.

Poor Charles! Unable to think, he made a—(*but wait a
moleskin-gloved minute here, Colonel, this isn't going to
work at all*)—he made a machi—(*but isn't this the same
blamed thing all over again?*)—he made a machine to
think for him and to—

Hold it, hold it! That's enough. Poor Charles was the
only machine that Albert ever made that was dumb
enough to do a thing like that.

Well, whatever it was, the machine that Poor Charles
made was in control of the situation and of Poor Charles
when Albert came onto them accidentally. The machine's
machine, the device that Poor Charles had constructed to
think for him, was lecturing Poor Charles in a humiliating
way.

"Only the inept and the deficient will invent," that
damned machine's machine was droning. "The Greeks in
their high period did not invent. They used neither ad-
junct power nor instrumentation. They used, as intelligent
men or machines will always use, slaves. They did not de-
scend to gadgets. They, who did the difficult with ease,
did not seek the easier way.

"But the incompetent will invent. The insufficient will
invent. The depraved will invent. And knaves will
invent."

Albert, in a seldom fit of anger, killed them both. But

he knew that the machine of his machine had spoken the truth.

Albert was very much cast down. A more intelligent man would have had a hunch as to what was wrong. Albert had only a hunch that he was not very good at hunches and would never be. Seeing no way out, he fabricated a machine and named it Hunchy.

In most ways this was the worst machine he ever made. In building it he tried to express something of his unease for the future. It was an awkward thing in mind and mechanism, a misfit.

His more intelligent machines gathered around and hooted at him while he put it together.

"Boy! Are you lost!" they taunted. "That thing is a primitive! To draw its power from the ambient! We talked you into throwing that away twenty years ago and setting up coded power for all of us."

"Uh—someday there may be social disturbances and all centers of power and apparatuses seized," Albert stammered. "But Hunchy would be able to operate if the whole world were wiped smooth."

"It isn't even tuned to our information matrix," they jibed. "It's worse than Poor Charles. That stupid thing practically starts from scratch."

"Maybe there'll be a new kind of itch for it," said Albert.

"It's not even housebroken!" the urbane machines shouted their indignation. "Look at that! Some sort of primitive lubrication all over the floor."

"Remembering my childhood, I sympathize," Albert said.

"What's it good for?" they demanded.

"Ah—it gets hunches," Albert mumbled.

"Duplication!" they shouted. "That's all you're good for yourself, and not very good at that. We suggest an election to replace you as—pardon our laughter—head of these enterprises."

"Boss, I got a hunch how we can block them there," the unfinished Hunchy whispered.

"They're bluffing," Albert whispered back. "My first logic machine taught me never to make anything I can't unmake. I've got them there, and they know it. I wish I could think up things like that myself."

"Maybe there will come an awkward time and I will be good for something," Hunchy said.

Only once, and that rather late in life, did a sort of honesty flare up in Albert. He did one thing (and it was a dismal failure) on his own. That was the night in the year of the double millennium when Albert was presented with the Finnerty-Hochmann Trophy, the highest award that the intellectual world could give. Albert was certainly an odd choice for it, but it had been noticed that almost every basic invention for thirty years could be traced back to him or to the devices with which he had surrounded himself.

You know the trophy. Atop it was Eurema, the synthetic Greek goddess of invention, with arms spread as though she would take flight. Below this was a stylized brain cut away to show the convoluted cortex. And below this was the coat of arms of the Academicians: Ancient Scholar rampant (argent); the Anderson Analyzer sinister (gules); the Mondeman Space-Drive dexter (vair). It was a very fine work by Groben, his ninth period.

Albert had the speech composed for him by his speechwriting machine, but for some reason he did not use it. He went on his own, and that was disaster. He got to his feet when he was introduced, and he stuttered and spoke nonsense:

"Ah—only the sick oyster produces nacre," he said, and they all gaped at him. What sort of beginning for a speech was that? "Or do I have the wrong creature?" Albert asked weakly.

"Eurema does not look like that!" Albert gawked out and pointed suddenly at the trophy. "No, no, that isn't her at all. Eurema walks backward and is blind. And her mother is a brainless hulk."

Everybody was watching him with pained expression.

"Nothing rises without a leaven," Albert tried to explain, "but the yeast is itself a fungus and a disease. You be regularizers all, splendid and supreme. But you cannot live without the irregulars. You will die, and who will tell you that you are dead? When there are no longer any deprived or insufficient, who will invent? What will you do when there are none of us defectives left? Who will leaven your lump then?"

"Are you unwell?" the master of ceremonies asked him quietly. "Should you not make an end of it? People will understand."

"Of course I'm unwell. Always have been," Albert said. "What good would I be otherwise? You set the ideal that all should be healthy and well adjusted. No! No! Were we all well adjusted, we would ossify and die. The world is kept healthy only by some of the unhealthy minds lurking in it. The first implement made by man was not a scraper or celt or stone knife. It was a crutch, and it wasn't devised by a hale man."

"Perhaps you should rest," a functionary said in a low voice, for this sort of rambling nonsense talk had never been heard at an awards dinner before.

"Know you," said Albert, "that it is not the fine bulls and wonderful cattle who make the new paths. Only a crippled calf makes a new path. In everything that survives there must be an element of the incongruous. Hey, you know the woman who said, 'My husband is incongruous, but I never liked Washington in the summertime.'"

Everybody gazed at him in stupor.

"That's the first joke I ever made," Albert said lamely. "My joke-making machine makes them lots better than I do." He paused and gaped, and gulped a big breath. "Dolts!" he croaked out fiercely then. "What will you do for dolts when the last of us is gone? How will you survive without us?"

Albert had finished. He gaped and forgot to close his mouth. They led him back to his seat. His publicity machine explained that Albert was tired from overwork, and then the thing passed around copies of the speech that Albert was supposed to have given.

It had been an unfortunate episode. How noisome it is that the innovators are never great men. And the great men are never good for anything but just being great men.

In that year a decree went forth from Caesar that a census of the whole country should be taken. The decree was from Cesare Panebianco, the President of the country; it was the decimal year proper for the census, and there was nothing unusual about the decree. Certain provisions, however, were made for taking a census of the drifters and decrepits who were usually missed, to examine them and to see why they were so. It was in the course of this that Albert was picked up. If any man ever looked like a drifter and a decrepit, it was Albert.

Albert was herded in with other derelicts, sat down at a table, and asked tortuous questions. As:

"What is your name?"

He almost muffed that one, but he rallied and answered, "Albert."

"What time is it by that clock?"

They had him there in his old weak spot. Which hand was which? He gaped and didn't answer.

"Can you read?"

"Not without my—" Albert began. "I don't have with me my— No, I can't read very well by myself."

"Try."

They gave him a paper to mark up with true and false questions. Albert marked them all true, believing that he would have half of them right. But they were all false. The regularized people are partial to falsehood. Then they gave him a supply-the-word test on proverbs.

"———— is the best policy" didn't mean a thing to him. He couldn't remember the names of the companies that he had his own policies with.

"A ———— in time saves nine" contained more mathematics than Albert could handle. "There appear to be six unknowns," he told himself, "and only one positive value, nine. The equating verb 'saves' is a vague one. I cannot solve this equation. I am not even sure that it is an equation. If only I had with me my—"

But he hadn't any of his gadgets or machines with him. He was on his own. He left half a dozen more proverb fill-ins blank. Then he saw the chance to recoup. Nobody is so dumb as not to know one answer if enough questions are asked.

"———— is the mother of invention," it said.

"Stupidity," Albert wrote in his weird ragged hand. Then he sat back in triumph. "I know that Eurema and her mother," he snickered. "Man, how I do know them!"

But they marked him wrong on that one too. He had missed every answer to every test. They began to fix him a ticket to a progressive booby hatch where he might learn to do something with his hands, his head being hopeless.

A couple of Albert's urbane machines came down and got him out of it. They explained that, while he was a drifter and derelict, yet he was a rich drifter and derelict and that he was even a man of some note.

"He doesn't look it, but he really is—pardon our laughter—a man of some importance," one of the fine machines explained. "He has to be told to close his mouth after he has yawned, but for all that he is the winner of the Finnerty-Hochmann Award. We will be responsible for him."

Albert was miserable as his fine machines took him out, especially when they asked that he walk three or four steps behind them and not seem to be with them. They gave him some pretty rough banter and turned him into a squirming worm of a man. Albert left them and went to a little hide-out he kept.

"I'll blow my crawfishing brains out," he swore. "The humiliation is more than I can bear. Can't do it myself, though. I'll have to have it done."

He set to work building a device in his hide-out.

"What you doing, boss?" Hunchy asked him. "I had a hunch you'd come here and start building something."

"Building a machine to blow my pumpkin-picking brains out," Albert shouted. "I'm too yellow to do it myself."

"Boss, I got a hunch there's something better to do. Let's have some fun."

"Don't believe I know how to," Albert said thoughtfully. "I built a fun machine once to do it for me. He had a real revel till he flew apart, but he never seemed to do anything for me."

"This fun will be for you and me. Consider the world spread out. What is it?"

"It's a world too fine for me to live in any longer," Albert said. "Everything and all the people are perfect, and all alike. They're at the top of the heap. They've won it all and arranged it all neatly. There's no place for a clutter-up like me in the world. So I get out."

"Boss, I've got a hunch that you're seeing it wrong. You've got better eyes than that. Look again, real canny, at it. Now what do you see?"

"Hunchy, Hunchy, is that possible? Is that really what it is? I wonder why I never noticed it before. That's the way of it, though, now that I look closer.

"Six billion patsies waiting to be took! Six billion patsies without a defense of any kind! A couple of guys out for some fun, man, they could mow them down like fields of Albert-Improved Concho Wheat!"

"Boss, I've got a hunch this is what I was made for. The world sure has been getting stuffy. Let's tie into it and eat off the top layer. Man, we can cut a swath!"

"We'll inaugurate a new era!" Albert gloated. "We'll call it the Turning of the Worm. We'll have fun, Hunchy. We'll gobble them up like goobers. How come I never saw it like that before? Six billion patsies!"

The twenty-first century began on this rather odd note.

KING HARVEST

GARDNER R. DOZOIS

Those of us who grew up in the late 1940s and early 1950s were labeled the Silent Generation by the image-makers; but the name seems a misnomer to me, because we talked ("rapped") all night, Kafka-Mann-Sartre-Trotsky- Schonberg. It's the present crop of under-thirties, seemingly having nothing more profound to say than "Heavy, man," and "Like wow," who sound like a Silent Generation to us, or at least like an inarticulate one. Gardner Dozois belongs to that generation, and wears its tribal ornaments—long hair, headband, steel-rimmed glasses, the works—but he's a welcome contrast to his peers, magnificently at home in the resources of our language. His moving, richly figured story, "A Special Kind of Morning," was for me the most important piece in the first **New Dimensions**; now, happily, he returns with another, more somber and much closer to home in theme, but no less eloquent.

On his way down to the dying ocean, Kagan came across some cops looting a grocery store. There were five of them, clustered around a prowl car that had been parked kitty-cornered to the curb to form a partial barricade. The prowl car was streaked with smoke and fire marks, half of the rear windshield was gone, and the shattered turret of the crash light gaped at the gray sky like a gouged, Cyclopean eye. The cops had just finished prying away the store's iron gates and smashing the glass from the window frame, and now two of them had stepped inside and were scooping canned goods into burlap bags. Almost as an afterthought, they broke the cash register open and fished a few wrinkled bills out of the till. Then they went back to stealing groceries. The other three cops remained outside: one sat behind the wheel of the idling prowl car, while the last two stood guard with riot guns. They all wore oxygen respirators—ribbed tubing snaked under their arms from back packs and connected to the blunt, ugly snouts of the masks. Blue smoke panted from the exhaust pipe of the car, and the noise of the big engine filled the street.

Kagan paused at the edge of the square. He watched the cops silently, standing hunch-shouldered, favoring his left leg. The muscles in his lined, exhausted face moved, shifted, played against one another—trying to express some violent, complex emotion: anger? disgust? fear? despair? They failed: his face registered only a huge weariness—it collapsed like a melting candle, slumped into puddled wax. His big hands came up, palms forward, pushed out, his fingers spreading wide, trembling, groping, trying to sculpt expression from the cindered air. Then they fell, slapping against his thighs, dangling bonelessly from the wrists. His shoulders slumped still further, collapsing into his chest. Words tumbled through his mind; he ran through them again and again without finding any combination that made sense—his thoughts tracked and scanned like a jukebox selector that cannot locate a certain record. This was too much—he could only define it with silence. Somehow this—*this*—focused the chaos of the last few days, brought it inescapably home: civilization was not coming back, it was all over. He listened to the sound of the looting: the crunch of broken glass under booted feet, the muted thunking of cans, slamming of drawers and cabinets, the labored breathing of the prowl car's exhaust. Then he shook his graying head, and his hands curled slowly into fists. He began to work his way around the circumference of the square.

A cop spotted him as he moved out of the cover of a building's shadow. The cop made a sharp, warning gesture with his riot gun, jerking the muzzle in the direction he wanted Kagan to go: away. He shouted something that was muffled by the oxygen rebreather. Kagan paused, instinctively drawing himself up. He found, to his surprise, that his skin was bristling, his gut pulled tight. His hands clenched, opened, clenched; he felt a vein start to throb in his forehead. The cop shouted again. Only his eyes were visible above the inhuman snout of the mask: They looked like wet rocks. The cop worked the action of his riot gun; the noise carried clearly across the square. Kagan felt his stomach turn over. Reluctantly, he turned and started to shuffle away toward the further rim of buildings. Behind him, the cop yelled a third time—a voice full of impatience and derision. Kagan began to walk faster, hobbling painfully, trying to keep as much weight as possible off his bum leg. But he wouldn't run. He pounded his fist against his thigh in rage and frustration. Christ send them all to hell and damnation, he wouldn't run. He'd paid taxes for twenty-five years— He laughed, suddenly, muttering under his breath at the absurdity of that. They had the guns—he could feel them trained on his back, along with those hard, maggot eyes. He could do nothing against them. But let them start shooting at him first, before he began to run. Okay? He owed himself at least that much pride, didn't he? After twenty-five years? So he told himself, counting each step, a long minute, two, and then he had reached the far side of the square, and no shots had come. He stood with one foot on the curb, feeling like a fool. He wasn't even important enough to kill: they'd known that they could scare him away. He didn't matter in the new order of things. Kagan limped up onto the sidewalk. He never had mattered, he realized, he never had at all. It was just that now the wraps were off, and nobody had time any more to pretend, to keep up the polite fantasy that an individual citizen counted for shit. He turned to look back at the cops. At this distance, it was hard to see the small areas of exposed flesh on their faces and hands—they looked like manikins made of leather and hard plastic and polished wood, rubber tubing and dull iron and blued steel: forbidding, martial golems. Now the golems were loading the prowl car with groceries, moving with efficient coordination, seemingly in time to some unknown, private music. One of them gestured at Kagan again—a contemptuous, shooing motion. Behind him, the dance went on.

Kagan selected a street and followed it away from the

square. The street dipped gradually down toward the ocean, curved: the cops were lost to sight, the sound of the engine faded. Buildings closed in on either side—rows of dilapidated tenements: tall, narrow, rotting, tilting and settling at odd angles, leaning against each other like tired old men. Faded brick and dirty plaster, rusted fire escapes zigzagging down the faces of the derelict buildings, sagging, clinging weakly to the walls, iron ladders hanging down onto the sidewalk in boneless lassitude. The street changed under Kagan's feet, becoming rougher, metamorphosing from asphalt into weathered cobblestone. The uneven footing accentuated his limp, threw his stride off, heel-toe-heel, *click-clack-click*. The dissonance echoed around the high, shuttered walls. Kagan walked more slowly, slower still, finally came to a stop. He stood, panting, weight on his good foot, listening to the echoes wash away. Anger had fueled him the first few hundred yards from the square, but now his fury had drained away, leaving only a scummy residue of futility. There was nothing he could do—it was too late for anything. All over the world at this moment, atrocities far worse than the looting of a store were taking place. He had seen some of them himself, the last two days. But before he had hung onto the delusion that there were sides to take, a struggle for something: authority against dissidents, order against chaos, preservers against destroyers. That was nonsense. There were no sides, no issues, no goals to this—chaos had already taken over. If he had a gun and a fast car he'd be doing the same thing—clawing desperately for survival, trying to bull his way through somehow, and too bad for anyone in the way. He laughed: disgust, self-contempt, corroding irony. So much for morality. All the civilized niceties were gone—there was no way to help anyone else when you could barely keep yourself alive, when every person you carried would only decrease your own chances of survival. It would be foolish to even try. Everyone was a stranger now; there was no way to fight that ultimate isolation. There were only two alternatives left: he could sit down and wait for the cold to kill him, right here, right now, or he could continue walking, aimlessly, directed only by murky, unverbalized pressures, vague yearnings—

even though he had no idea where to go to escape, or how to get there, or what to do once he had arrived.

Kagan pulled his coat more tightly about him, stuck his hands in his pockets for warmth, and shuffled off again, following the street down. It was nearing full darkness—the last traces of a sunset were fading behind the shabby buildings at the crest of the hill: deep gun-metal gray, somber purple and red, browns, bars of black. A grim, winter sky. The sun had only been visible at dusk, briefly showing a disk before it slipped under the horizon. The sight had not cheered Kagan, although he had been hoping fruitlessly all afternoon for a bit of sunlight: the sun had seemed without warmth, a cold, lidless red eye—distorted, filtered, and obscured by the foulness of the intervening air.

Night came down then like a cap over a candle: snuffing the day with unusual rapidity, all at once, as though the last rays of light had been swallowed, ·blotted up by the atmosphere. Kagan walked slowly through the darkness, taking it easy, trying to maintain a steady pace that wouldn't strain his leg. At the corner of an intersecting road, he stopped and looked around, trying to get his bearings. There was nothing to see, but plenty of it: black and smothering. No landmarks. He swore peevishly at himself for being lost. He had lived all his life within three miles of this spot in one direction or the other—moving around a lot but never leaving the general district, even when he got married, took his master's. The kids had moved upstate when they were grown, but he couldn't, though they'd said that he should, urged him to move—he'd never wanted to, not even for a moment, in spite of the muggings, the junkies, the noise, the filth, the crime, all the things the kids used as arguments, the things he knew as well as they and grieved over much more deeply than they ever could: but his wife was buried here, and his parents, and his parent's parents, and he couldn't leave. He was a city man, was all, and this area'd been his home as far back as he could remember. He'd even lived in the very neighborhood that he was groping through like a blind worm at the festering end of the world—lived, when he was a kid, on one of the steep streets that climbed up from the square, in one of the "new" postwar high-rises: more sterile and less squalid than the crumbling brick tenements, mostly bluff sandstone and whitewashed concrete, cement yards bordered by cyclone fences, the walls inside carefully painted half green and half white in accordance with sound psychological doctrine, a copy of the landlord's officious "regulations" posted at every landing of the stairwell—

Kagan jerked awake. He stumbled, almost fell, and staggered in a drunken swoop back toward the center of the street. Sweat blossomed in his armpits, the back of his knees. He shook with realization and nausea: he'd been walking in a daze, without volition, almost unconscious, his ankle pressed against the curb, mechanically following its curve—a wind-up walking toy that has bumped into the raised edge of the display table.

Cursing feebly, Kagan bent over and let his head hang below his knees, counting slowly to twenty. When he straightened up, blood roared in his ears and squiggly afterimages crawled over his eyes, but he felt steadier, more alert. He spat, sickness sour in his mouth. The air, he thought, roiling a murk of fear and outrage too articulate for words, the air. There was no sustenance to be had from it, little use in breathing any more; instead of renewing, it etched away the reason, numbed the spirit, drained the strength. It tasted foul—an actual taste, something between copper and clay, with a strong hint of rotten eggs—and it left a furry, cloying sensation in the back of his mouth, as if his throat had been stuffed with lint and bitter ashes. The air, he repeated. He felt—what? Betrayed. Yes. By whom? Helplessly, he started walking again. There was nothing else to do. Surely the air should be, was— Sacred? Basic and inviolable. Indivisible, with liberty and justice for all. He peered dully up at a lamppost; there were no street lights, and he couldn't make out the signs he knew were there, could barely see the pole itself, the hunched tenements that hemmed him on either side. He'd passed the cross street in his daze, still headed downhill, though only God knew where he was, and only the Devil cared. Damnation—the smothersoft rotting of living flesh. Maggots in blood, beating like hearts. Silence. He counted steps to stay awake, trying to keep his mind away from the fuzziness that waited to swallow it, to lap up and over like a whispering ocean of dust.

At one hundred, Kagan felt a change in the sound of his footsteps, in the quality of the wind behind him as it tore past and out. Ahead, the darkness opened up, a feeling of space and wet emptiness, the whistle of the wind changing pitch as it escaped from the narrow funnel of the street. Kagan picked his way out into this damp, echoing hollow, fumbling and tapping, until he could sense—not see: the objects hanging stubbornly at the edge of resolution, crimps in the night fabric, too indistinct even for shadows—another row of buildings somewhere in front of him. Then he turned at right angles to his old path and continued ahead, paralleling the unseen periphery.

This, Kagan told himself, inching through invisibility, must be the Avenue: the last major artery rimming this part of the city, at the foot of the hill he had descended from the square—further east, on the other side of the Avenue, was the maze of crooked, squalid streets that led at last to the docks, to the sea. If he followed the Avenue north, he should—he hoped—be able to eventually get to the bridge over the estuary, and then, on the further shore, he could turn west of north and so make his way upcountry. Hopefully that route would be the most devoid of traffic: the majority of the refugees had fled west, directly away from the sea. The slow dwindling of free oxygen from the atmosphere due to the death of its primary source, the phytoplankton in the blighted oceans, had started a desperate rush inland. Before the total breakdown of communications, a government scientist had announced his theory that survival would still be possible in the wilderness area rich in oxygen-producing vegetation, and although the theory had been assaulted by a dozen different experts, no one could claim to know exactly what would happen after the death of the sea, and even the slight hope conveyed by the scientist's message had been sufficient motivation for an exodus. "Orderly evacuation," the scientist had urged, invoking the ghost of Dunkirk, but it had soon become a panicked rout, helped along by the escalating chemical and bacteriological warfare attacks on population centers. The roads leading inland would surely be impassable, impossible, a disaster—clogged with human debris. But few people would think of following the shore line north. The streets around him bore out his speculations; they were deserted, lifeless, desolate—the parade had passed here hours ago, the inland rush leaving almost no one in the sections closest to the sea. Once he had cleared the city to the north, he could turn inland without having to force his way through the rotting metropolitan carcass, the twisted, ticking fragments of a clockwork mechanism finally overwound.

And then? Kagan refused to think about then—finding the Avenue and formulating even this scanty plan had awakened in him a tenuous hope, given him a direction in which to go, a sense of purpose to his activities, and he was afraid to examine any of it closely lest the whole shaky artifice vanish. Keeping his plan firmly in mind, clutching it, cherishing it, drawing a thin nourishment from it, Kagan made his way down the Avenue. It was a strange feeling, walking the river of empty asphalt in silence and darkness, deserted lanes rolling away on either hand. He felt oddly alien, fugitive, a mouse scurrying through vast and incomprehensible ruins, bright eye cocked for the cat. His feet made a hollow scuffing sound against the pavement. He began to count again, tallying the click of his heels. After he reached five hundred twice, losing count each time and starting again, he noticed that it was growing lighter, the surrounding landscape becoming hazily visible, as if a huge spotlight were being slowly increased in intensity behind the thick, smoky clouds—he could see the marching rows of buildings that rimmed the Avenue, ghostly gleams and glitterings from glass and steel and chrome, the white lines dimly discernible against the black asphalt under his feet.

Kagan wondered about the source of the new light for another ten or eleven steps, until, sluggishly, he realized that it must be the moon. Yes, it was the right time of month—somewhere above the scum, the poison clouds, rode a harvest moon, shining coldly down on a blighted, shrouded Earth: the land ripped, gutted, smothered with concrete under its rusty blanket, fungus whispering across its surface . . . ripe with decay; the sea finally killed by decades of pollution, sullied by massive oil slicks, sludge, raw sewage, industrial wastes, millions of tons of dead fish, scummed over by poisonous red tides. Kagan grimaced, feeling a return of desperation. *The plan,* he reminded himself, beyond irony. He allowed himself to drift across the lanes, closer to the opposite curb, on the seaward side.

This section of the Avenue had once been prosperous, but the second look caught the cracks in the stone, the chunks of missing mortar, the weeds forcing their way up through the sidewalk, the tangle of jury-rigged television aerials on the roofs. It had been a long time since the wealthy lived here, and now there was no one here at all—windows broken, glass scattered across the sidewalk, doors hanging open, swinging in the wind. Some of the houses were blackened, burned out, still smoldering. There were bullet holes in the façades of some of the buildings, and the acrid reek of smoke bit into his nostrils, cutting through the cloyed, sulphurous air, almost a relief. Kagan paced by, limping heavily, feeling nothing at all. Further along, the make-up of the Avenue began to change, dominated, after another quarter mile, by rows of newer—post-Depression—nondescript buildings: a gray anonymity of undistinguished stone structures, the ground floors of each devoted to commercialism, so that an unbroken line of small shops marched north, side by side—Kagan passed a florist, a drugstore, a meat market, a furniture store, a bakery. All had large display windows: some were shuttered by window gates, some were broken, most were both shuttered and broken—the rioting had proved more effective than the safeguards against damage. To Kagan, the buildings seemed topheavy, the ground floors hollow—scooped out, visibly, by the stores—while the blank, blind stories above seemed massively, overwhelmingly solid: stone teeth, eaten away at the base.

There were abandoned cars here, the first Kagan had seen since the square, a few still parked neatly near the curbs, the rest scattered across the width of the Avenue at random, as if by a giant hand: some parked diagonally across the lanes, others pointing north or south, most jammed together in odd positions—head to head, head to tail—to form rough triangles. The nearest car was just ahead, facing him: its windshield gave him his ghostly reflection as he approached, the dim, white face dancing crazily across the glass, sliding down as perspective shifted, finally staring up at him from the glossy finish of the hood as he stood by the driver's door. Tentatively, Kagan touched the roof, the door handle, the driving mirror—little, hesitant touches, almost furtive, snatching his hand back gingerly from the cold metal. It was hours since he had considered getting the use of a car: he had resigned himself to walking, grown accustomed to it, been absorbed by the rhythm of it, until he had almost begun to consider walking as an end in itself, perhaps more desirable than the actual reaching of any hypothetical goal. Now he found himself reluctant to change his pedestrian status, even if he could—driving seemed too fast, too hard-edged, too high-powered, somehow threatening the fantasy of escape by making it too overtly likely, too achievable: walking, with its greater physical exertion, its struggle, allowed him to delude himself that there was a way to get out from under this, if he just tried hard enough.

That was a dangerous thought. Kagan pushed it down. A car would help. He reached for the door handle, burned his fingers on the metal, wrapped a handkerchief around his hand and tried again—it was locked. Kagan limped around the car, tugging at the other doors, but they were all locked—evidently its driver had had time to be cautious. Kagan wondered if the man had seriously thought he would ever come back to claim his vehicle, if he had believed in the mystical "return to normalcy" that had been promised with increasing shrillness by the government until the radios went dead and society vanished. Kagan pounded once, futilely, on the safetyglass window, not even raising an echo—getting only a dull thump and a bruised hand. Then he turned away, his murky reflection seeming to grimace mockingly at him until it slid out of perception under the chassis. The next car was also locked. On the third try—a Volkswagen—he found an open door and stood blinking into the muskiness of the car's interior, a discarded sweater hanging limply over the front seat, one sleeve dangling down into the back, a jaunty straw hat with a feather perched on the dashboard: a museum of extinct trivia. There was no key in the ignition. He rummaged through the glove compartment— feeling a strong repulsion, feeling like a grave robber—but found only a pair of sunglasses and a faded AAA travel folder. Kagan knew that it was possible to start a car without a key by "jumping the wires," but didn't have the slightest idea how to go about this, and was disinclined to experiment: even touching the objects inside the car filled him with nausea and a slight panic. Cars seemed to be unnatural, even supernatural things now: remnants of an earlier cycle of existence, charged with the unholy, ancient presence of the Fallen. Kagan forced himself down the Avenue to the next grouping, a Dodge and a big Ford that had bumped heads; their fenders were snarled inseparably together. Twenty feet beyond that was a Chevy that had come to rest in the center of a mad swirl of skid marks, canted across the white lane markers. It was open, and there was a key.

Shuddering, Kagan slipped behind the wheel. The interior still smelled of old sweat, and the cushion sighed mournfully as he sat down on it. He slid his feet down, groping for the gas pedal. There was an empty Coke bottle on the floor; it rolled under his foot, and he kicked it aside with savage loathing, as if it was a snake. Blood roared behind his eyes and he almost passed out. He leaned against the wheel until his vision cleared, trying to slow his breathing. Steady, he told himself, you're falling apart. Yes. Why not? What did you expect? He twisted the key—the motor coughed, stuttered, died. He twisted again—this time he got only an incredibly final, metallic *thunk*. Five minutes of futile coaxing convinced him that the car was dead. Give it a minute and try again, he thought automatically, not really caring any more. He rested against the wheel, elbows propped, hands inside his coat, watching the dim glass faces of the dials on the instrument panel, the tiny numerals almost visible, almost visible, visible, and then he yanked himself violently up out of sleep, banging his head on the roof of the car. *Christ.* He turned the key violently—*thunk, thunk*—and then floundered up out of the car, staggering away, almost running, awash with superstitious terror.

There were four other cars in sight, but he ignored them, avoiding them by wide margins. He rationalized this by telling himself that he was too exhausted to drive anyway, that he would fall asleep at the wheel and pile up before he'd gone a mile. He needed the cold and the motion of walking to keep himself from oblivion. Another car. He circled it warily. He was shivering continually now, hugging himself, hands on elbows. The cars became more numerous, were packed closer together: here the collisions had been more violent—he saw his first real wreck, a car that had wrapped itself around a lamppost in an embrace of twisted metal, the post itself leaning drunkenly, the pavement around it cracked and buckled. There were puddles of oily, multicolored liquid: gasoline. And darker stains: blood. Beyond, a Mustang rested on the sidewalk, its rear end through the display window of a hardware store—glass had exploded out across the road; it crunched under his feet like brittle, crystalline snow. On the left, a mail truck had plowed into the back of a station wagon— the rear doors of the truck had given under the impact and large bags of mail had tumbled out, spilling letters into the street, where they tumbled and flapped with the wind, occasionally lifted by a gust and swirled up and out of sight with the fluid grace of birds. Ahead and to the right, three cars had tangled with a pickup truck, leaving a twenty-foot wake of oil slicks and broken parts that ended in a heap against a concrete wall. A few yards beyond that was a multiple crack-up that stretched halfway across the Avenue. Kagan turned, walked parallel to the wall of rubble, finally skirted around its edges, only to find, on the other side, the major disaster of which this first horror was only an echo. Five feet ahead was an unbroken rear windshield, resting on its outer surface so that it bowed up like a dish, sitting in the middle of the street with perfect, serene grace. Fifteen feet beyond that was what looked like a quarter mile of wreckage, rubble packed in curb to curb: Kagan could see an overturned bus, a huge tractor-trailer van on its side, cars nearly upright on their rear wheels, held high by the weight of dozens of smashed vehicles. Some of the cars had exploded, and large swaths of the wreckage were blackened by fire. This was why the other cars, further back, had been unable to get out of the Avenue: after the initial big crackup, the reaction had spread backward through the pack of fleeing cars, the disaster growing as more and more vehicles whipped unstoppably into the pile. Only the cars at the end of the procession had been able to stop with relatively little damage, some of them stalling and jamming as they tried to turn around, others managing to disengage successfully and flee back the way they had come, probably toward another, more distant bottleneck. There was a wind toward Kagan, off the ocean, across the wreckage, and it carried the heavy, oily, sick-sweet smell of death, the reek of burnt pork—trembling horribly on the verge of being appetizing. There could be no further progress along the Avenue, no path picked through the graveyard ahead: the drivers killed with their cars, both rotting, the men eaten by putrefaction, the cars by rust, etched away by the gentle inevitability of wind and weather (for there would be no scavengers now either, Kagan realized—no birds, no animals, maybe not even insects) until an indiscriminate tangle of weathered bone and metal lay under the dead, black sky. No. Kagan turned, moving quickly, but very carefully, like a tightrope walker, like a man carrying a case of eggs; he was aware of a growing horror but partitioned it off, also uneasily aware of the fragile thinness of the glass he used for that task. The plan was still feasible—all he had to do was follow the web of secondary streets down toward the docks and then back up, by-passing the carnage ahead and rejoining the Avenue where it became Bridge Street, just before the estuary. That wouldn't be too much out of the way. He walked faster, back the way he had come, convincing himself, wanting to believe. Almost eagerly, he turned onto a side street, away from the Avenue, down to the sea.

After a block, he found the body of a dead girl.

The cars had been here too, tearing down this narrow street in a jostling shark pack, the survivors from the big collision up on the Avenue. One of them had hit the child, glancingly but at great speed, the impact throwing her across the sidewalk and against the base of a wall—Kagan could read all of the incident in the skid marks that swerved up over the curb, the trails of burned rubber that weaved away into the night.

The incident, Kagan repeated.

At the first sight of the child, Kagan had stopped, all at once, feet faster than his body, so that his torso first spilled forward, then—jerking, the stomach muscles contracting—surged back and up, rocking onto his heels, as if he had been pulled up short by hooks imbedded in his shoulder blades. He still hung there, by the hooks; quivering, up on his heels, elbows hugged tight against the body, arms up, hands cocked sharply at the wrists and pressed against the base of his throat, fingers digging into flesh. Then, slowly, he let his weight back down onto the balls of his feet. He began to breathe again, sucking in the fetid air. He lowered his arms, his hands fluttering aimlessly until he tucked them into his belt for lack of anything else to do with them, his fingers curling around the belt, gripping hard, keeping hold. He took a slow step, then a quick nervous step, then another, then three, then four, quicker, knitting his footsteps into a fabric of echoes *click-click-click* that steadily increased in tempo as he circled the dead child until he came to a stop, *clack*.

The child was lying face down, one leg and one arm twisted unnaturally under her body, the leg nearest the curb stretched out straight as a pipestem, pointing unreproachfully back toward the street, her sock bunched down around her ankle, her shoe sitting upright about a yard from her heel, the upper portion of her body lodged against the base of the wall of a stationery store, tilted up a little on one shoulder, the arm furthest from the curb resting vertically against the wall as if nailed there, fingers pointed upward, her head turned away from the street, her face pressed somewhat closer to the brick than would normally have been possible.

Kagan watched her silently, coming no closer than ten feet, as if she was surrounded by an invisible wall, a semipermeable membrane that kept him out. He was not thinking of anything at all. The wind was rising, slashing dirt and gravel into his face. Slowly, still without thinking, without any volition, Kagan turned and made his way across the street, walking hunch-shouldered, tilted against the wind. There was a pizza and falafel stand there, decorated by a brightly colored striped awning that flapped and tugged against its iron frame in the wind with a sound like the beating of leather wings. Kagan jumped up clumsily, caught the loose fold of the awning and pulled savagely on it, again and again, throwing his weight onto it, finally ripping it free of the frame, the awning billowing out with the wind, flapping like a mad snake, Kagan taking a hitch of it around his waist and slowly rolling himself up in it, clawing at it while it slapped his face and battered around his ears, inexorably pulling it down, weighing it down, throttling it into submission. At last it was quiet in his hands. Working grimly, carefully, Kagan bunched the awning up into a manageable ball, taking care not to let the wind get another handhold on the cloth. Then he stood with it clutched to his stomach, staring stupidly into the ornate, gilt-painted window of the falafel stand. A large, printed sign blinked at him: *Pizza Heroes.* Yes, he thought, yes, we are, aren't we? He walked back to the body like a crab, hunched around the ball of awning. With tremendous difficulty, he managed to spread the awning out on the sidewalk next to the dead child, fighting the wind constantly, almost losing it once, finally finding a loose cobblestone and using it to anchor one end of the awning while he knelt on the other. Then he reached out gently and grasped the child by the wrist of her outflung arm (his fingers shriveled at the coldness of her flesh), and began to pull her away from the wall. There was resistance—she had become frozen to the brick, and he had to tug strongly to break her loose, her body thudding over onto its back at last with all the dignity of a side of beef. Her face: the expected horror. There were no eyes to close. He dragged the child over onto the awning, positioning her neatly in the middle. He took one side of the awning and pulled it over her, tucking her into it, like a blanket at bedtime. The child was about the same age as his granddaughter; she was of a size too. He rolled her body up in the awning, wrapping her in it as tightly as he could, folding the ends in snugly. There was a smeared red stain on the wall, crusted with frozen pebbles.

The incident, Kagan repeated.

He began to cry, hugging his arms, rocking back and forth on his heels as he squatted next to the dead child, finally overbalancing and falling, sitting then in the street, rattled by sobs that seemed to pick him up by the neck and shake him, ripping his throat raw, slamming his chest and stomach from the inside—as if his spine was trying to tear itself free of his body. After a while his weeping became quieter, and then—as if he had been suddenly frightened by the noise he was making in the hush of the graveyard earth—turned to silent tears, welling up in his eyes like blood in a wound, rolling with infinite patience down along his face, filling his mouth with salt. Then even that well ran dry, and he was abandoned: sitting in the street, sitting in his shabby body, back at the end of the world. He became aware of the cold again—his tears had frozen to his cheeks, gluing one eyelid closed, and he cupped and rubbed that eye until he could open it. The wind walked up and down his spine, kicked him in the back of the head, yanked impatiently at the tails of his coat. Yes, yes, he thought, in a minute. I'll get up in a minute, Mama. He curled up deliciously in the blankets again, until the wind knocked him over on his face and he banged his lip sharply on the cobblestones. His mouth filled with blood: a more astringent salt. Kagan got to his hands and knees—hugging the pain like a crucifix—and then forced himself back into a squat, feeling his bones crack, this time having to balance himself with a hand. Why don't you die? the wind asked. Not yet, he whispered, not until I've finished, not until I'm ready—don't be greedy; you've got all the rest of them. He found himself choking on the unswallowed blood and spat it angrily away, shaking his head to free it of cobwebs, finally getting to his feet.

His eye was caught by the bright cloth of the awning. The child. Operating his arms like a claw machine at a penny arcade—doing it by remote control, as if he was at a great distance away from himself—he grappled with the shrouded body, heaved it upright, rested it against his knee, then managed to get it up across his shoulder. He staggered under the weight of the body, but began to walk, wobbling with each step, feeling as if he was on stilts. He was weary beyond belief. What do you think you're doing? he asked himself querulously, genuinely irritated when he didn't get an answer—the child is dead, what difference can it make to her? What about the millions of other dead children in the world, some maybe a few feet away, inside the buildings? Who's going to bury them? Who's going to bury you? Would any of you be any less dead if someone did? Will she? Can you stop her from rotting? Why should you even try?

"A man has to do *something*," he shouted aloud, harried by shadows, baffled by pain. The street ate the sound of his voice. Shuddering, he came to a stop. The child incredibly heavy on his shoulders, like the sins of all the world since the beginning. *A man has to do something*, Kagan repeated, afraid to speak aloud again. His knees were buckling, but he would not leave her in the street, like rubbish. Damn you, she is human, she counts for something. I say that she does. He shifted her weight, hunching his shoulder under it, feeling the strain to his toes. He could go no further. The wind had continued to rise, and it snatched eagerly at his burden, almost toppling him. With the last of his strength, Kagan carried her up onto the sidewalk, tried the door of the first shop that he found. It was open. A meat market. Kagan didn't even realize the grisly irony of this until he had carried the child inside and was searching for someplace to put her. He began to swear, brokenly, in a low monotone. It was all going wrong. There was nothing here, but the doors into the interior of the building were padlocked, and he was too weak to break in. Finally he bundled her into one of the large display cases, latching it and pushing some chairs against the door to keep it wedged shut, thinking that it would protect her body against rats anyway, if there were rats any more—then, as he stepped away from the case, the inappropriateness of what he'd just done, the horrible, unconscious humor, the bathos, hit him like a fist over the heart. For a moment he staggered physically under the impact, sickened, the room seeming to squeeze in on him, close down, and then everything drained away, leaving him empty, and he stared at the body dispassionately, not understanding any more why he'd wanted to do that, too barren even for bitterness or despair.

Kagan hobbled out into the street, leaving the door open behind him. His brain seemed ultimately awake now—although he couldn't feel his body at all, except very faintly around the edges—working at twice its usual speed, his thoughts as clear, hard, and cold as ice. The plan was nonsense, a makeshift fabric of animal fear and wishful thinking. How could he have believed in it, why hadn't he seen through it before? Now he could foretell everything that would happen, all of it as unequivocal as a computer print-out. He wasn't going to escape. He was going to die. Everyone was going to die. It had all been for nothing—all the messy struggles of humanity from sea to jungle to city. It had never meant anything: all blind protoplasmic tropism, incidents, accidents of entropy. Now they had killed the sea, razed the jungles, strangled the cities. There was a wonderful appropriateness to it, a mathematical, cerebral beauty—it had the perfect, geometrical inevitability of a bacteriological culture overgrowing its slide. That's all it had ever been: a blind progression of matter expanding to the limits of a closed system, then stopping. Call it life, call it humanity—that would not grant it exemption from entropy. All of the distinctions between organic and inorganic, sentient and insensate were human conceits—there was no difference, the equation would work out the same if you used bacteria or men. There was no difference between the dead child and rubbish; there had not been even when she was alive.

It was all funny. Delighted with the solemn absurdity of the joke, Kagan skipped, executed a floundering dance step—his leg gave way under him and he cracked his knee sickeningly on the pavement, feeling the pain only as an unimportant, faraway twinge, buffered by a million thicknesses of glass and cotton. As he levered himself gaily to his feet, the wind reached its peak: exploding into a sudden rain squall that battered and blinded him, twirled him in a staggering circle, left him drenched and shivering in an instant. Somewhat sobered, he lurched across the street, tripping over the curb and sprawling forward, catching himself on his hands before he could bang his leg too badly—this time the pain was more insistent, closer. He groped until he found a building wall, and then felt his way along it, pressing his face close to the brick to shield it from the hammering of the rain. I won't die in the rain, he told himself slyly. A little comfort, please, a little civilization! An eternity of blind groping then, time measured only by the rutch of his fingertips over the brick, until his hand blundered into a brass doorknob: a change in geographical eras, a new continent thrust abruptly up from the muck. An aeon later, when he had been first satiated and then complacently bored by the texture of brass, he realized that the doorknob had a social function as well, and, after a pause of a few millennia to remember what the function was, twisted it. Resistance—he put his shoulder to the door, heaved, and fell rather than stepped into the building, taking the impact on his shoulder and cheekbone.

The place was a Polish delicatessen—had been a delicatessen, Kagan corrected himself, getting up on his elbows. Now it was nothing, a construction of wood and plaster, a fossil of artifice. It had already been looted: papers, torn signs—*hot pastrami* peered up at him from under a footstool, *Polish sausage* flapped slowly across the floor with the wind—cooking utensils, silverware, and money had been scattered around the room, trampled underfoot; furniture smashed, the overhead lights broken, the counter caved in, the sink basin torn out of the wall. Not looting after all—destruction: pettish, savage, desperate; it had gone beyond looting now.

It was comfortable to rest there, propped on his elbows and admiring the desolation, but the rain had followed him into the store, licking him like a cold, abrasive tongue. Kagan floated up, tilted himself carefully back to a standing position. Moving with exquisite, fussy deliberation, he pushed the door shut to keep out the squall, making sure that it closed tight, getting it right in every particular. He was annoyed when he continued to feel the bite of the wind: he was sure he'd done it correctly. Then he noticed that there was a broken window. Petulantly, he shrugged, and moved toward the interior of the store, obedient to the pressure of the wind, riding it lightly as a little poison spore, as a virus-and-vector. The floor tilted ponderously, first one way and then the other, with a restful rocking motion, like a seesaw. He drifted into a back room, darker, part of the living quarters—he could dimly make out a wooden table, a chair, a cupboard in one wall, an ivory crucifix on another.

The destruction had not reached this far. After some searching, he managed to find a small package of bologna wrapped in wax paper, a half-empty bottle of milk, and— after forcing the sticky bottom drawer of the cupboard and rummaging blindly through its dusty, cobwebbed interior—two cans of Sterno and three wooden kitchen matches. His hands did the work, scavenging efficiently while he watched, uninvolved, sardonically amused by their earnestness, not understanding what they were doing but not interested enough to interfere. At last his hands seemed to have finished—they had gathered together all the treasures they'd found, scooped the treasures up in a net of fingers. He smiled benignly at them: all done? When they didn't answer, only curling more possessively around their things, he smiled again and straightened up, letting them bring the treasures with them. The room was starting to spin around him in a circle, very slowly at first and gradually becoming faster, like a carrousel, like a record turntable before the machine has warmed up. He admired that too, appreciatively, although it was a little dizzying. Then his feet began to act up, stirring and walking across the room all by themselves, dragging him along behind them like a dinghy while he balloon-bobbed in the current. He smiled tolerantly at them too, being "understanding." How aggressively independent and self-assertive everyone was today! Still he had always been patient with children. His feet tugged him to the table, and he sat down in the single chair. He was gone for a little while then, and when he came back he found his fingers impatiently tearing away the wax paper, breaking the meat into small portions. He consented to this—let them have their rituals—amused when his mouth got into the game and surprised when he began to play himself, after a few pieces had disappeared. He ate and drank slowly, working hard at it, coaxing himself—a piece for Mama, for Papa, for Alice, for each of the children—with a guilty glance at the overhanging crucifix—for Christ. Eventually the food was all gone, but his hands still wanted to do something. They fumbled at the cans of Sterno, finally pried the lids open. This is what the matches were for! Proud that he had remembered, he scratched a kitchen match against the table top. The first one refused to light; so did the second. The third one ignited, and he managed to get both the Sterno cans going with it before it burned his fingers and went out. The Sterno smelled funny but not unpleasant—it hissed softly, and blue flame danced across its surface. He hunched closer to it, concentrating on its

sound to block out the hungry whine of the wind. The ar-
tificial light had shot his night vision: now he could only
see the flickering blue flames and a surrounding square of
table top. But the room was spinning again, even though
he couldn't see it, faster and faster, not to be denied this
time. He spun with it, around and around, being funneled
down an endless waterspout, the spiral tightening and descending into infinity. He didn't care as long as he could
hang onto the warmth of the Sterno, that warmth trailing
out behind him as he was sucked into the waterspout, a
tenuous connection, an umbilical cord. Whirling then,
whirling and contracting. Only the ivory crucifix did not
move, staring at him with sad, unreproachful eyes as the
rest of the room blurred and tightened, and went down.
And went down.

   Twenty-five years with the company
      count 910 lines on green, red slips separate
         measures have been
           "the state of the economy"
             form A, pc 54 or 85
               undue concern
                 CBW agents
                 of the sea
                    "stay in your homes"
                    incidents
                       temporary inconvenience
                     oil slick
                    alarmists
                  Father.

He talked with Alice. She was sitting right next to him,
but he was unable to take her hand: every time he tried
his hand would slide right over hers and off without ever
touching it at all, as if the air around her hand had become slippery to prevent the contact. It made him angry
that he was unable to take his wife's hand. He was trying
to explain to her that nothing mattered, that nothing
meant anything, but she wasn't listening. She had turned
her face away, disapprovingly, and she was hunching her
shoulders in that stubborn, I'm-not-listening way she had
when she was mad at him. He tried to tell her that they
were *incidents*, but faltered, because it pained him suddenly to deny her, and because she was fading away as he

talked, fading more quickly the more he tried to make her understand. He called her name and tried to grasp her by the shoulders, but already she was becoming transparent, becoming misty, and he still couldn't touch her. He stopped trying to convince her, suddenly desperate, unable to bear her going away again, feeling a huge, jagged surge of agony and loss. He pleaded with her to come back, telling her about that night he had come into the bedroom and found her dead, and how he had sat there in the dark and cradled her in his arms for hours, before calling the police, before telling the children, just holding her and stroking her hair and talking to her, gently trying to coax her into awakening, into coming back for even a minute or two so that he could at least tell her all the things that he would've wanted to tell her if he had known that she wasn't going to be there tomorrow, so that she would know and not have to go into the dark alone. He told her how he had held her until morning, until he could see her face in the cold, gritty light. She continued to fade, but she turned her face toward him and smiled sadly at him, and her eyes met his. Her eyes were enormous, calm, loving. Then she was gone.

His parents: he had been talking to them for hours, talking earnestly across the kitchen table, trying to explain the big dreams, the plans that he had. His mother, tiny, birdlike, her hands always darting and fluttering; his father, tall, gray-haired, listening with his arms crossed over his chest, shrugging skeptically from time to time. *I killed the world*, he told them. His father shook his head ponderously, shrugging, smiling wistfully. His mother's hands tangled like anxious birds, her lips moved inaudibly. *I killed the world, Mama. Papa. It's true. I did. So did you, Mama. So did you, Papa. We all did.* His mother patting his face in little darting touches, ruffling his hair, pressing his head to her breast. Her hands did not touch him. *We all did, Mama.* His father looking stern, then smiling, shrugging, his hand making an upward, releasing motion—forgiving him. *Do you forgive me then, Papa? Mama? Can I forgive you? The others? Do I? Is there forgiveness for this?*

Why don't you move away from the city, Papa? they asked him. They were not his parents any more. Somehow they had become his children—Stan, Jean, Carol. They were gathered around, looking at him concernedly, trying to talk him into it. He saw them as babies, as children, as young adults, all the millions of images superimposed over each other so that he saw all of them at once, without any of them being blurred or indistinct. Behind his children were his grandchildren, their images less crystalline and definite than those of his children, and behind them were still other figures, those completely unrecognizable—his great-grandchildren? But he didn't have any, yet. Would he have—still? There were four children in the foreground: one of them was the dead child, he realized, but somehow he couldn't tell which one of them it was, and it didn't seem to really matter. In the far background rose the crucifix: the eyes of the Christ were sad, calm, peaceful, ancient, and patient—his homely, human face said: First I had to forgive myself; there is no other redemption. His children pressed closer to him, began to drift around him in a slow, ascending circle. *Why don't you move away from the city, Papa?* they said in a communal voice that managed to preserve the individual accents of each. *It's not a good place for you, Papa, there's nothing here for you any more. Why don't you come away with us, Papa?*

"Why, I'm a city man," he answered gently. "It's too late for me to change. The new life—that's for you, that's for your children. You have the strength to start again. My roots are here. I worked for the company for twenty-five years."

Kagan woke up.

The wind had died. It was utterly silent. The Sternos had gone out, and it was very dark, and very cold. He blinked at the darkness. He had not expected to wake up. He was still very tired, and a part of his mind advised him to go back to sleep, to let it wait until morning. But there would be no morning. He knew: the world was so very quiet, so hushed and smothering, as if there would never be sound again. This was it. This was the end. He shrugged away the seductive temptation to sleep. *Can't sleep through Apocalypse; it just isn't done.* He smiled to himself in the darkness, a small, sad, weary smile. He felt inordinately composed for a sick, battered man about to witness the end of the world. The madness and despair had burned themselves out, and he was calm, almost at peace. He lifted his head from his arms. In spite of the cold, the room was stifling, suffocating, as if the air around him had congealed and sagged down onto him like a collapsed tent. He gulped hugely at the air, feeling on the razor edge of asphyxiation, but was unable to catch his breath. The air hurt his throat, his lungs; he could feel it all the way down, as if he had swallowed molten lead. He coughed, hawked, spat a thick gobbet of blood, and revised his estimate upward from *sick*: he was dying. He tried to moisten his lips, but his tongue was dry and enormously swollen. His lips were also dry and brittle, cracked, caked over with crusted blood, and his face was scorching, blisteringly hot even to his own hand. He was dying—from fever, from exposure, from the poison that he was taking into his body with every breath. Probably only the food and the heat from the Sternos had kept him alive even this long. Certainly he couldn't count on much more time.

I'd like to see the ocean again, Kagan told himself, *I'd like to make it down to the sea.*

He grasped the edge of the table and hauled himself to his feet, knocking over the chair. The world seemed to turn over three or four times, somersaulting with dreamlike slowness. Light novaed behind his eyes, wiping out his vision with raw, bloody red, red fading to luminous black, black slowly becoming the darkness of the room as sight returned. He became gradually aware of a hoarse, ugly sound, and listened to it for several seconds before he realized that it was himself gasping laboriously for breath. He swayed, tottering, leaning against the table, pregnant with death, feeling it in a cold, heavy lump in his stomach, like a stone fetus.

There was a patch of lesser darkness that must be the open doorway to the outer room, not so much light as the suggestion of light. Kagan pushed himself away from the table and staggered toward it, reeling, taking one long stride, two, three, four, and then his strength drained away and his legs turned to sand. He crumbled, pitching heavily forward onto his face. He hardly felt the impact.

I'm not going to make it, he thought, and then a giant

was stepping on him, grinding him into the floor, and the redness was back to swallow his vision, and there was an angry buzzing roar in his ears. This time the red tide took much longer to retreat, and when it did, leaving him limply strewn behind like driftwood on a beach, he rested for a few minutes and then began to crawl doggedly toward the door. It wasn't too bad, he found, if he took it very slowly, inching and hitching his way forward on his belly, like a snail. *At least let me get outside. You can do that much, can't you?* he scolded himself, piqued by his own helplessness, but at the same time strangely amused by it—the wry, scornful humor of the long-term invalid. *Let me get outside—I never liked mausoleums.* His hand encountered the doorjamb; he pulled himself over the lintel, wriggling into the big outer room of the store. The dim light was seeping in through the broken window. By it, he could see that the outside door was closed—he remembered closing it a million years ago, remembered jamming it tightly shut against the squall. He'd never be able to force it open now. There was another corridor, behind the counter, leading away into the interior of the building. That was the only chance. Painfully, he wormed his way around the counter, through the splintered wood and broken glass behind it—cutting himself deeply several times, although that hardly mattered now—and into the narrow corridor. After a dozen yards he was in complete darkness again, and could only crawl blindly forward, feeling his way, bumping into the angles of the corridor—fortunately it was relatively straight. A little while later he took a chance and cautiously got to his hands and knees. His head swam sickeningly and he had to rest for a moment, but then the dizziness passed, and it appeared that death was going to let him get away with that too. Now he could crawl much more quickly. Soon he could make out a lessening of the gloom ahead.

It was the back door. He had crawled all the way through the building to the other side, and somebody had left the back door open. When the light had become a definite grayish square against black, Kagan stopped and rested, gathering his strength. Then he crawled forward until his fingers found the doorframe, grasped it, and pulled himself erect. *Walk,* he told himself sternly, *you* crawled for twenty-five years. He rested for another second, then launched himself away, and he was reeling outside, concrete underfoot, away from the hateful enclosure of the building, childishly exhilarated. He blundered into a grouping of metal garbage cans, sending them flying, the clatter horrific and terrifying in his ears, staggering, regaining his balance, away from the concrete apron of the service area, his feet biting dirt, and then—fadeout—a dull red purgatory—fadein—and he found himself sitting on frozen mud, his head lolled between his knees, rasping like a blown horse. He had pushed it to the limit that time—if that hadn't killed him, then he would have a little while yet before the end. Still, he knew that he'd never have the strength to move again. This would be it: here in the mud. *Better than concrete,* he thought, disjointedly, *replenish the soil, kyrie eleison.* After a while he was able to lift his head.

The gray sea curved below him like a shield, like the crooked, gunmetal arm of a giant: the estuary. He had come to rest a few yards from a bluff that dropped the last twenty feet to the docks, to the sea. From here he could see a 180° sweep of the horizon: he traced the estuary from a misty point on the far right where it met the bulk of the Atlantic, close in to where it was a broad fan of water nibbled by docks, to the left where the bridge that had once been his goal bulked in the middle distance—beyond it was the other shore, the promontory of the mainland. The moon was going down behind the bridge, chopped in half by the line of the other shore: an enormous, blotted disk, wildly distorted by the atmosphere, seeming to take up a quarter of the horizon. The bridge was etched in stark black tracery against that leprous backdrop.

In the intense moonlight, Kagan could see movement on the bridge. Straining his eyes, he managed to make out a number of ant-sized figures on the span, some standing still behind the fingernail-sized glints that were abandoned cars, others running toward the figures in hiding, fanning out, dodging and scurrying. Suddenly, unbelievably, there was the distant sound of gunfire, and Kagan saw tiny, intense needles of flame flickering out from the running ant-figures, lancing back from the hiding ant-figures. They were men, and it was war. Even now, even in the ruins of the earth, they could find an excuse for war. Briefly, Kagan wondered what it was: maybe suburbanites trying to stop the flow of city refugees through their territory, maybe some political factionist's dispute, or maybe just because there was nothing better to do.

The battle lasted quite some time. Kagan saw several of the ant-figures fall and not move again, and once saw one fall from the bridge, a twisting black spot hurtling a hundred feet down to the water. Both sides had taken to the cars now, and there was intense guerrilla warfare among the wrecks. Eventually the swollen moon went down, and Kagan could no longer see the bridge. He didn't need to—he could see them clearly enough in his mind: the oxygen masks, the guns, the faces contorted with hate and fear and desperation. The skirmishing went on in the dark for another fifteen or twenty minutes—Kagan could hear sporadic gunfire, and the muzzle flashes flickered out over the ocean like heat lightning. The sounds of the shots was brittle and very tiny in the preternatural hush that shrouded the rest of the world—like children's penny firecrackers. Then there was silence. Kagan waited, swearing softly and bitterly, not knowing whether or not he hoped there were any of them left alive. The cold was starting to get to him—he could no longer feel his legs. After another ten minutes he heard the sputter and roar of starting engines and saw headlights blink on halfway across the bridge, three sets of big truck headlights, tiny and bitterly bright, like novas in faraway star systems. The headlights crossed the rest of the bridge, wound on up into the invisible hills of the other shore, seeming to climb up into the black sky until they dropped and disappeared; the survivors.

Watching them go, Kagan found, surprisingly, that he felt nothing at all—no hate, no envy, no resentment over his wasted years. They were the strong and ruthless, and it was their world now. It would be a savage world, done in primary colors, sharp-edged, no chiaroscuro, chock-full of incidents—it would have to be, for many years to come. There would be room only for large, simple things—no room for the small, complex things, like love or mercy or understanding or learning, the things that had made this civilization marginably tolerable, the things that had failed to save it from itself. Kagan's world was dead, and those things with it. And the things that had not deserved to survive that world lived on, indefatigable, indestructible. Back to the Stone Age. But Kagan was a city man—he loved them, loved the promise of them: he had seen them grow perverted and monstrous, seen them strangle the world. If there were survivors, some of them would be decent men—he couldn't discount the hope that his children or grandchildren might be among them. Maybe they would learn something on this trip back from barbarism, this time around. Maybe when they got around to it next time, they would know how to build cities as they should be built, as he would have had them be. Or maybe not. Probably not. Probably there would not even be survivors. Humanity had always been a long shot.

It had grown incredibly cold. Kagan now could not move his feet or legs at all, and it felt as if something very heavy was sitting on them. He was shaken by a spasmodic, racking spasm of coughing, bringing up blood, and when it passed he could feel the numbness creeping up from his legs, toward his chest. A race. He hooked his arms around the iron railing of the service apron, hanging on it, using it to keep him sitting upright. He wanted to watch the sea. He could see it, very faintly, by straining his eyes: a hint of gray in a sullen confusion of black earth and sky. He had loved the sea as a boy, eagerly walking three or four miles, whenever he could, to visit the then unspoiled coastline above the city. He still loved it, and though he watched the murdered estuary he saw that younger sea, that private ocean—radiant and eternally breathing, foaming against pale sand and humped, weathered boulders; periwinkles; whorled driftwood; mossy barnacles on rocks below the tide line; the vivid green of snaky sea grass; the sting of salt brine and the sour reek of exposed mud flats; a pocket of stranded water warmed to blood heat by the sun; the sideways scurry of a furtive hermit crab; a gray water rat blinking from a chink in the sea wall; a dog tearing down the beach; the scream of seagulls overhead, and always the foam-flecked Atlantic, stitched by white wedges of sails, waiting like an actor in the wings. He had loved to duck his head beneath the surface and open his eyes, looking at the wavy underwater plants that rolled off into mystery, into the green twilight, imagining that he could hear the bells of drowned ships and churches and empires ringing sonorously under the water—

Kagan pulled himself back to the world, floundering and confused—he had been talking to Alice again, and he looked around stupidly for her until his daze wore off and the agony of consciousness hit him. He had frozen to the railing, and the pain was indescribable. He made a helpless mewling sound and tried to yank himself away from the railing—

He woke strangling. The wind was rising again, hissing like demons, and he was swamped with atavistic terror. He clawed for life, struggling to get to his feet, collapsing, crying weakly. Then the terror passed. The pain was less intense now, and he had a moment of clarity, watching the sea, listening to the hungry insect chittering of the wind. *This is not an incident,* he told the wind, *it means something. I say that it does. And be damned to you.* The wind jeered, gusted, slammed him against the railing. The world seemed to split into two halves, slid out of focus. He felt a bottomless pool of fire-shot blackness open beneath him, felt hands close on his ankles and pull him down, felt his head slide beneath the surface—

He woke twice more, strangling and coughing up his lungs, choking on his own phlegm and spit-up blood, hanging from the railing like a scarecrow, somehow holding onto life.

The last time he saw a long red line across the ebony horizon.

As he recognized the dawn, he heard all the drowned bells ring at once, around the world, under the sea.

TAKE A MATCH

ISAAC ASIMOV

Does Isaac Asimov need introduction to this book's
readers? Must novels like **Caves of Steel, Currents of
Space,** and the **Foundation** trilogy be mentioned? Must
we cite his fifty-foot shelf of non-fiction, running the
gamut from **The Intelligent Man's Guide to Science** to
The Sensuous Dirty Old Man? No. No. Not a further
word about him, except to say that Asimov is writing
science fiction again after too long a lapse, and it's
good to have him back.

Space was black; black all around in every direction.
There was nothing to be seen; not a star.

It was not because there were no stars—

Actually the thought that there might be no stars,
literally no stars, had chilled Per Hanson's vitals. It was
the old nightmare that rested just barely subliminally
beneath the skin of every deep-spacer's brain.

When you took the Jump through the tachyon-Uni-
verse, how sure were you *where* you would emerge? The
timing and quantity of the energy input might be as
tightly controlled as you liked and your Fusionist might
be the best in space, but the uncertainty principle reigned
supreme and there was always the chance, even the inevitability, of a random miss.

And by way of tachyons, a paper-thin miss might be
a thousand light-years.

What, then, if you landed nowhere; or at least so distant from anywhere that nothing could possibly ever guide you to knowledge of your own position and nothing, therefore, could guide you back to anywhere?

Impossible, said the pundits. There was no place in the Universe from which the quasars could not be seen and from those alone you could position yourself. Besides, the chance that in the course of ordinary Jumps mere chance would take you outside the Galaxy was only one in about ten million and to the distance of, say, the Andromeda galaxy of Maffei 1, perhaps one in a quadrillion.

Forget it, said the pundits.

So when a ship comes out of its Jump and returns from the weird paradoxes of the faster-than-light tachyons to the healthy we-know-it-all of all the tardyons from protons down to protons up, there *must* be stars to be seen. If they are not seen nevertheless, you are in a dust cloud; it is the only explanation. There are smoggy areas in the Galaxy, or in any spiral galaxy, as once there were on Earth when it was the sole home of humanity, rather than the carefully preserved, weather-controlled, life-preserve museum piece it now was.

Hanson was tall and gloomy; his skin was leathery; and what he didn't know about the hyperships that plowed the length and breadth of the Galaxy and immediately neighboring regions—always barring the Fusionists' mysteries—was yet to be worked out. He was alone, now, in the Captain's Corner, as he liked to be. He had at hand all that was needed to be connected with any man or woman on board and with the results of any device and instrument and it pleased him to be the unseen presence.

—Though now nothing pleased him. He closed contact and said, "What else, Strauss?"

"We're in an open cluster," said Strauss's voice. (Hanson did not turn on the visual attachment; it would have meant revealing his own face and he preferred his look of sick worry to be held private.)

"At least," Strauss continued, "it seems to be an open cluster from the level of radiation we can get in the far infrared and microwave regions. The trouble is we just can't pinpoint the positions well enough to locate ourselves. Not a hope."

"Nothing in visible light?"

"Nothing at all; or in the near infrared, either. The dust cloud is as thick as soup."

"How big is it?"

"No way of telling."

"Can you estimate the distance to the nearest edge?"

"Not even to an order of magnitude. It might be a light-week. It might be ten light-years. Absolutely no way of telling."

"Have you talked to Viluekis?"

Strauss said, briefly, "Yes!"

"What does he say?"

"Not much. He's sulking. He's taking it as a personal insult, of course."

"Of course." Hanson sighed noiselessly. Fusionists were as childish as children and, because theirs was the romantic role in deep space, they were indulged. He said, "I suppose you told him that this sort of thing is unpredictable and could happen at any time."

"I did. And he said, as you can guess—'Not to Viluekis.'"

"Except that it did, of course. Well, I can't speak to him. Nothing I say will mean anything at all except that I'm trying to pull rank and then we'll get nothing further out of him. —He won't start the scoop?"

"He says he can't. He says it will be damaged."

"How can you damage a magnetic field!"

Strauss grunted. "Don't say that to him. He'll tell you there's more to a fusion tube than a magnetic field and then say you're trying to downgrade him."

"Yes, I know. —Well, look, put everyone and everything on the cloud. There must be some way to make some sort of guess as to the direction and distance of the nearest edge." He broke connection.

Hanson frowned into the middle distance then.

Nearest edge! It was doubtful if at the ship's speed (relative to the surrounding matter) they dared expend the energy required for radical alteration of course.

They had moved into the Jump at half light-speed relative to the Galactic nucleus in the tardyon-Universe, and they emerged from the Jump at (of course) the same speed. There always seemed an element of risk in that. After all, suppose you found yourself, on the return, in the near neighborhood of a star and heading toward it at half light-speed?

The theoreticians denied the possibility. To get dangerously close to a massive body by way of a Jump was not reasonably to be expected. So said the pundits. Gravitational forces were involved in the Jump and for the transition from tardyon to tachyon and back to tardyon those forces were repulsive in nature. In fact, it was the random effect of a net gravitational force that could never be worked out in complete detail that accounted for a good deal of uncertainty in the Jump.

Besides, they would say, trust to the Fusionist's instinct. A good Fusionist never goes wrong.

Except that this Fusionist had Jumped them into a cloud.

—Oh, that! It happens all the time. It doesn't matter. Do you know how *thin* most clouds are? You won't even know you're in one.

(Not this cloud, O pundit.)

—In fact, clouds are good for you. The scoops don't have to work so long or so hard to keep fusion going and energy storing.

(Not this cloud, O pundit.)

—Well then, rely on the Fusionist to think of a way out.

(But if there was no way out?)

Hanson shied away from that last thought. He tried hard not to think of it. —But how do you not-think a thought that is the loudest thing in your head?

Henry Strauss, ship's astronomer, was himself in a mood of deep depression. If what had taken place were undiluted catastrophe, it might be accepted. No one on the hyperships could entirely close his eyes to the possibility of catastrophe. You were prepared for that, or you tried to be. —Though it was worse for the passengers, of course.

But when the catastrophe involved something that you would give your eyeteeth to observe and study, and when you found that the professional find of a lifetime was precisely what was killing you—

He sighed heavily.

He was a stout man, with tinted contact lenses that gave a spurious brightness and color to eyes that would otherwise have precisely matched a colorless personality.

There was nothing the captain could do. He knew that. The captain might be autocrat of all the ship beside, but a Fusionist was a law to himself, and always had been. Even to the passengers (he thought with some disgust) the Fusionist is the emperor of the spaceways and everyone beside dwindles to impotence.

It was a matter of supply and demand. The computers might calculate the exact quantity and timing of the energy input and the exact place and direction (if "direction" had any meaning in the transition from the tardyon to tachyon) but the margin of error was huge and only a talented Fusionist could lower it. What it was that gave a Fusionist his talent no one knew—they were born, not made. But Fusionists knew they had the talent and there was never one that didn't trade on that.

Viluekis wasn't bad as Fusionists went—though they never went far. He and Strauss were at least on speaking terms, even though Viluekis had effortlessly collected the prettiest passenger on board after Strauss had seen her first. (That was somehow part of the imperial rights of the Fusionists en route.)

Strauss contacted Anton Viluekis. It took time for it to go through and, when it did, Viluekis looked irritated in a rumpled, sad-eyed way.

"How's the tube?" asked Strauss gently.

"I think I shut it down in time. I've gone over it and I don't see any damage. Now"—he looked down at himself—"I've got to clean up."

"At least it isn't harmed."

"But we can't use it."

"We might use it, Vil," said Strauss in an insinuating voice. "We can't say what will happen out there. If the tube were damaged, it wouldn't matter what happened out there, but, as it is, if the cloud cleans up—"

"If—if—if—I'll tell you an 'if.' If you stupid astronomers had known this cloud was here, I might have avoided it."

That was flatly irrelevant, and Strauss did not rise to the bait. He said, "It might clear up."

"What's the analysis?"

"Not good, Vil. It's the thickest hydroxyl cloud that's ever been observed. There is nowhere in the Galaxy, as far as I know, a place where hydroxyl has been concentrated so densely."

"And no hydrogen?"

"Some hydrogen, of course. About five percent."

"Not enough," said Viluekis curtly. "There's something else there besides hydroxyl. There's something that gave me more trouble than hydroxyl could. Did you locate it?"

"Oh, yes. Formaldehyde. There's more formaldehyde than hydrogen. Do you realize what it means, Vil? Some process has concentrated oxygen and carbon in space in unheard-of amounts; enough to use up the hydrogen over a volume of cubic light-years, perhaps. There isn't anything I know or can imagine which would account for such a thing."

"What are you trying to say, Strauss? Are you telling me that this is the only cloud of this type in space and I am stupid enough to land in it?"

"I'm not saying that, Vil. I only say what you hear me say and you haven't heard me say that. But, Vil, to get out we're depending on you. I can't call for help because I can't aim a hyperbeam without knowing where we are: I can't find out where we are because I can't pinpoint any stars—"

"And I can't use the fusion tube, so why am I the villain? You can't do your job, either, so why is the Fusionist always the villain?" Viluekis was simmering. "It's up to you, Strauss, up to you. Tell me where to cruise the ship to find hydrogen. Tell me where the edge of the cloud is. —Or to hell with the edge of the cloud; find me the edge of the hydroxyl-formaldehyde business."

"I wish I could," said Strauss, "but so far I can't detect anything but hydroxyl and formaldehyde as far as I can probe."

"We can't fuse that stuff."

"I know."

"Well," said Viluekis violently, "this is an example of why it's wrong for the government to try to legislate supersafety instead of leaving it to the judgment of the Fusionist on the spot. If we had the capacity for the Double Jump, there'd be no trouble."

Strauss knew perfectly well what Viluekis meant. There was always the tendency to save time by making two Jumps in rapid succession, but if one Jump involved certain unavoidable uncertainties, two in succession greatly multiplied those uncertainties, and even the best Fusionist couldn't do much. The multiplied error almost invariably greatly lengthened the total time of the trip.

It was a strict rule of hypernavigation that one full day of cruising between Jumps was necessary—three full days was preferable. That gave time enough to prepare the next Jump with all due caution. To avoid breaking that rule, each Jump was made under conditions that left insufficient energy supply for a second. For at least some time, the scoops had to gather and compress hydrogen, fuse it and store the energy, building up to Jump-ignition. And it usually took at least a day to store enough to allow a Jump.

Strauss said, "How far short in energy are you, Vil?"

"Not much. This much." Viluekis held his thumb and forefinger apart by a quarter of an inch. "It's enough, though."

"Too bad," said Strauss flatly. The energy supply was recorded and could be inspected, but even so Fusionists had been known to organize the records in such a way as to leave themselves some leeway for that second Jump.

"Are you sure?" he said. "Suppose you throw in the emergency generators, turn off all the lights—"

"And the air circulation and the appliances and the hydronics apparatus. I know, I know. I figured that all in and we don't quite make it. —There's your stupid Double Jump safety regulations."

Strauss still managed to keep his temper. He knew—everyone knew—that it was the Fusionist Brotherhood that had been the driving force behind that regulation. A Double Jump, sometimes insisted on by the captain, much more often than not made the Fusionist look bad. —But then, there was at least one advantage. With an obligatory cruise between Jumps, there ought to be at least a week before the passengers grew restless and suspicious and in that week something might happen So far, it was not quite a day.

He said, "Are you sure you can't do something with your system: filter out some of the impurities?"

"Filter them out! They're not impurities; they're the whole thing. Hydrogen is the impurity here. Listen, I'll need half a billion degrees to fuse carbon and oxygen atoms; probably a full billion. It can't be done and I'm not going to try. If I try something and it doesn't work, it's my fault and I won't stand for that. It's up to you to get me to the hydrogen and you do it. You just cruise this ship to the hydrogen. I don't care how long it takes."

Strauss said, "We can't go faster than we're going now, considering the density of the medium, Vil. And at half light-speed we might have to cruise for two years—maybe twenty years—"

"Well, you think of a way out. Or the captain."

Strauss broke contact in despair. There was just no way of carrying on a rational conversation with a Fusionist. He'd heard the theory advanced (and perfectly seriously) that repeated Jumps affected the brain. In the Jump, every tardyon in ordinary matter had to be turned into an equivalent tachyon and then back again to the original tardyon. If the double conversion was imperfect in even the tiniest way, surely the effect would show up first in the brain, which was by far the most complex piece of matter ever to make the transition. Of course no ill effects had ever been demonstrated experimentally and no class of hypership officers seemed to deteriorate with time past what could be attributed to simple aging. But perhaps whatever it was in the Fusionists' brains that made them Fusionists and allowed them to go, by sheer intuition, beyond the best of computers might be particularly complex and therefore particularly vulnerable.

Nuts! There was nothing to it! Fusionists were merely spoiled!

He hesitated. Ought he to try to reach Cheryl? She could smooth matters if anyone could, and once old Vil-baby was properly dandled, he might think of a way to put the fusion tubes into operation—hydroxyl or not.

Did he really believe Viluekis could, under any circumstances? Or was he trying to avoid the thought of cruising for years? To be sure, hyperships were prepared for such an eventuality, in principle, but the eventuality had never come to pass and the crews—and still less the passengers—were surely not prepared for it.

But if he did talk to Cheryl, what could he say that wouldn't sound like an order for seduction? It was only one day so far and he was not yet ready to pimp for a Fusionist.

Wait! A while, anyway!

Viluekis frowned. He felt a little better, having bathed, and he was pleased that he had been firm with Strauss. Not a bad fellow, Strauss, but like all of them ("them": the captain, the crew, the passengers, all the stupid non-Fusionists in the Universe), he wanted to shed responsibility. Put it all on the Fusionist. It was an old, old song, and he was one Fusionist who wouldn't take it.

That talk about cruising for years was just a way of trying to frighten him. If they really put their minds to it, they could work out the limits of the cloud and somewhere there had to be a nearer edge. It was too much to ask that they had landed in the precise center. Of course, if they had landed near one edge and were heading for the other—

Viluekis rose and stretched. He was tall and his eyebrows hung over his eyes like canopies.

Suppose it did take years. No hypership had ever cruised for years. The longest cruise had been eighty-eight days and thirteen hours when one of them had managed to find itself in an unfavorable position with respect to a diffuse star and had to recede at speeds that built up to over 0.9 light before it was reasonably able to Jump.

They had survived and that was a quarter-year cruise. Of course, twenty years—

But that was impossible.

The signal light flashed three times before he was fully aware of it. If that was the captain coming to see him personally, he would leave at a rather more rapid rate than he came.

"Anton!"

The voice was soft, urgent, and part of his annoyance

seeped away. He allowed the door to recede into its socket and Cheryl came in. The door closed again behind her.

She was about twenty-five, with green eyes, a firm chin, dull red hair, and a magnificent figure that did not hide its light under a bushel.

She said, "Anton. Is there something wrong?"

Viluekis was not caught so entirely by surprise as to admit any such thing. Even a Fusionist knew better than to reveal anything prematurely to a passenger. "Not at all. What makes you think so?"

"One of the other passengers says so. A man named Martand."

"Martand? What does he know about it?" Then, suspiciously, "And what are you doing listening to some fool passenger? What does he look like?"

Cheryl smiled wanly. "Just someone who struck up a conversation in the lounge. He must be nearly sixty years old, and quite harmless, though I imagine he would like not to be. But that's not the point. There are no stars in view. Anyone can see that and Martand said it was significant."

"Did he? We're just passing through a cloud. There are lots of clouds in the Galaxy and hyperships pass through them all the time."

"Yes, but Martand says you can usually see some stars even in a cloud."

"What does he know about it?" Viluekis repeated. "Is he an old hand at deep space?"

"No-o," admitted Cheryl. "Actually, it's his first trip, I think. But he seems to know a lot."

"I'll bet. Listen, you go to him and tell him to shut up He can be put in solitary for this. And don't you repeat stories like that, either."

Cheryl put her head to one side. "Frankly, Anton, you sound as though there *is* trouble. This Martand—Louis Martand is his name—is an interesting fellow. He's a schoolteacher—eighth grade general science."

"A grade-school teacher! Good Lord, Cheryl—"

"But you ought to listen to him. He says that teaching children is one of the few professions where you have to know a little bit about everything because kids ask questions and can spot phonies."

"Well then, maybe your specialty should be spotting phonies too. Now, Cheryl, you go and tell him to shut up, or I will."

"All right. But first— Is it true that we're going through a hydroxyl cloud and the fusion tube is shut down?"

Viluekis' mouth opened, then shut again. It was quite a while before he said, "Who told you that?"

"Martand. I'll go now."

"No," said Viluekis sharply. "Wait a while. How many others has Martand been telling all this?"

"Nobody. He said he doesn't want to spread panic. I was there when he was thinking about it, I suppose, and I guess he couldn't resist saying something."

"Does he know you know me?"

Cheryl's forehead furrowed slightly. "I think I mentioned something about it."

Viluekis snorted. "Don't you suppose that this crazy old man you've picked up is bound to try to show you how great he is? It's me he's trying to impress through you."

"Nothing of the sort," said Cheryl. "In fact, he specifically said I wasn't to tell you anything."

"Knowing, of course, you'd come to me at once."

"Why should he want me to do that?"

"To show me up. Do you know what it's like being a Fusionist? To have everyone resenting you, against you, because you're so needed, because you—"

Cheryl said, "But what's any of that got to do with it? If Martand's all wrong, how would that show you up? And if he's right— Is he right, Anton?"

"Well, exactly what did he say?"

"I'm not sure I can remember it all, of course," Cheryl said thoughtfully. "It was after we came out of the Jump, actually quite a few hours after. By that time all anyone was talking about was that there were no stars in view. In the lounge everyone was saying there ought to be another Jump soon because what was the good of deep-space travel without a view? Of course, we knew we had to cruise at least a day. Then Martand came in, saw me, and came over to speak to me. —I think he rather likes me."

"I think I rather don't like him," said Viluekis grimly. "Go on."

"I said to him that it was pretty dreary without a view and he said it would stay that way for a while, and he sounded worried. Naturally I asked why he said such a thing and he said it was because the fusion tube had been turned off."

"Who told him that?" demanded Viluekis.

"He said there was a low hum that you could hear in one of the men's rooms that you couldn't hear any more. And he said there was a place in the closet of the game room where the chess sets were kept where the wall felt warm because of the fusion tube and that place was not warm now."

"Is that all the evidence he has?"

Cheryl ignored that and went on. "He said there were no stars visible because we were in a dust cloud and the fusion tubes must have stopped because there was no hydrogen to speak of in it. He said there probably wouldn't be enough energy to spark another Jump and that if we looked for hydrogen we might have to cruise years to get out of the cloud."

Viluekis' frown became ferocious. "He's panic-mongering. Do you know that—"

"He's not. He told me not to tell anyone because he said it would create panic and that, besides, it wouldn't happen. He only told me because he had just figured it out and was all excited about it and had to talk to someone, but he said there was an easy way out and that the Fusionist would know what to do so that there was no need to worry at all. —But you're the Fusionist, so it seemed to me I had to ask whether he was really right about the cloud and whether you had really taken care of it."

Viluekis said, "This grade-school teacher of yours knows nothing about anything. Just stay away from him. —Uh, did he say what his so-called easy way out was?"

"No. Should I have asked him?"

"No! Why should you have asked him? What would he know about it? But then again— All right, ask him. I'm curious what the idiot has in mind. Ask him."

Cheryl nodded. "I can do that. But are we in trouble?"

Viluekis said shortly, "Suppose you leave that to me. We're not in trouble till I say we're in trouble."

He looked for a long time at the closed door after she had left, both angry and uneasy. What was this Louis Martand—this grade-school teacher—doing with his lucky guesses?

If it finally came about that an extended cruise was necessary, the passengers would have to have it broken to them carefully, or none of them would survive. With Martand shouting it to all who would listen—

Almost savagely, Viluekis clicked shut the combination that would bring him the captain.

Martand was slim and of neat appearance. His lips seemed forever on the verge of a smile, though his face and bearing were marked by a polite gravity—an almost expectant gravity as though he was forever waiting for the person with him to say something truly important.

Cheryl said to him, "I spoke to Mr. Viluekis. —He's the Fusionist, you know. I told him what you said."

Martand looked shocked and shook his head. "I'm afraid you shouldn't have done that!"

"He did seem displeased."

"Of course. Fusionists are very special people and they don't like to have outsiders—"

"I could see that. But he insisted there was nothing to worry about."

"Of course not," said Martand, taking her hand and patting it in a consoling gesture, but then continuing to hold it. "I told you there was an easy way out. He's probably setting it up now. Still, I suppose it could be a while before he thinks of it."

"Thinks of what?" Then, warmly, "Why shouldn't he think of it, if you have?"

"But he's a specialist, you see, my dear young lady. Specialists think in their specialty and have a hard time getting out of it. As for myself, I don't dare fall into ruts. When I set up a class demonstration, I've got to improvise most of the time. I have never yet been at a school where proton micro-piles have been available and I've had to work up a kerosene thermoelectric generator when we're off on field trips."

"What's kerosene?" asked Cheryl.

Martand laughed. He seemed delighted. "You see?

People forget. Kerosene is a kind of inflammable liquid. A still more primitive source of energy that I have many times had to use was a wood fire which you start by friction. Did you ever come across one of those? You take a match—"

Cheryl was looking blank and Martand went on, indulgently, "Well, it doesn't matter. I'm just trying to get across the notion that your Fusionist will have to think of something more primitive than fusion and that will take him a while. As for me, I'm used to working with primitive methods. —For instance, do you know what's out there?"

He gestured at the viewing port, which was utterly featureless, so featureless that the lounge was virtually depopulated for lack of a view.

"A cloud; a dust cloud."

"Ah, but what kind? the one thing that's always to be found everywhere is hydrogen. It's the original stuff of the Universe and hyperships depend on it. No ship can carry enough fuel to make repeated Jumps or to accelerate to near light-speed and back repeatedly. We have to scoop the fuel out of space."

"You know, I've always wondered about that. I thought outer space was empty!"

"*Nearly* empty, my dear, and nearly is as good as a feast. When you travel at 100,000 miles a second, you can scoop up and compress quite a bit of hydrogen, even when there's only a few atoms per cubic centimeter. And small amounts of hydrogen, fusing steadily, provide all the energy we need. In clouds, the hydrogen is usually even thicker, but impurities may cause trouble, as in this one."

"How can you tell this one has impurities?"

"Why else would Mr. Viluekis have shut down the fusion tube? Next to hydrogen, the most common elements in the universe are helium, oxygen, and carbon. If the fusion pumps have stopped, that means there's a shortage of fuel, which is hydrogen, and a presence of something that will damage the complex fusion system. This can't be helium, which is harmless. It is possibly hydroxyl groups, an oxygen-hydrogen combination. Do you understand?"

"I think so," said Cheryl. "I had general science in college, and some of it is coming back. The dust is really hydroxyl groups attached to solid dust grains."

"Or actually free in the gaseous state, too. Even hydroxyl is not too dangerous to the fusion system, in moderation, but carbon compounds are. Formaldehyde is most likely and I should imagine with a ratio of about one of those to four hydroxyls. Do you see now?"

"No, I don't," said Cheryl flatly.

"Such compounds won't fuse. If you heat them to a few hundred million degrees, they break down into single atoms and the concentration of oxygen and carbon will simply damage the system. But why not take them in at ordinary temperatures? Hydroxyl will combine with formaldehyde, after compression, in a chemical reaction that will cause no harm to the system. At least, I'm sure a good Fusionist could modify the system to handle a chemical reaction at room temperature. The energy of the reaction can be stored and, after a while, there will be enough to make a Jump possible."

Cheryl said, "I don't see that at all. Chemical reactions produce hardly any energy, compared to fusion."

"You're quite right, dear. But we don't need much. The previous Jump has left us with insufficient energy for an immediate second Jump—that's regulations. But I'll bet your friend the Fusionist saw to it that as little energy as possible was lacking. Fusionists usually do that. The little extra required to reach ignition can be collected from ordinary chemical reactions. Then, once a Jump takes us out of the club, cruising for a week or so will refill our energy tanks and we can continue without harm. Of course—" Martand raised his eyebrows and shrugged.

"Yes?"

"Of course," said Martand, "if, for any reason, Mr. Viluekis should delay, there may be trouble. Every day we spend before Jumping uses up energy in the ordinary life of the ship, and after a while chemical reactions won't supply the energy required to reach Jump-ignition. I hope he doesn't wait long."

"Well, why don't you tell him? Now."

Martand shook his head. "Tell a Fusionist? I couldn't do that, dear."

"Then I will."

"Oh no. He's sure to think of it himself. In fact, I'll make a bet with you, my dear. You tell him exactly what I said and say that I told you he had already thought of it himself and that the fusion tube was in operation. And of course, if I win—"

Martand smiled.

Cheryl smiled too. "I'll see," she said.

Martand looked after her thoughtfully as she hastened away, his thoughts not entirely on Viluekis' possible reaction.

He was not surprised when a ship's guard appeared from almost nowhere and said, "Please come with me, Mr. Martand."

Martand said quietly, "Thank you for letting me finish. I was afraid you wouldn't."

Something more than six hours passed before Martand was allowed to see the captain. His imprisonment (which was what he considered it) was one of isolation but was not onerous; and the captain, when he did see him, looked tired and not particularly hostile.

Hanson said, "It was reported to me that you were spreading rumors designed to create panic among the passengers. That is a serious charge."

"I spoke to one passenger only, sir; and for a purpose."

"So we realize. We put you under surveillance at once and I have a report, a rather full one, of the conversation you had with Miss Cheryl Winter. It was the second conversation on the subject."

"Yes, sir."

"Apparently you intended the meat of the conversation to be passed on to Mr. Viluekis."

"Yes, sir."

"You did not consider going to Mr. Viluekis personally?"

"I doubt that he would have listened, sir."

"Or to me?"

"You might have listened, but how would you pass on the information to Mr. Viluekis? You might then have had to use Miss Winter yourself. Fusionists have their peculiarities."

The captain nodded abstractedly. "What was it you expected to happen when Miss Winter passed on the information to Mr. Viluekis?"

"My hope, sir," said Martand, "was that he would be less defensive with Miss Winter than with anyone else; that he would feel less threatened. I was hoping that he would laugh and say the idea was a simple one that had occurred to him long before and that, indeed, the scoops were already working with the intent of promoting the chemical reaction. Then, when he got rid of Miss Winter, and I imagine he would do that quickly, he would start the scoops and report his action to you, sir, omitting any reference to myself or Miss Winter."

"You did not think he might dismiss the whole notion as unworkable?"

"There was that chance, but it didn't happen."

"How do you know?"

"Because half an hour after I was placed in detention, sir, the lights in the room in which I was kept dimmed perceptibly and did not brighten again. I assumed that energy expenditure in the ship was being cut to the bone and assumed further that Viluekis was throwing everything into the pot so that the chemical reaction would supply enough for ignition."

The captain frowned. "What made you so sure you could manipulate Mr. Viluekis? Surely you have never dealt with Fusionists, have you?"

"Ah, but I teach the eighth grade, Captain. I have dealt with other children."

For a moment the captain's expression remained wooden. And then, slowly, it relaxed into a smile. "I like you, Mr. Martand," he said, "but it won't help you. Your expectations *did* come to pass; as nearly as I can tell exactly as you had hoped. But do you understand what followed?"

"I will, if you tell me."

"Mr. Viluekis had to evaluate your suggestion and decide, at once, whether it was practical. He had to make a number of careful adjustments to the system to allow chemical reactions without knocking out the possibility of future fusion. He had to determine the maximum safe rate of reaction; the amount of stored energy to save; the point at which ignition might safely be attempted; the kind and nature of the Jump. It all had to be done quickly and no one else but a Fusionist could have done it. In fact, not every Fusionist could have done it; Mr. Viluekis is exceptional even for a Fusionist. Do you see?"

"Quite well."

The captain looked at the timepiece on the wall and activated his view port. It was black, as it had been now for the better part of two days. "Mr. Viluekis informed me of the time at which he will attempt Jump-ignition. He thinks it will work and I am confident in his judgment."

"If he misses," said Martand somberly, "we may find ourselves in the same position as before but stripped of energy."

"I realize that," said Hanson, "and since you might feel a certain responsibility over having placed the idea in the Fusionist's mind, I thought you might want to wait through the few moments of suspense ahead of us."

Both men were silent now, watching the screen, while first seconds, then minutes moved past. Hanson had not mentioned the exact deadline and Martand had no way of telling how imminent it was or whether it had passed. He could only shift his glance, occasionally and momentarily, to the captain's face, which maintained a studied expressionlessness.

And then came that queer internal wrench that disappeared almost at once, like a tic in the abdominal wall. They had Jumped.

"Stars!" said Hanson, in a whisper of deep satisfaction. The view port had burst into a riot of them and, at that moment, Martand could recall no sweeter sight in all his life.

"And on the second," said Hanson. "A beautiful job. We're energy-stripped now, but we'll be full again in anywhere from one to three weeks and during that time the passengers will have their view."

Martand felt too weak with relief to speak.

The captain turned to him. "Now, Mr. Martand. Your idea had merit. One could argue it saved the ship and everyone on it. One could also argue that Mr. Viluekis was sure to think of it himself soon enough. But there will be no argument about it at all, for under no conditions can your part in this be known. Mr. Viluekis did the job and it was a great one of pure virtuosity even after we take into account the fact that you may have sparked it. He will be commended for it and receive great honors. You will receive nothing."

Martand was silent for a moment. Then he said, "I understand. A Fusionist is indispensable and I am of no account. If Mr. Viluekis' pride is hurt in the slightest, he may become useless to you, and you can't afford to lose him. For myself— Well, be it as you wish. Good day, Captain."

"Not quite," said the captain. "We can't trust you."

"I won't say anything."

"You may not intend to, but things happen. We can't take the chance. For the remainder of the flight, you will be under house arrest."

Martand frowned. "For what? I saved you and your damned ship—and your Fusionist."

"For exactly that. For saving it. That's the way it works out."

"Where's the justice?"

Slowly, the captain shook his head. "It's a rare commodity, I admit, and sometimes too expensive to afford. You can't even go back to your room. You will be seeing no one in what remains of the trip."

Martand rubbed the side of his chin with one finger. "Surely you don't mean that literally, Captain."

"I'm afraid I do."

"But there is another who might talk—accidentally and without meaning to. You had better place Miss Winter under house arrest too."

"And double the injustice?"

"Misery loves company," said Martand.

And the captain smiled. "Perhaps you're right," he said.

$$f(x) = (11/15/67)$$
$$x = her, \ f(x) \neq 0$$

GEO. ALEC EFFINGER

Old-guard science-fiction aficionados have lamented greatly in recent years that there's no longer any science in the science fiction being turned out by younger writers. That thesis is neatly disproved here by one of the brightest and most gifted of the new writers, Geo. Alec Effinger, "Piglet" to his friends. His first story for NEW DIMENSIONS is science fiction in its most literal and antique sense: fiction about science, a graphic demonstration of the workings of the scientific method.

Oftentimes we speak of the "privilege of science." Now, just what does this phrase mean? "Science," our dictionary tells us, concerns the observation and classification of natural phenomena. Now, already we are losing touch with the personal involvement that enables each of us, as individuals, to identify and communicate with our environment and our time. "Natural phenomena." What does that actually mean, how are we to grab hold of such a nebulous concept (an idea which in two words encompasses everything that comes to pass within the confines of the universe) so that it represents a concrete and virtual process? I intend by no means to suggest that all such groups of jargon words be eliminated in favor of pragmatic terms, but I do wish, at the outset, to avoid creating a mistaken impression in the mind of the reader.

So, to begin. Over three years ago our department began an experiment. The whole idea grew out of a discussion we had been continuing during our lunch break for some time. Indeed, the head of our department was aware of the high caliber of insights that were made during the informal bull sessions. He guessed that it had something to do with the contrast between the rigorous hours of the morning and the relaxed surroundings during lunch. In any event, someone (I believe it was Dr. Green) made an offhand remark about what we could do if we had the proper equipment. I said that even with the facilities he envisioned it would be impossible. Dr. Nelson disagreed. For four days our staff argued, in ever more heated tones. Research was done in our spare time. Authorities were consulted for outside opinions. Analogies were constructed, attacked, and defended. All of this was done extracurricularly; never did our regular tasks suffer.

On the morning of November 15, 1967, I arrived at the lab early. Somehow I knew that it was going to be a special day. Though I went to my locker nearly half an hour before my usual time, I found almost every one of my associates already dressed and ready for work. The green blackboard in the locker room had been freshly washed (some black wet spots were still fading from view) and a mysterious quotation had been written high up on the board. The writing was a masculine scrawl, beginning in the upper left corner and slanting down to about the middle of the board. The message was: "Direct lies told to the world are as dust in the balance when weighed against the falsehoods of inaccuracy; and accuracy can be taught." Sir Arthur Helps.

I was mystified. "What does this mean?" I asked Dr. Johnson.

"I don't know," he said, stifling a yawn with the back of his hand. His wristwatch protruded from the sleeve of his lab coat and gleamed under the locker room's fluorescents. His other hand held his clipboard.

"Is he weighing lies against falsehoods?" asked Dr. Green.

"I suppose," said Dr. Johnson.

"Which would be heavier?" said Dr. Nelson. "What's

so significant about dust in the balance? A gram is still a gram."

"It's very strange," I said, shaking my head.

"Perhaps this will straighten things out," said the deep voice of the department head. We all turned around quickly, startled, and saw our superior standing in the entrance to the tunnel that leads to our work area. He was leaning against the doorjamb and smiling. His smile is an unsettling thing: small, forced, generally reserved for unpleasant occasions. But now we knew that he had an agreeable surprise for us. He held a large glass apparatus in his hands.

"A Fleischer retort!" said Dr. Green. "And a hypostasis unit! How ever did you wangle that out of the commissioners?"

"My secret, gentlemen," said the department head softly. "As you no doubt realize, this equipment is very sophisticated, very expensive, and very necessary to that project you've all been mooning about for the last week. I've received permission to suspend the current experiments for as long as it takes for you to gather your data. Have a good time, gentlemen, but be careful! These things are fragile." Surely he knew that such a warning was unnecessary to men of our background, but I suppose that he was actually suggesting that the future of our department might rest with our conduct and our results in this spontaneous enterprise. I know for certain that his own position was in jeopardy. But we could never let him down; this was not the first time that our department head had taken such a risk for us.

"This is the way that science operates," said Dr. Green musingly, staring at Sir Arthur's quotation.

"Co-operation," said Dr. Johnson, clapping him on the back and putting his other arm around my shoulder as we started down the tunnel to the lab. "If we work together, we can build something that will endure for all time. If we bicker, if we let our petty feelings in the way, it'll be pure hell."

"Let's do it," said Dr. Nelson behind us. "Let's do it for the department head."

"Right," said Dr. Green.

And that's the way the project began. Of course, as yet

we had little idea of the work before us, or even the general direction that it would be necessary to explore. Each of us had his own idea of the proper hypothesis or the proper method. Even though we wanted desperately to begin the actual experimentation, we knew from experience that that stage was still some months away. Now was the time for more research, serious contemplation, and independent study in our particular field of strength. Later our data would be collated and evaluated, and our department head would guide us in directing our energies along what appeared to be the most profitable avenues.

Imagination is the lifeblood of science, as research and experimentation are its nerves and sinews. The scientist as artist: no mere contradiction in terms, but a true picture of the necessary role of the creative spark in the pageant of technological development. At Science Seminary in Iowa we were trained in many of the techniques used by the other schools, particularly the liberal arts branches. We read by candlelight. We were made to stare blankly from attic windows, our instructors walking among us to position our fingers in thoughtful attitudes on our chins and cheeks. We learned to use hunger and frustration effectively. Perhaps this is the reason that today those of us who made it through the Seminary are apt to be more dependably erratic, or spontaneous, or whatever constitutes true originality. Though (no doubt, no doubt!) we are harder to work with.

How large a part imagination plays in the cavalcade of scientific endeavor: that which is not accidental discovery is instead the result of careful preparation. Careful preparation in turn is the product of thought and reasoned discourse, which proceed from a train of related insights, which develop from a single, momentary, creative inspiration. The continued encouragement of an open-minded, receptive (and, therefore, productive), and enthusiastic outlook is essential. For years I signed my letters with this exhortation: Do not stultify! until I realized that it was pretentious.

As we began our work our interpersonal relationships became more complex. We were all great chums as it was, but now again we felt ourselves to be members of the same team, all working together, pulling as one, co-operating in a true spirit of Christian fellowship. Then one day our department head introduced the new member, Dr. Short (or, as we all called her, Janet). Far from being resented, she was immediately welcomed and made to feel at home. We did our best to include her in our group feeling as well as in our work, pausing now and then to give her a chance to voice whatever opinion she might have.

Janet was beautiful; even in her white lab coat she was the loveliest woman that I had ever seen. Her hair fell about her shoulders like rippling waves of sunshine. Her eyes were twin pools of limpid blue, and I never tired of staring into them. And, fortunately, she enjoyed that too. We used to stand about the lab, each of us by his own gas jet, staring into her eyes from our scattered work areas. She would smile and turn slowly, giving each of us his turn at falling directly into her line of sight. Her features were finely shaped, classically beautiful. Her bearing suggested that she was accustomed to command. We all gazed wistfully at the way her pendulous alabaster globes strained at the thin material of the sweater beneath the lab coat. On those rare occasions when we caught a glimpse of her thigh, we noticed that it was as creamy white and smooth as we hoped. Not one of us failed to feel the stirring in his loins when she came in each morning to chat with us in the locker room. But it was given only to Dr. Nelson to enjoy her special favor. Not that we overly envied his fortune or thought ill of them. Indeed, we were overjoyed at their happiness, for it seemed to knot our little group even closer. We took delight in their joy, and often.

The process of maturing is the recurring task of learning discipline. This lesson becomes more and more difficult, for as we grow older and more set in our ways we become less willing to be refashioned in new molds for new outlooks. The final rigidity, the final inability to follow instruction, is death. Nothing else is worth worrying about. And so it is in science: the imagination is vital, of course, but only insofar as it is disciplined. We must recognize standards.

Was that Dr. Short's function? Was she the unifying touchstone of caution that held us together, that kept us from flying off like excited children lost among the phantoms of scientific speculation? Or was she rather a scheme of our department head, to maintain Dr. Nelson's shaky equilibrium? Surely Dr. Nelson's instability was no secret; we discussed it often enough in his absence. But with Janet—Dr. Short—Dr. Nelson seemed to find his spiritual anchor. And everyone knew his weakness for trim ankles and faint mustaches.

While the exotic apparatus collected dust and held down papers on the desk of the department head, we compiled our facts. One by one the hypotheses were abandoned as hard facts contradicted premises. We celebrated the death of each theory at lunch. Someone would bring a radio and we'd dance, drawing lots while Janet, the only partner, sat apart and smiled tightly. She had a light dusting of freckles across her nose; I'll always remember that.

During the summer of 1968, Drs. Nelson and Short became better and better acquainted. Janet bought him a pair of boots and he gave her several necklaces and pendants. It became a morning ritual to stand about the lockers with their pasted-up pictures of Jane Fonda or Johnny Bench and the color shots clipped from *Life*, blown-up photos taken through an electron microscope of a virus or refractions from molecular arrangements and comment on them (the various necklaces and pendants, one of which Dr. Short would wear each day). We would laugh quietly and some of us would smoke until the bell rang. Then we'd all start off down the tunnel, ready for another day at the slate-topped work tables. The department head spoke to us each morning, just as we reached the end of the tunnel and emerged into the laboratory proper. We would ply him with questions concerning the meaning of that day's cryptic quotation, but he never gave us a hint. He believed that his daily mystery aided us in expanding our horizons, increasing our mental agility, combating the creeping conservatism that is inimical to progress, and so forth. He was apart from us, being admin., but in his own way he was always truly one of us. We never did really resent him.

I believe that it was Dr. Johnson who first remarked on the parallel courses of our experiment and Drs. Nelson's and Short's burgeoning relationship. "Even as we grope blindly," said Dr. Johnson, and Janet blushed endearingly, "feeling about for new laws and old events, so too are you, our very dear colleagues, discovering the most charming and novel variations of the age-old 'love' situation. Certainly you realize that this has been done many times before, but are you not still amazed at how fresh and new it seems? We are learning as we go, creating the rules and discovering the operations as they become necessary. So are you. I am curious to see who will win."

And this was very true. Dr. Nelson ceased shaking and mumbling, habits which, good friend though he was, often made him impossible to get along with. He found security at last, after nearly fifty years in the field. Janet made sure to touch an elbow patch of his lab coat every time she passed his work table. Dr. Nelson would look up and smile, the familiar old vagueness gone from his eyes. And soon he began to make important contributions, just as he did long before I was born. And Janet—that is, Dr. Short—gained from their alliance too. She took to carrying a small spiral notebook with her, to copy down such vocabulary words or aphorisms as Dr. Nelson might pronounce. She began to wear tight blouses, unbuttoned in a suggestive manner.

And then, after a year, we came into the locker room on November 15, 1968. On the blackboard, as usual, was a quotation: *"There are not many joys in human life equal to the joy of the sudden birth of a generalization illuminating the mind after a long period of patient research." Prince Kropotkin.*

Dr. Johnson turned to me, his speckled face transformed with expectation. "Are you ready?" he asked.

"Gee, I don't know," I said. I certainly didn't feel any differently.

"But today's the day, apparently," said Dr. Green. "I wonder who it'll be."

Dr. Johnson looked across the room at Drs. Nelson and Short. "I sort of hope it's Dr. Nelson. That would vindicate the department head."

We all stared with Dr. Johnson, and the rightness of his sentiment was undeniable. I think that each of us secretly decided to shirk that day, in order not to deprive

Dr. Nelson of the opportunity of making the Big Break-through by himself. None of us wanted to beat him accidentally to the key discovery. Consequently, after filing into the laboratory, we pretended to work as usual, but spent a good deal of time tying shoelaces and sharpening pencils. Dr. Johnson and Dr. Green played "dots." I called the other six associates (whom I have yet to mention by name; they were very silent) together for a review of our previous year's work, ostensibly as an anniversary celebration. Dr. Nelson was so engrossed in his analysis that he failed to notice us.

About noon Dr. Nelson called out to Dr. Johnson, "Do you think that the reduced amount of ultraviolet let through by the denser atmosphere could have been the stimulating factor?" Dr. Johnson said that he wasn't sure. Dr. Nelson went back to his work. In an hour he announced that he believed that he had a unified hypothesis that covered every one of the contingencies that we had specified in the last twelve months. We congratulated him, and Janet led him away to get a bit of lunch. We didn't see them again for several days, but we were so relieved that the initial phase was completed that we just chuckled indulgently.

When circumstances had returned to normal we met with the department head. He appointed Dr. Green to become obsessed with perfection. I was to be the pessimist. Dr. Johnson and one other were to question our motives. Dr. Nelson and Dr. Short had made their contributions, but they were to do even more. We owed quite a bit to them. Without their continuing efforts and constant support, both intellectual and spiritual, our job could never have been accomplished. Now, our team scattered as it is to the four corners of the globe, we often think of our debt to those two oddly matched, dedicated workers. I doubt if I will ever see their like again. It would be a tiresome repetition.

Everyone but the experimenter himself has confidence in the results, for the technician is the only one aware of the amount of hedging that is done (yes, we all do it, even the noblest of us, for time is money). But the only one likely to be completely enthusiastic about a hypothesis is its originator. Thus, the department head tried to encourage us along lines which he himself believed to be best, while attempting to convince us that these choices were our own. We all knew what he was doing, but it made no difference.

When the working hypothesis was first put forward by Dr. Nelson (and soundly applauded), and modified by suggestions from Dr. Johnson and two of the others, we gathered together into a circle with the department head in the center. Those of us along the perimeter joined hands, and the department head made us promise that if the hypothesis proved unworkable we would not hold to it stubbornly. We gladly agreed. I recall very clearly walking back to my work area with Dr. Green. "Still," he said, "that does not mean that we must abandon the hypothesis after an initial failure or two."

"Right," I said. "As long as mere ideas do not take precedence over truths we shall be fine."

By this time, I believe, Drs. Nelson and Short were deeply and sincerely in love. They spoke to each other in lovers' terms, and with few actual words, but many sentimentalized looks and gestures. We watched them approvingly, and a little enviously, for we had all forsworn happiness at the Seminary. I always got a bit of a twinge when I saw Dr. Nelson put his hand on Janet's knee when he thought no one was watching. The shadows and planes of her knees worked together to give the impression that one was viewing a photograph of a bust of Poseidon. No one ever mentioned this, though. It may be that I was the only one of us who thought so.

The two were inseparable. They wandered about the lab together, they went out for a drink of water together, they sat together at lunch, he pressing his right calf against her left. They did little work, but we covered for them. Perhaps the department head realized that this was happening, but he said nothing as long as our tasks were completed according to our voluntary schedule. Dr. Short, when included in our conversations, would at one point or another remark on how brilliant Dr. Nelson's hypothesis was, and how much time it saved the entire project. Dr. Johnson reinforced his earlier observation thusly: "Our project is heading off in a definite direction now. We don't know yet if it is the correct one exactly, but the work we do will give us that information in just a matter of time. The structure is sound, built on sufficient mature thought. And so is your relationship. You are applying what you have learned about each other to form a long-lasting, internally consistent, mutually profitable arrangement."

Shortly after the actual research began we were stunned one morning to find two quotations on the board. I do not recall the uppermost sentiment (the one put there by the department head), but below it was scrawled in Dr. Nelson's hand: "We must never be too absorbed by the thought we are pursuing." Claude Bernard. We were shaken. Was this a denial of the significance of our work? Was it, even worse, an indication of his waning interest in Janet (Dr. Short)? We asked him about it at lunch; he denied putting it on the blackboard. We pressed him, and he admitted writing it there. But he was surprised at our outrage and curiosity. "I don't necessarily mean what Bernard suggests," he said, smiling. "It's just food for thought, gentlemen." We shook our heads in wonder. Even as old as he was, Dr. Nelson's mind moved through devious channels.

Research is to the progress of science as everything after the shuffling is to a game of canasta. There are two types of research: research done for its own sake or for the sake of knowledge (ad maiorem gloriam Dei), and research done to solve a particular problem. Our present work was neither. "Is this applied research?" I asked.

"No," said Dr. Johnson, "I don't believe so. There is actually little commercial value in what we're doing."

"But does that mean then that we're doing straight abstract stuff?"

"That should follow," he said with a puzzled expression, "but in this case it doesn't."

"Perhaps we have stumbled on a third sort of research," said Dr. Green.

"Maybe that's it," said Dr. Johnson, dismissing the matter with a wave of his hand.

At the Science Seminary we were instructed in game theory, according to the supposition that proper scientific experimentation had its own strategies, as much so as any game of chance. It does not take much alteration of viewpoint to see science as competition between the researcher and the inscrutable forces of nature. There is even a sort of "box score" that may be used to outline the degree of success enjoyed by an experiment. Science has its teams, its goals, its penalties; reason is its referee. The war against disease, poverty, ignorance, and intolerance is being won on the playing fields of Cal Tech.

Well, the sides had been chosen, the ball field prepared, the coin tossed, but there were no spectators. Ours was a silent struggle. No bands played, no girls in blue and white shorts cheered us on. Just the long walk from the locker room through the tunnel to the "dugout" (the lab), where our "manager" would give us our daily pep talk. We, the home team, *Science* carved in big rock letters like the ads for *Ben Hur* out on the Seminary lawn so many years ago, we started out half an inning behind the opposition. But we would bat last. What a silly way for adults to spend their lives.

We were like children! It was like Christmas out of our distant past; we set up the delicate glassware in preparation for the first of the test runs. Flasks, retorts, induction coils, copper tubing, rubber tubing, glass tubing, stoppers and petcocks, all joined together like a malformed Xmas tree for chemists. Banks of electrophoresis apparatus stood ready to analyze the products of the experiment. Cables ran underfoot, twisting through furniture and doorways to end with red and green plastic viper heads. It seemed to me that I was transported back to my youth, trying to synthesize amino acids in the high school lab, with sparks in a piece of glassware simulating lightning. Again, we played God.

"Building, always building," murmured Dr. Green. I happened to be standing very near to him at the time.

"Dr. Nelson and Janet?" asked Dr. Johnson, who stood very near to Dr. Green on the other side.

"No," said Dr. Green, "I meant us, here, with all this. In a little while we'll have learned something."

"I suppose," said Dr. Johnson. "But those two," indicating Drs. Nelson and Short, "are building much more, and at a greater rate than we can hope to match. *They* are the ones doing beautiful things."

"Perhaps we should give up here and go out and do likewise," I said jokingly.

"Not so facetious a suggestion as you might think," said one of the other scientists.

"Just keeping ourselves open to whatever options present themselves should suffice," I said. "Have a goal, but take what comes."

"With dedication the password to success," said the voice of the department head. We turned around, startled and amazed at his unusual appearance in our realm so late in the day.

"Dedication," said the wheezing voice of Dr. Nelson, "ah, dedication is less than illusion. It is a fallacy." We all gasped at his contradiction of the department head. Dr. Nelson had struck at the very foundation of our belief. "No matter," he said, "I don't really mean that, either. The important thing to remember, though, is that someone does." Could he mean me? I thought anxiously.

Perhaps it was only my guilty mind that insisted that Dr. Nelson had directed his curious attack at me. I was guilty, because I worshiped Dr. Short. I was blind then. I did not see those shortcomings which became so painfully evident later on, after the reviews were printed: I was not aware of her pathological needs which masqueraded as concern, or the malleable, almost mercuric nature of her personality, which provided her with emotional camouflage. We never wondered why she avoided large groups of people; she could not assume a personality that would be proof against the potential threats of all the others. But, as I say, I saw none of this. I was entranced by the pellucidness, the apparent guilelessness, the graciousness, the exuberance that was merely immaturity. And I loved her and felt guilt, for she was not my woman.

"*What is observed depends on who's looking.*" W. H. George. That was the quotation on the blackboard for November 15, 1969, the second anniversary of our project. Naturally, when each of us came in that morning we expected to be greeted by news of some major development that the department head had planned. It was one year ago that Dr. Nelson had made the necessary synthesis to begin our actual experiment. I felt that today might be the day when we would detect those products that signaled the final phase. But the quotation gave us little hope of such a step. In fact, the more we discussed it, the more it seemed to be actually negative in nature, as though we had been overlooking something vital and would have to begin again.

Dr. Green did not agree. "No," he said, "I think you're wrong there, barking up the wrong tree, so to speak. Your interpretation does not hold water. You're too quick to look at the gloomy side. I believe that the department head intends for us to see today as a rebirth of devotion, in a slightly altered direction. That is, if you take my meaning, that our outlook must no longer be so parochial, so narrow. We must grow with the project, if you follow me. We are in danger of getting in over our heads, and our only salvation will be to push back the frontiers of our trepidations, so that we may operate comfortably even though we're unsure what we're doing."

"That's very interesting," said Dr. Johnson.

"But aren't we all observing?" I asked innocently.

"Precisely," said Dr. Green.

"And aren't we all taking notes independently?" asked Dr. Johnson.

"Exactly," said Dr. Green.

"Well?" said Dr. Johnson.

"We're all approaching this wrong," said Dr. Green. "We're viewing the thing passively, jotting down each development when it happens and not trying to anticipate. Something happens and we say, 'Look at that!' We should be trying to predict what will occur, and then watch for justification."

"Is he right?" I asked Dr. Johnson.

"Perhaps," he said.

So that day we began doing just that. It must have been the correct thing, because the department head beamed proudly. Later, Dr. Green told me in confidence that he was inspired to his singular interpretation by his observation of Drs. Nelson and Short. They had ceased to be astonished by their relationship; not to say that the wonder had vanished, but that they had enough confidence in themselves now that they could rather make plans with some assurance. The future, of course, was still unknown, but it worked within a framework that they had discovered within themselves and within each other. The two of them had gladly replaced the fire of their early passion with a mature and quiet faith.

Some days later Dr. Johnson was staring into the huge central apparatus. The contents of the glassware were bubbling and shifting as they had begun to do recently, sliding through color changes in no apparent pattern. The liquid contents roiled and surged in a thick, sexual way, while the gaseous products hung in slowly shifting clouds, occasionally rising out of or falling into the liquid. It was an incredibly gorgeous thing to see, and I wonder if the beauty of it didn't seduce our eyes from the purely scientific observation for which we were employed. Dr. Short, that is, Janet, came over to the central work area and stood beside Dr. Johnson. He never took his eyes from the huge glass bubble, but he knew that she was there.

"These are the words that I have for your love for Dr. Nelson," he said. "Opalescent, sustentative, radiant, crystalline, epicene, vibrant, adamantine, chatoyant. The devoutly-to-be-wished consummation."

Janet was silent for a moment. Then she laughed. "Golly," she said, "If you only knew!" She twisted a button on her blouse for a few seconds, then turned around and walked away. She went back to her table with Dr. Nelson and put her arm around him and called him "honey."

It was now early summer of 1970. We had formed a softball squad to play the research team from across the hall. At the first game I stood at the backstop with a few of the fellows from the opposing group. Dr. Short was taking her practice in the batter's box and was doing pretty well, hitting line drives over the infielders' heads and sending the outfielders back in astonishment with some fairly long flies. One of the other group of fellows remarked on her surprising talent. I smiled and told them that she was involved with one of our number, and that the experiment we were conducting seemed to be paralleling their love affair. My audience chuckled, but stopped when I angrily repeated my strange statement. I was told that such a thing was very common, that they had had a similar experience themselves a few years ago. I said nothing more to these cloddish fellows. I watched Janet, now taking fielding practice in her long white lab coat. She seemed to me to be still afraid of hard ground balls.

Near the end of the summer things began to go bad. The first sign was the day we arrived to find no quotation on the blackboard. Hurrying worriedly through the tunnel, we discovered Dr. Short sitting at her work area, crying.

"What's wrong?" I asked her.

"Can we do anything?" asked one of the others.

Dr. Short (Janet) pointed in the direction of the experiment. Still weeping, she took Dr. Nelson's hand. "I don't know," she said, sobbing. "I don't know if I love you because of that thing or in spite of it." The department head had been summoned and now stood on the outside of our circle. We looked like Snow White and the seven dwarfs. He told her that she could have the rest of the day off. She shook her head, but followed him back down the tunnel to the locker room. We all told Dr. Nelson that everything would be all right. He watched helplessly.

Again the next day there was no quotation. We said nothing, but it was obvious that something terrible was happening. It was frustrating not to know what. The next morning I arrived half an hour early, so that I could write the quotation for the day. Someone already had: "The patient investigation and accurate methods required to obtain desired results in the school of experimental and technical science cannot fail to impress, refine, and ennoble the characters of those who work in this direction." Sir William Mather. It was not the handwriting of the department head. It seemed to have been put there by one of the nameless others. It certainly was the wrong sentiment; I was enraged. I took up a piece of chalk and printed "UP YOURS!" in very large letters. We were all feeling the effects of the tension.

It was learned that afternoon that the experiment was slowing down. There seemed to be less material in the glass bubble, although this seemed hardly possible. There was no way to measure the quantity of the contents without interrupting (and thus ending) the process. We could only observe anxiously. Weeks passed. It became definite: the liquid and gas in the bubble were somehow disappearing. We talked little, even at lunch. The department head spent a lot of time walking between our benches and silently patting our backs. We saw no more quotations.

At the same time we noticed that Drs. Short and Nelson also had little to say to each other. This was the most heartbreaking part, I believe. We had come this far, nearly three years, and we were committed to seeing it through. This was the test of maturity we had been warned about at the Seminary. I always thought that I could handle it; in theory I knew what I would do, that it was foolish to let adolescent emotions confuse your actions. But somehow I found myself as helpless as the others. There can be no preparation.

The third anniversary passed, officially unmarked. No one cared to mention that sad fact. More weeks passed; the contents of the glass bubble had dwindled to a few lumps of red-gold matter about the bottom and just a hint of greenish haze. I spent the days writing letters. Dr. Johnson and Dr. Green brought their guitars. Some of the others built models or touched each other secretly. On January 30, 1971, it was all over. A Saturday morning, bright and cold; we came into the lab and dressed wordlessly. When we passed through the tunnel we found the experiment completely dismantled. An old cleaning lady was just finishing up. The flasks, retorts, tubing and special equipment rested upside down, washed and drying on the slate-topped table. We were taken aback; there was nothing else to do but turn around. We returned to the locker room, hung up the lab coats, and went home. I have never seen any of that gang since.

Science, now—well, science has its rewards. But it requires a certain detachment, I suppose; they tried to drill that into me at the Seminary, but I was too idealistic to believe it. You have to be able to keep your identity. These things don't always turn out to be grand *Scientific American* coups (how seldom they do!). And you have to be able to pick yourself up and clean out your crusted test tubes and do it again: "*The love of life and the love of science are nearly indistinguishable, as science is the willing pupil of life. Thus, the science of life, which is after all the purpose of all learning, and the science of love, the latter only just less than equal to the former, follow in their courses as the night the day.*" Robert W. Hanson.

WHITE SUMMER IN MEMPHIS

GORDON EKLUND

Gordon Eklund lives in Berkeley, California, where the twenty-first century has staked out an outpost on the mainland of our era. He is an Air Force veteran, a father, a trustworthy member of the under-thirty conspiracy (membership expires in 1975), and, as of recent evidence, a writer of considerable power and promise. His first short stories were published in 1970; the following year brought a well-received novel, **The Eclipse of Dawn**; here now is his latest work, strange, haunting, memorable, and completely typical of his output so far, by which I mean that it's like nothing else he's written.

He had lain with this woman, this woman Marie, for a very long time, but since nobody knew he was there and nobody had seen him enter the apartment and nobody had heard him make or utter a sound since, it did not greatly matter. The length of time, that is, did not greatly matter.

But still: he had lain with this woman for a very long time.

She said, "You are through. You are through, aren't you through? You ought to be through by now, and if you are through, then would you get up? Would you please get up? Please."

But the man would not get up. He would not move. There was not a flickering of movement to show that he had even heard her speak. The man continued to lie quite

144

still, exactly as he had lain for a very long time. To Marie, the pressure of the man's teeth against her shoulder was like a never-ending succession of dull pinpricks. It had hurt her badly at first, his teeth that is; his nails as well, they too had hurt at first, but Marie was a woman well conditioned to pain. She could not remember a time in her life when pain had not been a motivating factor in her existence. Marie without pain: that would be like a prince without wealth, or an athlete without agility. Perhaps Marie needed pain; perhaps it needed her. (Perhaps.)

"Are you dead? You're not dead, are you?"

She pushed at his shoulders, and although he was a big man, she succeeded at last in freeing her shoulder from his teeth. There was blood there, she knew, blood with the pain, but again it did not seem to matter greatly. But she did want him off her. There was something about when a man remained inside a woman a long time after completing the business at hand, something wrong in it, for Marie had become so conditioned to the presence of pain that pleasure, in her mind, had assumed its place. She was a confused woman, and a pretty one (in some lights), with her coffee-tan skin and lips that pouted as easily and sensuously as others smiled, and her long brown legs which she exercised daily in her work, and her flat trim belly with its leavings of three children born. There was something about a man who lay inside a woman a long time after he'd done. It was a metaphor of love, and there was one thing Marie knew for certain about this man. He did not, could not ever, love her.

He was a white man.

"Please, I wish you'd get off me."

This time, the man moved, raising himself on his palms, as if exercising, and he peered straight down at her face. He seemed to like what he saw, and it was not something he had seen before, for this was the first time he had ever so much as looked toward her face. He smiled, and Marie smiled with him too, and he rolled off her body and lay at her side in the narrow bed which was even too small for her alone, but this, too, did not greatly matter, because Marie (no matter what others might think) was not in the habit of lightly sharing her bed with strange men.

But, in that case, why had she brought him here to her home? And why, too, had she allowed him to approach her so obviously in the street in the open where anyone—her father, mother, older brother—could have known and seen?

He was a white man, to be sure, but that certainly was not reason enough. When Marie had been younger, when she had been sixteen and twenty, she had had her times with the white men (or boys), but there hadn't been much of that. This man, though, he was different from those others. He had not approached her with the thought that she was black. Instead, he had come to her with the thought that she was a woman. And that, she realized, did make a difference, because hardly anyone had ever approached her with that in mind. No one, in fact, since her husband, who had left or died or whatever.

She turned her head and looked at the man, liking the way he was able to lie at her side hardly moving, certainly not gasping or panting like they always did (but not this man), nor did he smoke, or ask for a drink, or turn self-consciously toward the wall. If nothing else, this man was different, and Marie wanted that difference more than she wanted anything else.

When she returned from the bathroom, he was standing at the window, watching the street below. She had not heard him move, and she had listened, and he had drawn his worn pants over his legs. His back and shoulders glowed with a crisp white light of their own. Marie had never seen such a man before. Such a white white man.

Without turning, he asked, "How much?"

Marie laughed at him, not offended or angry or repelled, but amused. "I don't charge," she said, and that amused her also, so she laughed again and said, "Believe it or not, but I'm a waitress. I get my money there, and I don't share my bed with strange men."

He heard her out, then turned to face her. Harsh neon slanted through the window, bathing his chest with orange and crimson. There wasn't a trace of hair on the man's chest, Marie noticed, not even around the nipples where it almost always grew. His flesh was white, grandly white, like clean sheets in a good hospital.

Marie stood and watched the man, half leaning against the bed with her knees. The way she stood, she could see three tiny holes in her left shoulder and blood. She watched as the man reached slowly toward his head. His hair was worn very long, particularly in the front where it dipped past his forehead, nearly concealing his eyes. He raised both hands toward his head and slowly, cautiously, carefully, as though examining rare diamonds, he removed his hair.

His head was not only bald. It was bare. Like an egg, she thought, wondering if the eyebrows were real. The man pointed at his forehead. There was a mark there which the low hairline had concealed. It was a red mark, and it cut deeply into the white flesh. A hot iron had been used to make the mark, to carve a circle in the man's forehead, a circle with a bent cross at its center.

The man pointed at the mark, touched it, and smiled.

"You're . . . one of them," said Marie.

The man nodded.

"You're not a man."

"That," he said, "is up to you to decide."

Marie watched and stared, unable to speak but recovering from her shock. He was, she decided after all, a man. The answer came from a recollection. A preacher, a Sunday in the park, a hot summer day. The preacher had said, "For the first time since Adam's fall, men walk the face of this earth and do not bear upon them the mark of Cain." But that wasn't entirely correct, she could see that now. This man before her carried his sign more plainly than other men, but his sign was not that of God; his sign was a sign of man.

"You don't care?" said the man.

"Could you tell me your name? At least that much."

"My name is John," said the man.

She nodded, watching his face intently, seeing now all that she'd been unable to see before. She saw the perfection of his features. His ears and nose: neither too large nor too small. And his eyes—as blue as polished jewels. His face, unmarked by the passage of time, too perfect for handsomeness. He was a plain man. Indeed, he was the plainest man she had ever seen.

He said, "I want to stay here."

"You can," she said.

"Why? Why are you so sure? There are people after me. If they find me, they'll kill me. If they find me here, they'll kill you too."

She shook her head as she spoke, and she moved toward him, only partially realizing that this man was the first she'd known since . . . since she was twelve . . . whom she did not fear. She did not fear this man at all. And a white man too, she thought.

Her arms circled his back and held him tightly. "I don't care," she said. "Nobody knows I'm here. Stay if you want. I don't mind."

He slapped her across the face, and she fell, landing painfully. She looked up at the man, and he towered above her.

"I still don't care," she said.

"I'll sleep on the couch," he said.

Fitting the wig to his head, he reached down and helped her to stand. She took his hand, unafraid.

"I'll get you some blankets," she said.

The Sportsman's Club was the life of the side. Every morning of the week at six o'clock, the club opened its doors, and when it did, there was a crowd outside, standing and waiting. Some said the crowd had been there since the night before. But who knew this for certain? The faces of the crowd were never the same, but they were always there, at six o'clock in the morning, every day of the week.

On Friday nights, the club took on the density of a crowded lifeboat after a bad shipwreck. If the walls of the club had come equipped with hangers, there would have been people dangling up there every Friday night of the year. It was that kind of place.

There was even a well-established procedure for obtaining a drink. One waited until his current drink was nearly half gone, then started in the direction of the bar, drinking slowly, very slowly, talking or mumbling the whole way. With the aid of a little luck, one reached the bar at the exact right moment, with just one shallow sip remaining in the bottom of one's glass. That last sip was held, simmering in the glass, until the bartender's attention was engaged. Then one ordered one's new drink, and when the bartender went away, slowly, very slowly, with cool precision, one drank and swallowed that last sip. The refill arrived. New drink, same procedure.

And so it went, Friday after Friday, and this Friday was much the same as any of them. The juke box rattled joyously with the slow sadness of soft blues. Couples filled whatever floor space they could find and bounced, rocked, and rolled to the rattling rhythm of the juke. In the far corner of the stage the house band tuned their instruments—electric guitar and bass, drums, and two tenors—knowing that at nine o'clock they'd be going on, watching the clock, waiting and tuning.

Buttram Barkley had his own place at the bar. He had occupied that place at six o'clock and he had not moved since. Buttram was a huge black man with facial bones the size of an average man's fist. He drank his liquor straight, without ice, and he liked to watch his reflection in the barroom mirror.

The man at Buttram's left, the man whose hand actually touched Buttram's huge wrist, was a dude. Sharp, very sharp clothes, and neat, very neat hair. Buttram could not remember the dude's name. Buttram did not like the dude. The dude did not hold down a steady job.

Buttram held down a steady job. He worked for the city of Memphis as a street cleaner with his own personal route of nine square city blocks. Four times a day, five days a week, Buttram cleaned and scrubbed every square inch of those nine square city blocks. He knew the streets and alleys of those nine square blocks better than he knew anything else in the whole world, except his own face. Buttram knew his own face very well indeed, much better than most men, for he'd watched and studied it most intently in the barroom mirror at the Sportsman's Club every Friday night for fifteen years.

Buttram was not married, nor had he a steady girl friend.

The dude was speaking. The dude said, "I tell you, man, I seen him myself. He's a great big man, looks like a boxer. Remember Gene Fullmer, about twenty, thirty years ago? Well, this guy looks a lot like Fullmer in a way, except he's a whole lot better-looking and a whole lot bigger. Fullmer now, he was a middleweight, but this guy's got to be at least one-ninety, maybe more."

Buttram shook his head. He had come to the Sportsman's Club for two reasons. He had come to drink, and he had come to watch his face in the barroom mirror. He had not come to talk. He had especially not come to listen.

"I seen him heading into her place with a bag full of groceries, and I thought, Oh, Jesus, that's old Buttram's sister's place. What's this white man doing, going in there like he owns the place?"

Again, Buttram shook his head. It was, he decided, about time to move along. A Friday night was not a Friday night for Buttram unless he hit at least three clubs. He turned his head and looked at the band. He did not like the band, nor did he approve of their kind of music. What he liked was station WRTY-FM, which played uninterrupted computer tapes of instrumental standards, old stuff from the fifties and sixties, a quiet and relaxed kind of music, a kind that made one think. Yes, it was time to move along.

He swallowed the last of his drink and said, "Going."

The dude said, "Hey, wait a minute, man," and he grabbed at Buttram's sleeve. "I tell you your sister's living with a white man and you don't say nothing."

"You get your hand off my sleeve, boy," Buttram said softly.

"Living with him like man and wife. Lizzie, she says it's been going on a whole week. She seen the man a whole week ago. I just wanted to tell you, man."

"You told me," Buttram said. "Now get your goddamn hand off my sleeve."

The dude let go of Buttram, who spun quickly away and disappeared into the crowd.

"That Buttram," the dude said. "He's got something wrong with his head."

Another man said, "It's that garbage he's got to work with. It's got to his head."

While the two men were laughing, a third man, one who'd been standing near them for some time, slipped into the spot Buttram had vacated. By this time there were one hundred and eighty-three men and women in the Sportsman's Club, but this new man, he was different from all the others. He was a white man.

"Hey, Riley Oakley," the dude said when he noticed the new man, "where've you been hiding lately?"

"I've had me a job," Riley Oakley said, "and what's new with you guys?"

"Not much," the dude said. "How about purchasing us all a round?"

"I'll do that," said Riley Oakley.

It was Friday night eight o'clock, and the glare of bright neon light slanting through the bedroom window seemed greater than ever before. John had been there a full week now, but Marie wanted to go out.

"We could go to the Sportsman's Club," she said. "It's only up the street and round the corner. Wouldn't take any time to get there."

She sat in a straight-backed chair in the very center of the bedroom, hands clenched in her lap, like an expectant mother in a doctor's waiting room. John stood against the wall, glancing occasionally toward the window. Marie still wore her work clothes, clean and starched, white like those of a nurse.

John said, "I'd rather not."

"Why? You don't have to worry none about the Army. They can't come into our part of town unless we give our permission, and we never give it."

"I know that," John said. "Why do you think I'm here?"

"And the police. Don't worry none about them. They won't bother you, except maybe to ask to see your card, because you're white, but you said you have one that'll pass."

"I have one that'll pass," John said, "but you don't understand. I don't want to go out."

"Then why'd you run away in the first place if you're not going to do anything with your freedom? That's the part I don't understand. Why didn't you just stay where you were?"

John turned away and crossed the room. He stood in front of her chair, his shoulders towering above her. He hadn't struck her since the first night, and thinking back to that time, Marie often thought her memory was mistaken. John wouldn't have hit her. He was such a quiet man, a gentle man. Marie had known many violent men, but John was not one of them.

She said, "Lay down on the bed, I'll rub your back for you."

"There's nothing wrong with my back," he said, regarding her with amusement. "I'm a perfect man. I suffer no bodily aches or pains. With luck and avoiding a violent end, I ought to live to be a couple hundred years old."

"Wouldn't that be something?" Marie said. "Here now—lay down and let me rub your back."

He lay down on the bed, compliantly. The blankets were tightly stretched over the mattress, and the weight of his body did not wrinkle them. He unbuttoned his shirt, and Marie eased it off his shoulders.

She regarded his back, so thickly muscled that when she touched it each inch of exposed flesh seemed to ripple and move. Her hands worked together, down and up, up and down. John's face pointed toward the window, and the neon touched it, red, then blue, orange, then red.

"Feel better?" she asked.

"I feel fine," he said.

"Want to tell me something about yourself?"

"Such as?"

"Oh, about when you were a kid. You know. I told you a lot about me."

"So you have," John said.

"Just like when you were a kid."

"I could tell you about that, yes."

"Then do."

"Are you certain you want to hear?"

"I want to hear; sure I'm sure I want to hear."

He sighed. It was the first time Marie had ever heard him make such a sound. She increased the speed of her strokes, using the blunt edges of her hand. She wanted to be forceful, but she was unable even to ruffle the flesh. It seemed to her as if John were a rock. Or carved from marble. Or ivory. That was more like it. Ivory, white and hard and everlasting.

"It was known as the Hall," John said, "where we lived

as children. All of us were there, and the Hall was run like an army barracks. We were given inspections, arms training, and military courtesy and discipline. At first they only intended to use us as soldiers. It wasn't until later that they realized that our minds were fully as advanced as our bodies. They were worried then, and frightened. They didn't want to alienate the public, so they made soldiers of us anyway. I was a genius," he said, "and I was a private first class."

"Why'd they make you so smart," she asked, "if they didn't like you being smart?"

"Because," John said, "they were stupid. It was because of the genetic materials they used. There would have been no point in growing a crop of average men. Anybody can do that naturally. No, they had to grow us better than anybody else. They did. We were stronger and we were faster and we were brighter."

"But you're not in the Army now," she said.

"No," he said. "I ran away."

She stopped rubbing his back and moved her hands away. She liked the act itself, but she did not like the associations it produced, images of power and violence. She moved her hands away and crouched at his side, her head near his shoulders.

"When'd you run away?" she said. "You never even told me that."

"I ran away one year and eight weeks ago."

"That's a long time," she said.

"I've been hard to catch. Only this"—he tapped his forehead—"only this sign is proof of my condition. Which, I suppose, is why it's there."

"I'd like to see it again," she said. "That other time, I didn't really get a good look at it."

John said no.

Marie accepted his answer. She had never known him to change his mind. It was as if there were only one possible answer to any given question. Once John found that answer, there was nothing left for him to say.

Marie got off the bed and went to her chair. "Can you have babies?" she said, seated again.

John rolled to his stomach and looked at her.

"No," he said.

"Because you were made, not born?"

"No," he said. "I don't think that's it. I think they operated on me, when I was young. They made me sterile."

"Are you sure that's it?"

"Why? You're not worried, are you?"

"No," she said. "I'm not worried. I just wondered how you knew for sure. Knew for sure you were sterile."

He laughed, and after a moment she decided to laugh with him. He said: "It's only logical. They wouldn't want us to reproduce. We could create something that would wipe them out."

"But that's silly," Marie said. "You're human too. You can't wipe out what you are."

"No," John said. "That's one thing I can't do."

There was a long moment of silence, and then Marie said, "You want to go out now?"

"No," John said. "I told you before, and I never change my mind."

Marie nodded. That was true. That was one thing John never did. Change his mind. Not ever.

Beneath the heavy sleekness of her uniform, the heat was oppressive. So hot in Memphis this July, and there were food stains, like polka dots, sprinkled here and there amid the overpowering whiteness of her uniform.

Only one block to go, she told herself, and then she would sit at the open window, as naked as decency permitted, fanning her face with an old movie magazine. The heat never touched John—it wouldn't bother him to wear the uniform—but nothing ever seemed to touch John. He was oblivious, John was, as if this world were not his world at all, as if he lived in yet another land, one where it never grew too hot or too cold, where it was always perfect, always just right.

"Hey, you, Marie."

She halted at the sound of her name and turned, following the voice with her eyes. He was standing on the opposite corner, waving his arms over his head, arms that protruded from his heavy red jacket like stiff wooden clubs. She knew he'd been waiting for her, waiting for at least an hour since she'd had to work late, but she did not care. She did not want to cross that street, and if he had been anyone but her brother, she would not have done it. But Buttram was her brother, her only brother, and she did cross the street.

She said, "What do you want with me, Buttram?" (He smelled today, smelled badly, but he always smelled, not always, but after work he always smelled badly.) "I have to get home."

"Home?" he said, twisting his face to display his outrage. "You say, you say home. Home to your white man. Got to get yourself home before the white man gets himself pissed."

"Shut up, Buttram," said Marie.

"I won't shut up," he said. "I won't because you're a fool, fool to buy this man his food . . ."

"That," Marie said, "happens to be my business." Her uniform was soaked now with perspiration. The heat, the anger, the frustration, they had proved too overwhelming for the sleek softness of the white cloth. "Who's been talking about my business?" Marie asked.

"Nobody had to talk," said Buttram. "It's all over this side, and you know it. You got to know it, unless you're a fool. I'm surprised your mom and your dad, I'm surprised they haven't heard tell of it."

"You're not to tell them, Buttram."

"I won't tell," he said, "but somebody else, somebody I don't even know, they might tell. Nobody likes this fellow coming down here, messing with us like he is."

"He's not messing."

"He's messing with you," said Buttram. "You're my sister, and that means he's messing with me too."

Marie leaned forward, her hands on her hips. She leaned far forward, tilting at the waist, and she said, "You stand clear of my life, Buttram. You know I'm me and you're not me. There's other white men living on this side and nobody's bothering them. There's Riley Oakley. Nobody bothers Riley Oakley."

"That's different with Riley," Buttram said. "Riley socializes, and he doesn't care much for women."

"You just stay out of my life," Marie said with finality. She had succeeded in what she had set out to do. She had turned the conversation from herself to the other man. Now she turned to go.

Buttram shouted after her: "You watch yourself, lady. You best watch yourself, or there's going to be trouble. I'm not warning you again."

Already halfway to the end of the block, Marie smiled when she heard the shout. She heard the shout, but she did not listen to it.

Two children were playing a game of catch on the sidewalk in front of him, and Riley Oakley stepped off the curb so as not to interrupt their game. This was Riley Oakley's way, and even if it meant an extra step or two, he would go out of his way to avoid interfering with other people. This was how Riley Oakley had lived to the age of forty-one in a hostile environment, one that would always consider him the outsider.

Reaching the street he wanted, Riley stopped and looked both ways, even though there wasn't any traffic on the street, no traffic within miles, hadn't been any traffic for ten years. It was just past habit, Riley would say, a past habit he shared with nearly everyone who looked both ways before crossing the streets, the streets in which thick foliage had sprouted and grown.

It was a cool morning for this time of the year. Riley Oakley was not used to cool mornings, nor was he overly familiar with mornings in general. He seldom got out of bed before noon, only when he was working, and when he was working, he tried to get himself a night shift. But this morning Riley had risen at nine, he had risen with sleep still in his eyes and slipped past his astonished landlady, who'd shaken her head and said, "What are you doing running around this time of day?"

"Doctor's appointment," Riley had lied, even though he couldn't truthfully say that he ever believed in doctors. Riley was a farm boy, a product of the Alabama cotton belt, and he was still at heart a country boy. He'd lived in Memphis for the past twenty-two years, but he was still at heart just a country boy.

Riley did not like to lie and so, as he walked, he turned his lie into a truth. He told himself that he did indeed have a doctor's appointment (of sorts), for he was going to see not about his personal health, but about a medical problem of greater dimensions, one that pertained to the entire community as a whole. The continued well-being of his adopted community, that was what Riley Oakley was about early this morning, the health of its people and their lives.

Riley reached the apartment building he sought, and before he had an opportunity to get afraid, he pushed through the open front door and climbed the four flights of stairs, each seeming just a little higher than the last, until he found the right door. Then he knew that he had not walked quickly enough, for now he was scared, already he was scared, and there wasn't any reason for him to be afraid, that much he knew, but he was afraid. Trying to prove himself wrong, trying to do it fast before it was too late, he stuck out his finger and rang the bell. Almost at once, the door opened.

And there stood the man Riley was seeking, and that was all right, but this man was not only white, which Riley had expected, but he was white, so white that Riley felt instantly brown and dirty by comparison.

Before the man had a chance to shut him out, Riley said, "May I come in?" He said it carefully, proud of his deep and strong voice, one which was only slightly tainted by his years in the South. He'd worked hard to keep the cracker out of his voice, feeling that he had enough problems without the added weight of a redneck voice, but there were some things Riley did not know, and one of them was that, even though he no longer talked like a redneck, what he did talk like was a redneck straining hard not to talk like a redneck.

The stranger seemed to take in all of this, and much more, with a single glance. He said, "What do you want here?" closing the door slightly, so that only his right eye showed through the narrow crack. "You want me?"

"Yes, sir," Riley said quickly, wishing the man would open the door a little bit more. He wanted to see all of him, not just that single staring white eye. "I've got to talk to you, tell you about something."

"Who are you?" said the voice behind the eye.

"Oakley, sir. Riley Oakley, and I ..." But the words weren't there any longer. Riley had spent six hours rehearsing the previous day, preparing a speech that would say everything he had to say without giving unnecessary offense. But the words just weren't there any longer; they'd gone, disappeared somewhere. And Riley knew he was the only one with the right to talk to this man, which was why he had come here, but the words just weren't there any more. He said again, "Riley Oakley, and I . . ."

"Come on in," the man said. "Come on—we can talk inside."

Riley, saved from embarrassment, passed gladly through the door and dropped to a couch in a heap. It had been a long walk from the boardinghouse, up those four flights of stairs, and Riley, not a young man any longer, was tired.

The stranger sat in a straight-backed chair directly across from Riley. He sat stiffly and firmly in the chair, as though a part of it.

"Now," he said, "what's this all about, Mr. Oakley?"

"Call me Riley," said Riley.

"All right," said the stranger, with a hint of amusement in his tone, more than a hint of it in his eyes, "and you can call me John."

"John," said Riley, "well, John, it's like this. You and me, we're sort of two of a kind, you know that. That is, we're the only two white men living on this side here, and I thought it would be good if we sort of got together, just you and me, and talked things out. You see what I mean?"

The stranger nodded slowly. He said, "I see, and I'm glad you came. It's a fine idea. I wish I could offer you something, but there's nothing here. Marie ought to be home soon. She'll probably bring something with her."

Riley was truly amazed at the calmness of this man. Hadn't he any realization of the danger he was in? And if not, if the man was that ignorant, then why was he here in the first place? Riley, now Riley, he knew what was going down. Down in Alabama, ever since, he'd lived among the colored people, and he knew them so well it now made him nervous to be around whites. This white man, he made Riley more nervous than all the others put together. He was calm, too, and that made Riley even more nervous.

"You don't know these people," Riley said.

"I don't?"

"These people you're living with. Marie and them."

"I am living with Marie," the man said, "but not with anyone else that I'm aware of. Marie asked me to stay with her. You don't object, do you?"

"No," Riley said. "Of course not. It's just ... well, I don't think you understand these people you're living with. I've known them for forty-one years, known them well, and in those forty-one years there's one thing I've learned for sure. They're good people, pretty free people, and loose. They'll take you in, feed you a drink, talk to you, but there's this one thing. Not for a long time, not for a lot of years, they don't like us messing with their women. I've always known that, and I leave them alone. It started mostly with that integration thing. You remember that?"

"Yes," John said.

"You're too young to remember, but I'm not. What they did was, they tried to take them and us and make us live together, but it didn't work, because we didn't like them, and they didn't like us, and putting us together, like peas in a pot, it only made things worse. So, ever since, we've lived apart, separate. Now, we were separate before—before the integration thing—but it was different then, because we always said, 'Yeah, we white men are better than those blacks,' but after the integration didn't work, the blacks turned around, and they said that too, they said, 'We're a lot better than you whites in a whole lot of ways. We want you to keep away from us, and we'll keep away from you.'" (Riley had rediscovered his prepared speech now, and he was enjoying the feeling it gave him to have these words pouring out of him without the least effort. And, too, there was John, the first white man with whom he'd spoken in over ten years. There was that, too.)

John said, "I know all this."

"And," Riley said, "I expect you're here on this side for the same reason I'm here on this side. You like these people, don't you? The way they're so free and easy. I tried once about twelve years ago, tried to go on the other side and live where I was supposed to. It didn't last long. It's bad over there. Me, I haven't got much education, and I couldn't find any work over there. With those people, a man hasn't got work, he's like dirt to them. Plain dirt."

John, who had not moved even to shift since he first sat down, said, "Plain dirt."

Riley took this to mean he should continue, and he said, "But there's one big difference between you and me. I live by myself in a rooming house, and you're living with this woman. Now think about that, in line with what I just told you. You're living with one of their women, and, man, they just don't like that. I figure I've got to warn you. What I think is you want to settle down and live peaceable over here, and I'm telling you the only way you can do that is to get out of here. What I want to say is there's room in my boardinghouse. You can leave here right now and move on in. You don't have to drop this woman, if that's what you want. You can go right on seeing her, but while you're living here, sharing this roof with her, people are going to know, and people are going to get angry."

Riley stopped then and waited, but the stranger gave him no sign. So far as Riley could tell, the man had not heard him at all, and if he had heard, he had not understood. Riley decided he would have to start again at the beginning.

The stranger shook his head gently.

"What's that supposed to mean?" said Riley.

"I'm not leaving here," the man said.

Riley felt his frustration pushing at the edge of rage. This man had not understood a word that he'd said. All that work preparing himself, and for nothing. "Didn't you understand me?"

"I understood you," John said.

"Well?"

"I like it here."

"I . . ." Riley decided to try another path with this man. "Look here. You're going to have to get yourself a job pretty soon, right? And I'm telling you, nobody is going to give you a job, not on this side, or the other side either, not if they know about you. I'm telling you straight, man, they just don't allow nobody to come around and mess with their women."

"I have a job," the man said. "Whenever I need it, it's there."

"Oh, yeah?" Riley said, not believing the man. "And

what kind of job is that, that just sits there and waits for you?"

"Army," John said.

"Army."

"The United States Army, and since Marie ought to be here any minute, I'll have her cook—"

"No, thanks," Riley said, getting to his feet. He didn't like the way things were going. "I've got to go. I just came here to give you fair warning." He headed for the door, hoping he could reach it before anything bad happened. "Let you know of the possible consequences of your act." Riley opened the door. "Let you know you had a friend." He started to pass through the door, but turned once more to look at the stranger.

And the man, seeing Riley's eyes on him and grinning from ear to ear, the man tipped his hair. Not his hat, for the stranger wore no hat, but his hair, he tipped his hair and he held it in the air a full six inches above his head.

Riley stared at the hair and at the stranger for five seconds. Then he lunged at the man's throat. He said, "Goddamn you, goddamn, goddamn—"

The stranger struck Riley in the throat with the flat of his hand, and Riley fell into the hall, gasping, and the man slammed the door.

Riley was alone in the corridor, holding his throat. He got to his knees, still gasping, and held his head. There was something stuck in his throat. Riley swallowed and swallowed, but it would not go away.

He remembered the girl. Remembered that she was coming back. He forced himself to stand and, staggering, he plunged down the stairs.

He reached the street. He swallowed again, but the obstruction was still there. Looking both ways, he started across the street, and as he crossed, a woman passed him, a black woman, a pretty woman. She was carrying a bag of groceries in one hand. She started to say something to Riley, but he turned his head. He did not want to talk to this woman. Her kind. That was the last thing he needed. The very last thing.

"You told him. I know you told him. I could tell just

walking past him yesterday. Why? Why did you have to tell him? I want to know why you had to tell him."

John was sitting in the chair. He said, "I didn't tell him. I showed him." From the shadows of the chair, he lifted his wig and held it over his head. Outside, it was dark, and inside, it was darker. He tossed the wig on the bed, and he said, "Turn on a light."

Marie turned away and found the light switch. She said, "There I was at work today, and this woman comes up and says there's a man living on this side, and he ain't a real man, and I know she knows who he is and what I am, and what am I supposed to say? Knowing she knows so much and knows about me. I asked you yesterday when I saw him and you said he wasn't even here."

"Be quiet," John said. "I have to think."

"You should have done that before you did your showing. You should have done your thinking before. It's like you wanted him to know. Don't you know why he came over here? He came over here because he's jealous of you doing what he's too damned scared to do himself."

"That," John said, "is why I showed him." He sat in the chair, so calmly, like a flag on a still summer's day, not moving at all, and his head bald and smooth as an egg.

"I killed a woman once," he said.

Marie nodded. She'd guessed something like that all along. A year he'd been running free, and she knew there was more to it than just that. Marie sat on the bed, wearing only her slip, its pale whiteness like ice against her dark skin.

"After I was through with her," John said, "I lifted my hair and showed her, like I showed you. She looked at me for a long time, not saying anything, and then she turned over and went to sleep. I laid next to her, and I didn't sleep or move until dawn. Then I must have fallen off, because the next thing I knew it was noon. I opened my eyes, and she was sitting at her desk, and she was writing a letter with her big quill pen. She was writing to the government to see if she could buy me from the government. She wanted to know if they'd let her have me, since I'd run away from the Army and would run away again if they ever took me back, and nobody else wanted me. I'd

lived with other women before this one, and whenever I
got tired of them, it might be the first night or it might
be a month, I'd pull off the wig and show them my sign,
and they'd know what I was, what they'd let between
their legs, and they'd tell me, 'Monster, get out of my
house.' But this woman with whom I'd lived for two
months and told everything and now shown everything,
she wanted to buy me. A couple hours later, I slit her
throat and she was dead."

"A white woman?" said Marie.

"Yes, in Greenville, Mississippi, a white woman. She
lived in a big white house overlooking the town, and you
could see the Mississippi River from the porch, and trees,
more trees than you'd ever seen in your life, and a bridge,
and across the bridge, it was Arkansas and even more
trees. She came from the North, down with her father to
live after the war, and her father died, and she stayed until that night when I killed her."

Marie said, "Yes," neither disgusted nor surprised nor
afraid nor anything. She knew John had acted right. John
had killed this white woman because this woman had neither been afraid nor disgusted nor surprised nor repelled.

"Did they find out you did it?" she said, on the bed,
raising her eyes so that she looked right straight at him.

"They did," John said, "because after she was dead I
went into town, and I went to a beer place, and I waited
there till it was full, and when it was full, I pulled off my
wig and showed it to them, and then went outside and
stole a car and came here."

"John, I'm not afraid of you," Marie said.

"I know that," he said.

"Should I be afraid of you?"

"I don't know," he said. "I think you should, yes, because you and the woman are both human beings and I'm
not. Black and white, that doesn't matter when you're human and you're up against something that isn't human."

John rose from the chair and walked across to where
Marie sat slumped on the bed. The neon played tricks
with the whiteness of his skin, and Marie looked up,
looked up at his forehead, and the red mark gleamed in
the harsh light, gleamed and danced and smiled at her.

"I'm sorry," John said.

And Marie—not yet, still not yet, she was not yet afraid. Marie was never afraid. Not ever.

In Riley Oakley's room in the boardinghouse owned and operated by Mrs. Jenny Hayes, there was a bed and a dresser. There wasn't a rug on the floor, nor were there curtains on the window. The dresser had things in its drawers, but there was nothing on top of it. On the bed were two dirty socks, a single brown shoe, and Riley Oakley.

Riley was looking toward the door. He had heard the sharp knocking, and he was wondering if he ought to tell whoever it was to come inside. He was wondering about it, but he knew that he wasn't going to say a thing, not a word. He also knew that it wouldn't make the least bit of difference.

The door opened, and two men came into the room, and the first man was the older man, the one with the white mustache and the look of wisdom in his eyes, and the second man was the big one, the one with the fists that hung at his sides like black cantaloupes.

The older man said, "Hello, Riley."

Riley nodded but said nothing and did not move.

"You know why we're here," said the older man. "You were expecting us." The big man moved over and leaned loosely against the wall.

"I know," Riley said.

"Why didn't you come to us?" the older man said.

Riley shrugged, then looked toward the big man. But the big man had not moved. Riley said, "I should have come to you, Lieutenant."

"That's right, Riley," said the older man, the lieutenant. "He killed a woman in Mississippi, a white woman, you didn't know that, but he did. You should have come to us."

"I know that," Riley said.

"You should have done it right away, because we went there just now, Riley, and she's dead, her throat cut. He killed a white woman in Mississippi, and now he's killed a black woman in Memphis."

"He's . . . not human."

"That's right, Riley," the lieutenant said, "he isn't human, and that's why you should have come to us. Why didn't you come to us, Riley? You told everyone, you told them he was living with Marie and what he was. You knew we'd hear about it eventually, you knew that, didn't you?"

"Maybe," Riley said.

"And do you know why you didn't come and tell us?"

Riley said nothing. He was looking at the big man now, and the big man was moving, shifting his big body. Riley had heard of this big man, this detective sergeant, and Riley was afraid.

The lieutenant said, "I'll tell you why you didn't come to us, Riley. You didn't come because the man was a white man and because you're a white man too. You told everyone, knowing we'd find out eventually, but you wouldn't come to us and tell us that the white man with Marie was not a human being."

Riley said, "That's not true."

The lieutenant said, "It is true, Riley, and you know it is true, and now you know what we're going to do to you. We're going to hurt you, Riley, just a little bit, and we're going to take you to the wall, and we're going to leave you, and, Riley, you're not ever coming back on this side. You're going to live with your own kind from now on out, and that's the way it's going to be."

Riley still said nothing, but he shook his head, and he looked at the big man's fists.

"You're not going to kill me?"

The lieutenant shook his head. "Perhaps we ought to kill you, but we're not going to kill you. We're the law, and the law does not kill, only when it has to kill. It's those outside the law that kill, Riley, those like your friend."

"He's not my friend," Riley said.

The lieutenant turned away. He looked at the big man and said, "Okay," then he headed toward the door. He did not look back, and Riley did not see him leave. Riley was watching the big man, and he was watching the big man's fists, but he wasn't thinking about that. He was thinking about life on the other side, and he was wishing the big man would make a mistake, that his hands would slip, and that Riley would die. He was wishing for that, but down deep, he knew it would not happen, and he was sorry about that.

It was a new car, brightly electric, and it stopped just like that and went into reverse. It stopped at his side, and John looked through the window and saw that the driver was white. The driver said, "Get in quick," and John got into the car, which surged immediately forward even before John got the door shut.

The driver said, "Christ, man, what are you doing down here?"

"My last ride dropped me here," John said. He leaned back in the plush, warm seat, savoring the smoothness of the ride and the calmness of the music which came from the dashboard. John felt well now, he felt very well indeed, for the first time in weeks he felt alive. He took a deep breath and exhaled slowly.

"What was he thinking of?" the driver said. He was a small man in a clean suit. A small man with a quick staccato voice. "The last ride you had, I mean. Even if the guy was colored, he should have known better than to let you off on this side. I'd never drive through here myself, except I'm in a hurry this time. I was supposed to be home two hours ago, and my wife's probably mad as hell."

John said, "Yes." He did not want to talk, nor did he want to listen. He did not know what he wanted to do, but he closed his eyes and shifted his head on the seat. John had long ago learned that the best way to avoid unwanted conversation was to close one's eyes. Whether asleep or not, the talk would cease.

But this little man, this driver of new electric cars, did not stop. In his fear, he could not stop. He had to talk, he had to say, "Cops stopped me about three miles back. Searching my car, Negro cops. Don't know what they were looking for, but I can't get out of here fast enough. You're lucky I came along."

John kept his eyes shut, stifling as best he could an overwhelming urge to raise his wig and show this small and fearful man a slice of life he would not soon forget, show this white white man that one who he thought his equal was in reality lower than the lowest. This was John now, thinking though he did not want to think. Thinking that the blood that flowed through his veins was neither white nor black but brown perhaps, brown like mud, and that he was neither here nor there, neither better nor worse. Fear and disgust were the only emotions John wanted to feel from them. Fear, yes, and disgust. Fear because he was better than they, and disgust because he was lower than they.

The little man was still talking. He was saying, "I hate being out here alone. If I was on foot, good God . . ."

John thought about Marie and how he had known he would kill her from the first moment, when she had looked at him neither afraid nor disgusted. Black and white, John had seen them both now, and he would keep looking for that fear and that disgust, keep looking till they killed him.

"There it is," the driver said. "Thought we'd never make it."

John opened his eyes, and he regarded the wall which rose in front of the car, six rigid feet of bricks and wire and concrete.

The car pointed toward the hole in the wall, and even when the black soldier stepped in front of them, the driver did not pause. He swore under his breath, but he did not pause, and the soldier jumped out of the way, and the car went through the wall, and another soldier on the other side watched them pass, shaking his head.

"Jesus Christ," the driver said. "That's it. Never again am I going through that place. Did you see that soldier? He wanted me to stop."

And John closed his eyes again. He closed his eyes and he drifted. He said softly, "They're all like that," he said. "All of them just like that."

And the driver nodded, though John did not see, and he pointed the car at the road. The radio played and John thought. John thought: It won't change soon. It's still here and it won't change. Kill them all and they won't change.

And so on, John kept thinking, and so on into the summer's night.

LAZARUS II

MIRIAM ALLEN DE FORD

A grim, harsh vignette by a veteran storyteller: a scientific experiment is its ostensible subject, the pervasiveness of deceit its deeper theme.

He fought to breathe. He could feel his heart pounding, so he was still alive.

Time must be distorted at such a moment. Perhaps only a second had passed since the cyanide egg was dropped into the bucket of sulphuric acid beneath the green-painted metal chair. It seemed forever that he had been fighting to get his breath.

Suddenly he wondered if Jennie had struggled so while he was strangling her. For the first time he felt a twinge of remorse.

Then, like the shutting of a door, the end. Nothing.

• • •

Somewhere a woman screamed at word of the deed. Not Jennie: he had strangled her. His mother.

• • •

The termination of Edwin R. Mahotney, murderer. Of no importance except to himself. And his mother. And once to a girl called Jennie.

• • •

They were ready and waiting, the three distinguished surgeons and the attendant nurses. They were high enough in the scientific and political hierarchy to have unraveled infinities of red tape. The few—the warden among them—who must know were sworn to secrecy. This was Top Secret not only from the newspapers and the people of America but from all the world. It would remain so in the case of failure. In that of success, it would be America's free offering, its expiation for historic sins.

As soon as the gas chamber was cleared of fumes, the corpse was hurried to a nearby room transformed into an operating theater. It was placed in a modified iron lung, the heart was opened and electrical stimulation established, the poisoned blood washed out, hyperoxygenated blood poured in. Massive doses of methylene blue were injected, until blue tears rolled down the dead cheeks and blue urine stained the table. They worked fast, against time, pausing only to have the sweat wiped from their faces with sterilized towels.

Under the sharp preoccupation of their work, half-conscious thought drifted. "Poor devil," thought their leader, "he won't thank us if we succeed." Perpetual imprisonment? He could not be freed.

"Human detritus," thought the second man contemptuously. "The only contribution he can ever make to the world's welfare." He thought of three dead cosmonauts in their fatal spacecraft.

And the third: "We are Galileos, Copernicuses, of a new dispensation. Or we are life's worst bunglers."

• • •

An old woman forced her way into the warden's office. "I have come to bury my son," she said.

"I'm sorry, madam," the warden lied, "but he is already buried."

"I had to raise the money," she wept. "I couldn't let you know beforehand. Can I see his grave?"

"They are unmarked," he answered stiffly. And again, "I'm sorry."

"My boy couldn't help it," the old woman sobbed. "That bitch wouldn't let him go, she wore him down."

"We have to bury them at once, by law," the warden said. It was a necessary lie: he had no choice, but his eyes were troubled and ashamed. He led the shaking woman gently to the prison entrance.

•   •   •

The heart quivered, then feebly began to beat in rhythm. The mechanism expanded and depressed the lungs. New blood rich in oxygen ran in the arteries and veins.

They placed metal disks on the shaved skull. The needle began to write.

The exhausted men straightened, the nurses took over. All this had been rehearsed many times. The crucial moment was now.

The being was carried to a hospital bed. It breathed, its heart beat, it could move its limbs.

The encephalographic record ran in an unwavering straight line.

"Coma," the leader murmured. "Comas end." But he shook his head.

•   •   •

Was it a living man at all? Was it the same man as before? Had this human vegetable on the prison hospital bed, fed intravenously, bathed, catheterized, massaged, by sulky convict orderlies, suffered "cruel and unusual punishment"?

Was it—he—a warning against further attempts, or a signpost of dangers to be avoided? Did the potentialities of scientific research justify such meddling?

They did not know. They did not speculate. These are questions for theoreticians, not for working scientists.

•   •   •

The old woman wept in her lonely room. "If only my boy was alive and here!" she lamented. She shook with hatred for the bitch Jennie who had driven him to desperation. "He was such a good boy till he met that Jennie!" she cried bitterly, not caring that even she knew it was not true.

* * *

It was autumn when men had killed the murderer and other men had brought him back to something they were pleased to call life. It had been winter, and now it was spring.

Did he know? Did any dream or feeling cross that smothered mind?

The three resurrectionists met again. The powers that had authorized the experiment now demanded a formal report that would serve as a basis for future action or inaction.

They stood around the bed where the creature lay. It breathed, through a stethoscope they heard its heart beating, it could turn its head on the pillow and move its arms and legs restlessly. There were no peaks or dips in the encephalogram.

They were alone, the four of them: the three surgeons and their—patient? victim? laboratory animal? The prison doctor and his inmate aides were banished for this private consultation. The three stood in silence for long minutes.

Then the leader fired a piercing gaze on the living corpse and commanded harshly and peremptorily: "Look at me!"

The dull eyes continued to stare vacantly into nothing.

"Can you see us? Can you hear me?" the surgeon persisted. There was no response.

The leader glanced at his two colleagues.

"If I were alone with him now—" one of them murmured.

"Euthanasia?"

"Illegal."

"No more illegal than what we have done. We have negated the law that prescribes capital punishment for murder. He was condemned to die. If we undo what we have done, we shall only be carrying out the sentence."

They eyed one another like conspirators.

"The Hippocratic oath—" the third man muttered. The others ignored him.

"The experiment has failed," said their leader. "When an experiment fails we clean the mess away."

"Then perhaps another subject?" one of his colleagues ventured.

"Would you take the chance of making *that* out of a good human being?" the leader cried passionately. The third man nodded.

As if by an unspoken order one of them moved to a window and gazed out on rain streaking the prison yard. The other of the two associates stationed himself at the closed door. He shut his eyes.

Quietly, his face intent, like a compassionate physician ending pain, the leader drew from his bag a hypodermic syringe, dipped it in boiling water, broke an ampule, and filled the plunger.

As the needle went inexorably in, suddenly the thing on the bed was galvanized. The unseeing eyes blazed, the head jerked.

"I died once!" the intolerable voice croaked in terror. "Let me live!"

Then the lethal dose reached his heart. He collapsed.

The man at the door retched. He at the window clutched the sill to hold himself upright.

The leader, gray-white, returned the syringe to his bag.

"I shall set a date for our first meeting to make the official report," he said through clenched teeth. "Notify the warden. We were all present when this man slipped imperceptibly from coma into death."

THE MEN INSIDE

BARRY N. MALZBERG

In the old days, when a writer's luck or skill or productivity resulted in his having two stories in the same issue of a science-fiction magazine, the editor would almost always insist on hiding one of the stories behind a pseudonym. This was something that used to happen to me quite frequently, but I never understood why it was so: perhaps the editors feared to be caught displaying undue favoritism, were afraid of charges of kickbacks, nepotism, or simony, or sincerely felt that the readers would rather see one unknown name on the contents page than see the same familiar name twice. In any case, I cheerfully abandon the quaint custom here. It happened that two among the eleven stories I liked best while reading submissions for this NEW DIMENSIONS were by Barry Malzberg; and so he appears for the second time in this volume, with a story which in some ways resembles **Fantastic Voyage** as it might have been written by Dostoievsky rather than Asimov, but which carries Malzberg's own idiom of brilliant despair and bleak, shattering joy.

In Memory of Herbert Finney

I

COMPREHENDING HULM: In the night after his first Experiment, Hulm has a dream. In that dream, at last, the process has been perfected. Institutes bearing his name have opened all over the world, staffed by trained workers to speed relief to the millions, and now, as he hovers cloudlike over his agglomeration, all of the workers turn to him: to Hulm. Reduced by the process to seven six-hundredths of an inch, they mass, an army of elves speaking in chorus, their little lances poised deftly in tiny hands, and what they are saying is: YOU ARE A VAIN MAN, HULM, A VAIN AND STRICKEN MAN BECAUSE NONE OF IT TURNED OUT QUITE THE WAY YOU THOUGHT IT WOULD. NONE OF IT, NONE OF IT: CORRUPT, CORRUPT! and turn from him then to assault a phalanx of patients; patients are all around them now: they are lumps of flesh which heave under their little feet. The landscape of patients trembles under the thrusts of the lances and Hulm recoils.

"No," he says, rising, raising his fists, "no, it isn't that way; it wasn't my fault; it had to be a corporate entity to survive. I didn't want it but they made me!" Somehow it seems that he has gotten the whole gist of the argument from his tiny messengers, none of whom pay any attention to him as they dive towards pockets of metastasis. "Oh yes, you did," one of them calls back, the lone muted voice fluting in the dark, "yes, you did, indeed you loved it; you saw it all even then, the potential and the reward, and it was profit-making and it was the money more than anything else which drove you through your mad researches. Not to cure but to prosper, you old bastard. But the joke is on you, Hulm; it's on you, kid, because it's all been taken away, every single part of it, and only your name remains. You were a cripple; you had the greed of the entrepreneur, but none of the devices," and the Messengers march giggling away. Hulm screams, screams from his cloud, bellows himself to frenzy, but none of them are listening, no one, it seems, wants any part of him, and he says, "I wanted to do good, that's all I wanted; how did I know that it would have this effect on you?" and comes, awakening, to realize that he should have given it some thought, a lot more thought to the Messengers, because these were people who were going to make it work; better give some consideration to the psychic mechanisms of this thing but no time for that, no time ... stretched in ice, freezing in his bowels, Hulm has awakened dying to the dawn and before anything can be done for him it is late, far too late.

Only the Experiments and their notations can be saved. He had carried them to his bed, to sleep over them.

Poor old bastard.

II

TELLING IT ALL TO THE PRIEST: So I killed him, which is true, but that was later on and an anticlimax. It means nothing, the killing. Soon you will come to see that. This is no apologia. The act is its own reward. I enjoyed it. I did it well.

The night I graduated from the Institute, I went to the Arena. Perhaps it was disillusionment; perhaps sheer perversity, but I got drunk then and destroyed a Priest while only trying to make my position clear. Later on, when all the factors coalesced, I discovered that things were almost that simple; I had not had to destroy in proof. By then, however, the Priest was done. So, for all I know, was my sensibility. The peace which passeth understanding, etc., comes after the fact.

Which is not to say that the job is good. The job is a disaster in every conceivable way. But it is bad in a fashion which I did not understand; good in ways which I could not have suspected. One learns. One cultivates perspective. One turns twenty-one and begins to see implications. By then, however, damage has been done. The night I ripped the priest, I thought I was dying. Conventionally dying.

"Let's face it," I said to Smith, who had come with me that night, not because he was my friend (no Messenger has friends, ever) but because he was one of those off whom I could bounce the rhetoric without back talk, "and let us understand. We're menial laborers. Hod carriers. We swing our pick in the gut; all colors and flashes around. The lowest of the low in the post-technological age. In truth, we spent four years in the most dreadful training imaginable simply so that we could jive in mud. Disgusting. The whole thing is for a fast buck and it was dreamed that way. It's profitable and they've got fear working."

"Oh," he said, "oh, Leslie," and finished his drink one-handed, his dull eyes turning wide and large in the after-taste, looking around helplessly for a servant, "Leslie, I can't argue with you, you're so much smarter than the rest of us, but do you think that this is so? The work is so important. And it's dedicated. Scientific."

(I should point this out: I am changing Smith's name for the purpose of making these notes publishable. Like most of the people from his Downside, he had a long unpronounceable ethnic name which sounded like a curse. Your correspondent, however, has given his true name and you will find him useful and creditable throughout, not a trace effeminate despite the misfortune of his name.)

"Pick and shovel," I said. "Move that caboose. That's all. They've trained us four years their way to make the optimum profit; now we're to breathe religion. On a five-year up."

The Arena, of course, is dedicated to the most practical pleasures but there is a small anteroom of a bar where serious drinking may be done and it was there that Smith and I had gone. I knew that it was only a matter of time until I left him for activities more situational ... but we were stupefied with drink and I had still to say what was on my mind. Whatever was left there. No Messenger can really handle liquor; we are not trained that way. The kind of mind which can be manipulated into a Messenger's would adapt poorly to drink.

"You're an orderly," I said. "Be realistic."

"Cancer. Cancer, Leslie! Just think of that instead. We're going to cure! Fifty years ago no one knew the answer and now people like you and me can make it. We are the answer. And think of the free education."

"They'll get it back tenfold. It's all calculated. Don't you understand the factor of turnover?"

"Education! It's all education and free; we've made something of ourselves. We're going to be people. They can't keep me down. The gut isn't afraid," Smith said and lurched, fell toward his feet. Alas, drinking Messengers! Alas, incoherency! He fell tablewards to land in a sighing heap.

"Stupid," I said. "They didn't have to hook you in; you were a sale when you were born."

Those fine Smithian hands that would soon cleave out

colons twitched and he muttered, "Leslie," in a high guttural. I decided to leave him where he lay. In due time— there is always due time except in our business—he would come back to himself and deal with the situation and that would be enough. There were five years ahead of him. In the meantime he was entitled (or this was the way I really thought at the time) to all the oblivion he could find. I could only envy his low threshold.

I left him.

I left the drinks too, went into the corridor and toward the fluorescence of the Arena. The attendant caught me at the rope and decided that I looked safe. She asked me what I wanted. She did not ask this graciously but then Smith and I were not in Clubhouse. Grandstand is the habitat for Messengers.

"I want a Priest," I said.

"A confession machine?"

"A Priest they call them, don't they? That's what I want."

She looked at me with some puzzlement on her fine, middle-aged face. (I could see a wart that would flower into metastasis in five or six years; one could see the intimation of filaments casting: burn it out fast and horrid with the deep knife.) "We don't get many requests for those now."

"People don't want to confess?"

"Not that way. Others."

"I want it that way."

"It's not working too well. It's an old model."

"I'll take my chances. Do I have that right?"

Something must have caught her or only, perhaps, the frenzied caper of my hands moving as if in bowels. She looked, shrugged, pressed a bell. "I'll have an attendant," she said. "You aren't just from the Institute, are you?"

"That's right. Graduation."

"I know about the graduation. I just wasn't sure for a minute, that's all. Most of them you tell right off."

"I'd get that wart looked at. I see desiccation."

"What's that?"

"Desiccation, death, intimations of waste. It could go rampant any time, break the seals. Get it checked," I said helpfully and went off with the attendant, a girl of twenty-four or -five who looked at me strangely and held me off as we eased down a corridor. From closed doors I could hear moaning. The attendant dragged me into an alcove halfway toward a door and, putting her hands on me, asked if I wanted some flesh.

"No," I said and laughed. "I'm neutered."

"Neutered? I don't understand that." She squeezed. I laughed some more, under this guise could feel the horrid pressure of her rising breasts under a layer of silk, whicker of lips deadly against the ear. "Come on," she said. "I can tell. Most of you can do it. We'll take it right on a table. Private rates."

"Don't touch me," I said, pushing, feeling her resilience cave to waste under pressure, all yielding, devastation, loss. "Don't touch me, I'm contaminated."

"Are you crazy?"

"I'm a Messenger."

"I know that. Oh well," she said with a shrug and took my hand wearily, "I can't give you confidence."

"Nothing."

"Oh, it isn't all that bad," she said, her features congealing toward an asexual slant, perfect for celibates and lunatics. "It can be a great thing, Messengers. Besides, you should be proud. The contribution—"

"No contribution," I said, leading her down the corridor. "Give me to the Priest."

"It's in there," she said. "Don't talk any more. I can't stand this all of a sudden." She gave me a slight push into the room, closed the door.

I looked at the Priest for a while and then took a seat down front. It was an older model all right, no reclining chair, just stiff wood, no color. I put the machine on receive, waited until the green cleared, and said, "I have come to you, Father, for I have sinned."

"You have come unto me, for you have sinned," the machine said in a pleasant tenor, the voice only creaking a little.

"I wish for you to hear me; my sins are dark and grievous."

"Confess and be blessed," it said, rasped, came to an effeminate yowl on the *blessed*. Gears ground in the background. I inspected the small plate on the front which said 1993. A very old one. "Be blessed," it said again and clicked. "Confess and be known."

"I have just graduated from the Hulm Institute where I completed Messenger training."

"A fine undertaking. Messengers—"

"The Institute is a profit-making organization run under medical sanction as a monopoly. It exploits its one stroke of genius and the terror of its dependents for crude gain. It is destructive."

"Messengers feel this way in the beginning. Go on, relieve yourself."

"It is in the hands of greedy men who, having acquired the rights to the Hulm Projector, use fear as a means of maintaining power."

"How long have you felt this way?"

"Listen," I said, "listen to me. I have not come to this lightly; I have learned. I know the three causeways of metastasis, I know its lesser and greater pathways, its colors and symbiosis. I learned the seventeen manual and forty-five automatic means of incision. I learned of filaments, mitosis, and the scattering of cells. I saw demonstrations, I performed my own tasks, I learned of the history and implications, I—"

I went into the cadaver, the surfaces collapsing around me, and walked through the arches of death, toward the spot which had killed him; confronted it there, a dome a thousand feet high, and looked upon it in awe, then, bringing the fire from my lance, ground it to bits. They took me from the cadaver screaming, bits of cancer still dribbling from the lance. "Don't worry," they said. "It is always the worst the first time. That is why we give you poor dead ones to enter. They were doomed anyway."

"That all sounds very interesting. However, you have not yet detailed your problem. Speak loudly and clearly as you detail your problem."

"You're not even giving me a chance to finish."

"Confess and be blessed."

"I could have come here for anything, you know. Who needs confessors in a whorehouse? Show some consideration."

"Why personify?" the machine asked rather petulantly. "Why this compulsive need for iteration? The important thing is to come to terms—"

The new confessors have special circuitry. Even though demand for the machines is nil (who needs guilt any more if there is a cure for cancer?) connections are available which block the Priest at certain points so that you can finish a statement. (I have read much on Priests; I still believe in guilt.) There seemed no possibility of dialogue here. Also, the machine was hooked into a vintage Freudianism which is completely outmoded.

"Impossible," I said. "It's impossible."

"I beg your pardon?"

"Let me finish," I said. Rather desperately. One last time. There was no point in getting exercised about machinery: this is the basic understanding. "Let me conclude. I learned all the means of Reduction, to say nothing of the splendid history of the Hulm Projector, a beautiful piece of equipment whose commercial application began only after the sudden death of its inventor and the full details of whose functioning remain suppressed. I learned of Hulm himself, the poor old bastard: I learned about the vision which drove him in darkness toward a sense so enormous—"

"You are sweating. Your pulse is extremely rapid. Why do you react to this cold data with such excitement?"

"I don't want to be calm. Calm reasonable men got us into this."

"You cannot confess unless you are calm. You must suppress—"

"How do you know my mental state?"

"Why do you ask?"

"Why not?" I said. "I took the oath. I came from the Institute. I have been educated to all the greater and lesser evils into which the corrupted Messenger may stray and I have learned the ways of their avoidance. I received a drill and beam, I received a lance. An engraved diploma and memory book will be mailed me, the cost of which will be deducted from my first salary check. I will make thirty-nine thousand dollars a year before taxation and this is only the beginning; soon I will go to fifty if I keep my

lance straight. I have all the advantages of which I would
have otherwise been deprived in Downside."

"What do you think of this?"

"I think nothing of Downside. I had no future: the Institute nourished me. I had no possibilities, the Institute
made them manifest. I had no hope, the Institute gave
me a profession."

"So you must have gratitude."

"But this is not my question. You must listen to me
now. All of this has been done to me, just as I have established it for you. If this is so, and it is indeed, why do I
hate them?"

The Priest blinked. "Pardon me," it said, light waver-
ing. "I am now on automatic. There is an overload in the
circuitry. This is only a slight problem which can be
swiftly corrected. An attendant will come."

*I felt the walls were going to come in around me; I felt
that I would perish in slick, dark flesh, an invisible mote
struggling against entrapment, enveloped by decay, and I
must have screamed then; rung my little alarm for assis-
tance; they dragged me out on the attached string which
is part of early training and falling through, past uncon-
sciousness, I woke into a dream where I stood on a table
top, expanding, now three feet high, and said, "I cannot
stand this. I cannot possibly take this any more." "You
will," they said. "You will."*

"My circuitry is now overloaded," the machine said.
"Please be patient. There is a small problem. An attendant will come; all will be corrected. Very little time will
elapse until I am again functional."

"Listen to me," I said, pounding metal. "You dull son
of a bitch—"

"Do not personify. Circuitry overloaded is. If you
will—"

"I paid my money and this is my confession: *I want to
kill.* Not to cure but to strike. All my life I have been
maimed, burned, blasted, sullied, and turned off by deprivation, now they have taken me from those streets and
told me of a future ... but I do not want a future, I do
not want the Hulm Projector or to clamber inside people

like an itch to burn out cancer. I hate it. I will not—"

"I am not functional. My circuitry overloaded is. Patience and mendacity, lying quietly signals quietly and looking for an attendant soon will pass and then well again all must speak for now but it be coming now attendant overload is sing the circuit panel open dark—"

"And kill," I said. I rose to my full, delicate height, possessed of liquor and intent, five feet three inches of power (Messengers are treasured for this; one must not only be a Downside denizen but a *tiny* D.D.), and hurled myself against the metal, battered my tiny hands into the walls. Smashed my little feet against the damned iron couch and began to work on it in earnest application then, spinning controls, wrenching dials, moaning. "You too!" correspondent shouted. "You're just like the rest of them. All of it is machinery!"

Oh, correspondent! he was drunk indeed. Drunk so that I wished my hands were stone so that I could smash the Priest, smash while the whore-attendant returned and saw what I was doing, came to embrace me in a clutch as fierce and warm as death. "Don't worry," she said, "it's not so bad, you only think it is, but then you learn to live and live with it." And nuzzled me with lips like steel, this sweet machine of the Arena. Causing me to faint.

If you want Inside you can suffocate.

Correspondent paid for a battered Priest, vintage 1993. Eight hundred and sixteen dollars and forty-five cents, payable in ten percent salary deductions. The machine was a souvenir and here it sits, right here this moment before correspondent, right in his foul little room where he continues to transcribe these notes.

He has, at the present time, so little else to do that he might as well turn to writing. He could stroll through a window, of course, or phone the Protectors. This is useless speculation; correspondent has no plans, has come around to the belief that all energy is merely a cover for The Void; has bigger and better things on his mind as well he might. Circumstances will get better or maybe worse depending on one's point of view; the important thing is to maintain a caution and open-minded reserve.

Dwarflike but vigorous, correspondent sits in the highest room of the Clinic, behind barricades, and decides exactly what he will Make of His Life. No hammering in the corridors yet. I am glad he did it. He deserved to die. That is a constant.

III

REDUCTION: It hurts. It hurts, it burns, it is a feeling of compression and helplessness coming over in slow, thick waves of illness and impotence; from scalp to toes the body curls in upon itself, the flesh becoming desiccate and sickly and then folding in a series of snaps like a ruler. Disproportionate it is, terribly so; the limbs are already gnomish when the shoulders and head have not yet begun to gather and the feeling is one of foreshortening: gloom and extended concentration then, the kind of emotions which, I understand, might be known in sexuality or gymnastics when the body, sighing, departs from its humors and takes a more ominous direction. And throughout . . . throughout the pain, the pain which sears and rends, the helplessness of irreversibility. You cannot stop it, once it begins. The wish to supersede . . . but nothing to be done.

My God, my God (but Messengers cannot pray), can they not understand? This is being done to people! At the tormented center, the fuse of a soul. (A Downside soul but nonetheless sacred for all that or so we are taught.)

Are the souls of patients larger because they contain us? At the core of my fuse, a light as wicked as death, as constant as night. It lights my lance.

IV

HOW THEY LIGHT THE DOWNSIDE: I think he screamed once as I killed him. Or perhaps it was my own scream in his chambers. Two screams then, melded to darkness. Did both of us die then? If so, why are they out to get only me?

Better talk of Downside.

The way that they work it is this: flyers are pasted all

through there, always vandalized of course, but repasted the same day ... and you grow up with them. Grow with pictures of the Institute and songs of the Messengers and six times a year there is an enormous recruiting campaign, complete with festival and band. Politicians will venture in during these campaigns, enclosed in glass, to talk through megaphones of the virtues of dedication, the power of paraprofessionalism, and although there have been one or two really spectacular assassinations through the years, by and large the technique is effective. Obviously it is effective.

I love to this day, for instance, to meet celebrities, particularly politicians: it is the sense of connection they provide which is so exciting. Everyone from the Downside understands this right away. Ask them.

It seems that the bare facts of the case are enough. No invention in the recruiting campaigns has yet been noted. Since there is a certain paucity of returned Messengers anyway, the pitch proceeds without difficulty. Be a Messenger and Make Something of Yourself. Come to the lance, be a man. Enlist in the war against cancer. Fight a fighter; it takes one to know one.

My old man didn't know about the bonus. That is the best indication of the kind of seed from which I sprang.

Even without the question of a bonus, however, it appealed to him. For my eighteenth, as a coming-of-age present, he pulled me from a pocket Arena and took me to the enlistment office. There they told him of the bonus and their gratitude as well; he wept for humility, he took the bonus and attempted to hit the multimutuels for everything that they had taken from him in the forty-odd years intervening between Transfiguration and Death.

He did not succeed.

Were this my father's story rather than mine, I would now go into the particulars of his failure ... but the hell with him, the hell with all of them; center stage to Leslie, please. Leslie overtakes all, even his father ... because I learned through channels recently that the old bastard had applied for admission, as a subsistence patient, to Clinic #5 in Houston for the removal of his cancer. A subsistence patient! Charity! Of special value! He claimed relative privileges, of course. Somewhere in the recruiting bulletin this is promised and it had been read to him.

He found out, I am sure, the value of the Institute's promise.

But at this moment, even now, even writing these notes, I am convinced that that collection of angles and systems which he had accumulated through four decades—four!—stood him in good stead when confronted by the ninth race and that, even at the odds, he could have beaten the game. Do not bet fillies against colts. Never bet maidens in a mixed field. Watch for sudden drops in class. How painfully acquired, how preciously, he submitted these dicta to me! They were my only legacy.

This hardly matters. My tentative postmurder maturity assures me that ninety-nine percent of life is sheer abstraction and the remainder, all of it, can be handled as if it were. Nothing matters. None of it. All lies and small entrapment, manipulated cunning in the dark.

(A speculation for old time's sake: I see him lying on his bed somewhere in the last of the miserable, furnished apartments in Downside which have been his life. His eyes glint, his face sags, he looks through drugs at the ceiling. He is finally aware that he is dying and can even bring himself to say it—*the game is up, my laddie, the machines have now locked, it is now post time*—but inescapably, at some corner of consciousness, he is not sure of this. He wishes to think differently. Perhaps it is a final elaborate hoax rigged by the Telegraphics to test his innocence.

(Three or four insects scuttle across the sheets. They chat with one another, wander on his palm. His eyes flutter, screams of children outside, the noise of Downside flooding the room in an expiring moan. *Watch for sudden drops of weights.* He gathers to absorb that sound, rises, gasps, air comes into his lungs. *Look out for lightly raced three-year-olds in allowances for threes and up.* Now he feels pain; pain in filaments and fragments, pain working through him at all levels, and he tries to hold it off. He shakes his head, mumbles, the noise rises, his breath sags. He falls. *Watch the condition factor carefully.* He expires, dreaming of four figures on the tote, rolling gracelessly from bed to floor then; exhibiting an acrobatic he has never shown previously.

(All reverence to this discovered grace of a father whose limbs insects now occupy. Insects and metastases. Cancer and apprentice jockeys.)

"Be a professional," he said to me in chronotime, "and make something of yourself. You're nothing now, you and me both, but you'll really be something if you're lucky enough to get into the Institute."

Lucky enough to get into the Institute! "You don't understand, Father," I said (I was only eighteen), "the Institute takes everyone. Everyone. Why do you think they push it all the time? Why the campaign?"

"Because that gives them the widest and finest selection of young men to choose among; that way they can sift for the cream of the crop."

"No. They'll take anyone."

"No sir, no sir," he said and fairly leaped for emphasis, "there you are wrong. They want you to feel that it is easy when it really isn't. The requirements are high, the processes, testing, and some of the very best do not make it. You'll be in by hundreds if we can get you in there."

I was not naïve, after all—a childhood in Downside, while no real preparation for Messengery, is an education against vulnerability of a different sort—but his intensity was alarming. "I don't know," I said. "I hear stories. I don't want to be a Messenger."

"What's that? Not a Messenger! Coward, you take me, the old man who has raised and nurtured you. I'm too old, too cold, got bold but slack in the limbs, got no potential any more. They wouldn't take me now. If they had had this thing when I was your age, it would have been the making of me. I'd enlist in two seconds. If only they had it when I was younger."

So I went down, we downed, through the corridors of Downside, holsters at ready, two steps behind my old man, into the main sector and right to the booth, which was hot and cramped and smelled of ozone. On the wall were posters showing Messengers twelve feet high advancing on a battlefield, lances at ready. The Messengers were clean and solemn, bright faces washed to vacancy by commitment, and in one of the posters a Minister was delivering a blessing under the line YOU'RE REALLY SOMETHING

WHEN YOU'RE A MESSENGER. The booth was occupied by a fat man who breathed poorly; every time he exhaled, the papers on the walls and desk jumped. There was something about the aspect of the office which indicated that he had not had company for a while. Small marks of vandalism around the door hinted, however, that in its own way Downside kept him in mind.

"Take him, take my son!" my father said with a series of antique flourishes resembling those with which he encouraged horses by teletape. "Take this boy; he's just a young lad now with a streak of cruelty and bad manners but he's my own son and he has potential. I told him that you'll make something out of him, bring him to his purposes. It's all in the training; training is a wonderful thing when it works with the young animal. He wants to serve humanity, sir, he only needs a director."

"Of course," the recruiter said, "he looks like a very promising lad; indeed he does, and his height is good too. He has wonderful height."

"I told him, told him that smalls were tall," the old man said and winked. "It's grace, that's what it is, and entrance into small alleys, moving the good way."

"I have to ask a few questions, of course," the recruiter said. "It isn't automatic; we have a selection here. Firstly, to whom should the bonus be made payable?"

"Bonus? Bonus! You say there is a bonus?"

"It varies as to the conditions, the length of enlistment, qualifications and so on. You mean you weren't aware?"

The old man put his hand on my shoulder and I felt the grip move toward pain. Of simpler stock than his son, he showed emotional reactions in blunt physical ways. "Of course I knew that," he said. "You're not meddling with an old fool and his tiny son; I just wanted to make sure that that came front."

"You mean you didn't know that?" I said. It occurred to me for the first time then that my father was insane. He had driven me toward the Institute not for money but for commitment's sake; this was inexplicable.

"I said I knew it, didn't I?" he asked sullenly and looked at his nails, uneven and green in the pastel light. "I know all that stuff."

"You don't think they'd get people into this for nothing, do you?"

The recruiter gave me a look, an expression strangely paralleling my father's, and I took the papers he handed me, began to sign them indiscriminately. My insight had changed my life. I had not realized until that instant how badly I needed to get away from him. There is no future in being influenced by a man who believes that the Institute can get voluntary admissions.

"It should be several thousand dollars," I said. "Make sure of it. Large money in Downside."

"Several thousand dollars; that's just what I expected and one of the very reasons I brought my boy down this morning. He's a fine boy, brought up to be of high quality, and in these filthy circumstances that is not easy, of course. When do I get these thousands of dollars? It should be today, right?"

"Why should you get it?" I said. "Then, on the other hand, why shouldn't you? Let it be my gift to you."

"It's only a small return on my investment in you."

"We still have to get the questionnaire complete," the recruiter said, moving one palm against the other palm, "and we can talk out these arrangements a little later. If you'll just take a few inquiries now—"

"Just give me the dough," the old man said, having settled on the essential thread of the interview. "Just pass it over to me, for I'm entitled. It's all mine for raising him. The boy isn't of age anyway but there'll be some good investments for him too. I think of everything. I have plans."

The recruiter and I looked at one another in some horrid comity of understanding and then, perhaps, put all that to one side. "Your history," he said, "your biography, the details if you will. It's not necessary but a good option to tell the truth. Hold back on nothing; the Institute wants to know the best way to train any problems which might come up sooner or later."

So I filled out the forms. Filled them out in three minutes in their full complexity and meaning and was then rewarded with a moist Recruiter's Handshake, a winsome Recruiter's Wink and a deft Recruiter's Check, postdated.

The check I turned over to my old man, the others I kept. He took the money.

What I am trying to make clear is that money did not interest me, then or now. My motives are never mercenary. Life in Downside is always the same, money or not, and the Institute is a way out. If he wanted money to color the question of his existence, my old man was entitled. This is the kind of thinking which one can entertain at eighteen. It lingers. I never did anything for money.

So I took my travel orders and went.

There's no waiting at the Institute, a new cycle begins every month, and in the meantime they give you a fine dormitory to lie within and interesting puzzles to perform. This is a Good Thing, at least from the point of view of the Institute, because one is provided a long waiver with lots of subclauses and qualifications and, thinking of this waiver, having time to consider it at home, might turn a speculative soul around. The waiver contains phrases like "irreversible reduction" and "accidental mortality" and "disclaim infective contamination" and even though faithful correspondent could not read or write well at this time (imagine that!) he took note of some of them with interest. "Don't worry," the recruiter had said, "it's purely routine, just a routine little waiver. No one ever gets injured on the job, not really. Nothing ever happens."

Recently, there were riots in Downside. Seventeen of the booths were bombed or burned out; one unfortunate recruiter happened to be working late when this occurred. (But, unfortunately, not mine.) Since then recruiting is allowed only at certain times of the year and in special circumstances: this means only that instead of being empty most of the time the booths, when they are opened, draw huge lines. Still, a few things have changed: a different quality of man was entering the Institute, a kind of Messenger who might be inclined to dance in the intestines. Consequences seem less final. Still, superficial change is still superficial: they will still not recruit women, Hulm's inheritors being a proper sort. Not that women have shown undue eagerness. They are still a minority of the patients.

Clatter of wood in the distance. Definitely they are on to me now. It is only a matter of time, but time enough to continue. They will not spare me. I will have to write it all down before this ends.

V

LIFE AT THE CLINIC: If only I had killed the first case, I would have been spared all of these convolutions. Confronted by simplicities, we do not act; we circumvent, we come back to it only much later and at a scuttle. The purity of the solutions before us is something we cannot grasp. Still, I am relatively content; I could have not done it at all.

Matters settled in at Clinic #4. Much of my revulsion was of the long-term variety, not to be confused with apprehension. Clinic #4 of the Hulm Institute for Metastases, Easterly Division, deposit in full upon admission. Landscaped grounds: an aura of green for brief, recuperative walks. Private toilets for all patients. Erected in only 2019, it was a modern facility. Diamonds glittered in the lobby fixtures.

Correspondent was given a private full at the end of a corridor a mile long and half a mile high, a full plug into the music system. Correspondent was given full access to the employees' courtesy shop, the employees' lounge, the employees' cafeteria, the employees' recreational facilities. No possessives, of course. No mingling with the patients. Enough contact is enough. Correspondent was given a uniform with his house name stenciled thereupon in red, he was given with all due ceremony his own Projector. Mine to keep and treasure forever, liable to pay for the damages for the duration of my term as Messenger. My house name was Jones. I had requested but been denied a Hebraic. There is no sense of humor in the Institute. Imagine a tiny Goldstein in your gut!

I was given a tour of the facilities and an orientation lecture by Miss Greenwood, head of employee services, who made an obscene suggestion· to me in an alcove. "I like Messengers," she said. It is impossible for even a Miss

Greenwood to understand that Messengers are function-
ally neutered. If it is not congenital, it is nonetheless effective for all of that. Neutering is not, strictly speaking, a
requirement of the job (and some Messengers have been
known to flex their tiny limbs in copulation) but it usually works out that way. Sex too is a mystery and how
many mysteries can we sustain?

(Perhaps the process is a metaphor for Entrance and
that most basic of entries denies any other. Or it may only
be a repressed homosexuality of which I am aware. The
power of certain urges! The rage! The need! Messengers,
even the least of them, are complex people: do not hasten
to understand me.

(Also, I have a low threshold for exercise. Also I have
never been able, during my few moments of sexual attempt, to avoid scatological images, clownish fantasies,
dwarfs scampering in mire or seizures of deflation.)

The tour did not surprise me. I was not disconcerted, I
was prepared for all of it. The only thing that I learned
was that all of them—patients and doctors, nurses and attendants—treated us like orderlies. Perhaps they thought
we were orderlies. This they had not readied us for in the
Institute. They spoke only of the unusual status of the
Messenger and the special and privileged position he occupied in the War on Death.

The Institute prepared us for very little, outside of the
technological questions. The rhetoric was poor: "Dedication is the first obligation of the Messenger, respect his reward, paraprofessionalism his outcome. Full professionals
then work together in unified and sanctified accord under
this benevolence of technology in an atmosphere of pro-
bity." The religion was puerile: "Purgation of the body
and the blood, the holy lamb, the divine spirit. Cast your
lance against doom like a prophet of old." The sanctions
were dull: "Remember this, gentlemen, we are soldiers
and must give no quarter. We are in the front line of the
battle."

(I do not mean to down it entirely. Believe it or not, I
came late to cynicism, despair in the early years being
only the opposite coin of belief. The rhetoric was effective, they taught machinery well, the two came together
and kept the Messengers in line. Whatever we expected

of the job when we moved in, we knew this, for they had told us: we would be treated with a dignity upon which our skills were incumbent. They had their reasons. I can see them now.)

Nonetheless. Orderlies. We were treated like orderlies. In fact, at odd moments, it was possible for one to think that one was an orderly; a certain kind of grinning shamble seemed to overtake the walk, a certain vacancy around the eyes. The Downside stupor: seeing everything, registering everything, understanding nothing, rising only through small humiliations and grief to rage. One could well have been an orderly, of course, had it not been for the Institute. This was kept in mind.

Part of the patient problem was that we were introduced in exactly that way. Messengers and their function are not, after all, particularly appealing and it suits the public relations and policies of the Institute to make things as aseptic as possible. One does not go in (at the price they are paying) to have cancer burned out; one goes in for "a little job," something made you "a little tired," and one rejoins the world joyfully, having acceded to cosmetic change. This is the thrust of the Institute's public relations; a stay with the Institute is a happy stay; cancer is a happy disease. So, then, one met the patients very much out of role: This is your helper, Mr. Jones, your personal-needs technician, or whatever lie the effusive Miss Greenwood had in mind at that time. The fact that this grinning, genial, nicely miniaturized little helper would shortly go crawling inchwise into their guts was something to come by only peripherally, after the relationship had been established. Even then there was little interest: the thing about the patients was that they were perfectly willing to function as if the little job, the little problem, took care of itself and attending the Institute were essentially a social obligation ... like an obligatory party.

(A certain dislike for patients seems to have filtered through. Let me make it clear then that I bear no grudge; the possession of money or status has never struck me as a basis for hatred of itself. The patients are manipulated; they come from the only group who can afford the Institute, they do the necessary for the Institute. One must look nearer or deeper to get into the matter of culpability.)

Reinforcement on the employee end to be sure. Rule seven: a Messenger may never divulge to a patient the nature of his responsibilities. A certain modesty of demeanor is recommended should there be inquiries. (Rarely are there inquiries: who cares?) A Messenger is technology's servant; it is not his right to call upon himself particular reverence. Humility is the source of strength.

Policy and procedure; procedure and policy. All of it carefully conditioned. Even now the manuals fall quickly into the mind's eye: regulation and ordnance, containment and meaning ruled neatly on the lined paper, the printing very large for the functional illiterates among us.

Little were we prepared, however, for being orderlies.

It was something else; the one thing perhaps, that we (or at least faithful correspondent) allowed ourselves to believe and that was what we would be: benign priests of reduction, striding through the wards to the awed gasps of doctors and nurses, nurses and attendants, performing our green and terrible tasks in an oozing isolation of ease, under rich beams of fluorescence to occasional gasps and whimpers of applause. (Like a tennis match, perhaps.) It was the Hulm Projector which made us go; still, even the Projector's Tools were entitled to a little common respect. We had struggled years to learn to play our motions against the body's cave; we had practiced in a hundred corpses so that we could take on the husks of the World's Best; weren't we entitled to applause?

Gentlemen, the question is rhetorical: do not answer. Neither peer through the cracks in these doors in an attempt to see; Leslie has shrouded himself in smoke and haze, towels stuffed in all crevices. There is no way that you can get at me unless you break the door or I let you in and I am not ready, not quite for either, thank you very much. How my little fingers tremble on these notes! How my eyes bulge, my brow emits its antique and chiseled beadlets of sweat! Time, gentlemen, time! Everything will come to its conclusion.

I will even tell you why I came to kill. Presently, presently.

Correspondent's visions were incorrect. Things did not work out in that way. Disillusion is the condiment of the reflective life: nevertheless, I suffered. Bedpans were the lot of the tired Messenger, bedpans and strange prosthetic devices. This enamel was poor enough reward for four years of study but there were also changes of clothing to be made, rollings over and regurgitation, pattings in the night (post-operatives became nauseous from the recollected need to expel us), heave and retch, claw and moan, pat and wonder, the small activities of the postmetastatic patient being conducted in the smells and tightness of their rooms which for all the highly vaunted décor of the Institute still had a twentieth-century cast. Amorphousness and sleek panels of doom, overlaid on the emptiness. In the dark they would grasp at us to whisper horrid confidences. "I'm afraid," old or oldish people would whisper, bending their arms to crook's edge, staring from luminous eyes, the pall of cancer bringing strange knowledge to their faces, "terribly afraid, you see; I don't think that it can work out. I just don't see it."

"The process is infallible. Just relax. It's like a toothache, as antiquated as diabetes. Be reasonable. Be calm."

"But the pain," they would murmur, "still, the pain—" and I would not have the heart to advise them that the pain was mostly illusory, encouraged by the preoperative drugs administered by the Institute so that their gratitude at its vanquishment would be that much more profound, the process through which they had been that much more dolorous. Instead of telling them the truth (Messengers never tell the truth) I would assure them that it would work out, everything would work out; no problems at all. It was only a question of machinery and technique, calm and patience. The days had, I would say, already shaped themselves into a pattern that would see them strut from the ward, easy and freed . . . but still the Institute counseled a certain amount of fear in lieu of credit agencies and while I could deal with the men, most of them, the women defied me. I could not deal with feminine emotions: no neuter can. And then there were younger ones too; even some children of the rich whom I found particularly trying, and then there were the semi-informed who had picked up knowledge on the side ... and these were the ones who suspected the true function of the Messengers, and they were apt to be the worst of all because when you came in the night (always the night) to do the Process, one might find them sitting at terrible ease, drugs discarded in a washbowl, peering through ominous eyes as the Projector was repaired. These were the ones the nurses had to condition with needles and it was difficult, difficult.

Illuminate if you will: a scene. A patient. A Process. "Boy," he said to me, "boy, I'm really sweating. You'd better clean this stuff up, I feel like I'm sitting somewhere in a pool." A middle-aged man, verging toward senility since his cancer is deep into the liver and lungs; I understand that he is the founder of the largest manufactory of masks in the nation. He provides masks for all rituals in the major Arenas. Still remaining then is the founder's Sense of Command.

"I've already done that," I say, reading (*Journals of a Nihilist: A Romance.*) "I've cleaned you three times today. Already. You've got to rest now." I think I'll kill you tonight, I decide.

One transmits the full picture: the book is poised flapping in my hand, an unopened magazine for good measure on my little knee; I am sweating quietly myself in the strange heat of the room, neatly drenching my attendant's whites. Not five hours from now I am to go inside and remove it from him, a glowing filament which stretches from here to there, localized by X ray, painted and gleaming for me. A nauseating operation: many capillaries to be by-passed. Preoperative and pained, he is restless. "I'm not comfortable," he says, "you've got to show some consideration and care. You're paid for that. Clean me up."

You will be the one I kill; I have waited too long, I think. "It's been done. Time and again. Why don't you try to rest now?" The request can only move him the wrong way, of course. A slight edginess wavers into my tone; I am entitled to apprehension. The Process is safe, very safe (the Projector has, after all, never lost a Messenger and it has had thousands of opportunities by now), but it is taxing, very much so. Hours after reduction, one still feels a sense of compression in the joints, liquid unease, a feeling of disassembly. Also, there is the question of archetypes to be posed: this is not respectful work we are doing. Perhaps the body needs to become cancerous and we have made it the other way; by preserving against devastation we make things more difficult in the Other World.

Still: one must stay with the patient through the end of the conventional shift, apprehensions or not. One is obliged to maintain the full responsibilities of the Messenger. This is policy. The patient must be soothed, relaxed, must have utter confidence in one. Only the Messenger may be the patient's attendant; only he can train him to his insights. (It also cuts the overhead.)

"You don't understand," I say. "I can't be in the service of your every whim. I'm tired."

"I don't care if you're tired, boy," the patient says as if he were ordering a consignment of greens, "you've got to make me comfortable. What am I paying for if not my care?"

Oh, how one would like to pity him now! He is after all a potential murderee. Pity his ravaged frame, pity his fear; one senses that in health he would again be wistful, gentle, attracted to picture books and small children, but the illness and its syndrome have made him cantankerous, have thrown upon him fully the aspect of the senile fool he would, due to prolonged life, become. It is hard to maintain tolerance in the face of this understanding; I could kill him now in the sheets for joy. "You're my orderly," he says, "and it's my right."

I stand. It is not easy and the book flaps uncomfortably floorward but nevertheless it is done. A pity in light of all this impressive effort that my height can hardly be calculated to close the gap. "Listen," I say, "you can't order me around like that. I'm not an orderly, I am a Messenger." (Knowing I will kill him should have been enough. Why I lost my temper I cannot say. Perhaps it is balancing action.)

He shrugs and says, "I know all about that part."

"In five hours, maybe six, I am going to crawl inside, slither in your gut like a fish, and take the matter out. Can't you show a little respect? What do you think is going on here anyway?"

"That's disgusting," he says. "You made me sweat all over. You're never supposed to tell me what you're doing. What are you, anyway?"

"Come on now," I say, picking the magazine off the floor and tossing it toward a corner of the room. (It is one of our trade journals, full of glistening equipment and helpful hints to the voyager, written by advertising copywriters and largely involved with two-toning Projectors.) "I can't take this much longer. There are limits to everything. I can't clean you up; I can barely clean you out."

"You're frightening me," he says, rearing in bed, and I think of his little liver quivering, the cancer already knocking it down to one fifth of its normal size, the accretion of acids, the lava of amino; he is only making my job that much more difficult.

"Lie down, you ass," I scream, in another mood, "don't you understand that you'll make it impossible by infiltrating your gut that way?" I pummel pillows, slap sheets at his side, and begin to talk to him in a high-pitched but comforting tone, taking another line entirely. I have, after all, been a fool: isn't murder enough for me? I will make his alleyways impassable; I will never get the lance in. He must be calm, calm, for me to murder; I snatch alcohol from the bedstead and begin to rub, pummel, converse, his flesh like slate under my hands, his heart puffing and ticking in the distance.

"You frightened me," he says. "I didn't mean to say those things but you did frighten me."

"Forget it," I say, "the stakes are too large. Just be calm." An orderly's whine creeps into the assassin's tone: is it possible that one can become what they say?

I apologize, skulk to the relief room to urinate, light glittering before me, light shuddering and receding, the filaments of his gut weaving their way past my stricken consciousness and toward some deeper center. Push, pull, pummel, knead. And murder him that night. Why? Well, why not?

My father sent me one letter during training, the only letter I ever got from him, the only letter he ever wrote: THE SISTEM WURX, he said, ITS ALL QUESTION ENGLES IS ALL I SHOULD KNOWN IT A LONGA TIME AGO. I filed it a away. Three months later he contracted cancer. I should known it a longa time ago.

Now they are pounding at the door. Finally. Their voices rasp insistent in the hallway: it would be interesting to know what they are saying. I have toward this the kind of clinical interest that toward the very end I was able to sustain toward murder. But only toward the end.

Eventually they will become forceful, try metal and hooks, but long before that all of this will have been finished, all of it placed inside the drawer with the sock and I will await them with the dull, glazed assassin's smile, eyes narrowed, arms folded, a hint of arch in one brow, all quizzicality and compunction as they come to extract their due.

I have formulated what I will say to them; the first words, that is, before they begin to ask their foolish, hammering questions. "Gentlemen," I will say to them, "gentlemen, please listen to me and you will understand. I wanted to change lives. I wanted to change the way in which people regarded their situation. I wanted to prepare for large deeds, terrible shifts in circumstance, a different kind of person.

"And found only that it was all a lie and that ripeness, ripeness, gentlemen, is all."

VI

THE PROCESS: "But," a voice says, somewhere in the distance, "but." (I think that I have externalized my father.) "But you still haven't made yourself clear. For one thing you haven't made it known what it's like, and secondly, the motives are still shrouded. Who can care about this?"

One hastens to answer. Correspondent hastens to answer. The point is elegant, meaningful, well taken, clear. A word then about the Process. A word about how it

works. Keep on pounding, you sons of bitches, you'll
never get me alive. I am going to finish this.

The Projector. You stand before the Projector. It is
cold in the dark, cold and damp; one stands shuddering,
wet in the crevices, wet to the bone of nakedness, only
the huddle of the patient deep into anesthetic omnipo-
tence hints the possibility of connection. Catalepsy moves
from the trembling pores. In this night the noises of the
hospital overwhelm. Tick of generator, wailing scream
down the hall, patter of night nurses tossing scatology at
one another. The singing of electricity, power in the coils.
It is possible at this moment to conceive that one is no
longer in a hospital at all, nor is this a patient. One is
standing instead, perhaps, in one's own room; one is eight
or nine years old, alert toward the dark and attuned to
that very sense of possibility which seems to stream
through the windows. The gasping of the patient is now
only the sound of one's own dear parents fornicating in
the hall, forcing fluid from one to the other in that slick
dark transfer which we are told is love ... and then one
touches the Projector. The Projector, at least, is there, and
it brings one back to some sense of origins, destiny, the
fishlike twitches between.

One touches the Projector, the slick, deadly surfaces of
Hulm's obsession, and comes to know then that it is a different quality of experience here. It is not the same as
being eight or nine in the darkness. Here, one does not
refract possibility but history. One had known this before,
many times, of course. But each is a new onset. The Projector knows no history.

Hit the starting switch. (It must begin somewhere, although it really started so terribly long ago.) The batteries
hum, pulse with energy; Hulm's madness seems to call
upon the familiar of its inventor and issues his whine: a
strange, characteristic clang. Lights flicker, the Projector
is working. One hopes that it is working. One knows that
there has never been an authenticated case of a machine
breaking down in Process ... but there are rumors,
rumors which circulate through any population, and then
too, there is always a first time. The thought of reduction
continued or the thought of partial restoration within a
capillary is enough to keep even the limited imagination

of a Messenger hopping. Hop and hop; skip and connect. On schedule reduction begins. It is all automatic from the time of ignition.

It begins slowly, then accelerates. The Geometrical Progression of Diminution, it is called at the Institute, and they concede that they do not themselves know why it seems to work in this fashion . . . but it has long been graphed that, while it takes five minutes to lose the first foot, it takes merely another five to lose all but the necessary percentage of the rest. It is during this time then as during none other that the mind blanks, the corpuscles run free and there comes the slow, wild onslaught of epiphany. One sees things, one senses the dark. Reduction is narcotic, this being a theory I have, but it is based less on physiology than on the involved sense of anticipation.

Anticipation! One never knows, after all, what one might find inside there, what differences might be uncovered. I am led to understand that less committed men obtain the same reaction from sex. (I know nothing of this.) One thinks of the Ultimate Metastases to be discovered in the blood, the biggest fish of all.

And talks. Something must be done, after all, to make the moments and exhilaration go by; to seal off the fear and the wonder, and besides, the patient is so deeply narcotized that for once almost anything can be said without it sounding strange. We have so few pleasures. Most of us have no vices and must take satisfaction where we may. One perches on the edge of the chair and finally the center, exposing the body to the rays of the Projector, and raves onward, a tiny voice in the still night. "You do not understand what you put me through, you stupid, rich son of a bitch, and you ought to show some appreciation, which is why I'm going to kill you," or one will lapse into neologism and rhyme such as "Hitch, twitch, litch, itch, rich to the body's bitch and ride the rising blood" or "Faster metastases" or, more simply, "I'm going to kill you because I hate too much and they couldn't burn that out of me the way I can burn out cancer."

And so on. And so forth. And in the meantime, reduction is working away; working away all the time so that the voice, even in the process of address, becomes gradually higher-pitched, moving from a fine, adult rumble to an adolescent whinny and then bottoms into a childish squeak, squeak from the Messenger, squeak for remorse, the voice finally taking up residence somewhere below the jaws and then at last—

At last one is something less than an inch tall, dancing angelic but upon the head of no pin and then preparing for entrance. One makes haste. One slinks into the body.

(How entrance is accomplished will be my only secret. I will not say, nor will any Messenger, no matter how great his disillusion. You will not find it either in any of the popularized essays, articles, or books on our splendid trade; you will see it in no procedural manual. It is expurgated, it is our one professional secret blocked by the oath. I cannot break the oath to reveal. Not even I, not even now.)

Into the bloodstream we stalk, little divers carrying our lances, the lance also reducible for crises. Now in the body's fever at last the noises have changed; sharpened, heightened, strange whines and sirens in the distance, a clanging and receding, flicker and thud, as we stroll our way with surprising casualness up the alleys and toward the appointed spot.

The spot: ah yes, the spot; it has been localized for us, brushed red by radiation in the morning, turned orange by nightfall, nevertheless it does not show up clearly in that darkness, a thick, atmospheric haze descending like the soot of Downside, and illumination, cleverly provided by the tip of the lance (make of that what you will!), is necessary. In this cave, then, one can feel not only the humors but the instances themselves, the very seat of personality is here. Twitches of culpability, seizures of continence, revelations and platitudes, even a fanatic shriek here and there, and the corridors seem to curl in spots as if impaled. The siren rings faster, a bell knocks, we move upon the designated spot.

Oh, it is cold, cold! Temperatures are not adjusted through reduction and so one must shudder within one's little outer garb until reaching that designated spot. Stalk then, skitter, run, jump, sway, stagger, perch to a corpuscle and finally, finally, to the heart of the orange, now gleaming in the proximity. Doff the garments swiftly, hang them on some tissue.

Gloves, indicator, goggles: all gone. They flap on a filament in the chill, the strange intestinal wind moving them, and then the lance is carefully brought to fire through the old method, one droplet of heat applied. And burn, then, burn, burn! Mumble curses, eviscerate, quiver, until at last the burning, bright bulb of cancer emerges at the end of the lance.

One looks at it then in the light: one can see the whole of the lovely, lovely tumor, reduced to centimeters. It seems to have features; some of them mimic the faces of animals or men. Slash of mouth, wink of eye deep in the pocket, holding it then at little arm's length to avoid contamination, remove the tag from the lance and slap it in there. Don the goggles again, whisk the bag into the coat, and then off into the turbulence again. A boulevardier. A stroller out for his evening's pastime, the wind a bit damp, but what to make of it?

One shuffles much faster this time. Reduct exists only for a certain stated interval and after that one is known to enlarge, whether the patient can contain or not. Physics and Hulm cannot be embraced by simple wilfulness. It would not necessarily kill the Messenger, enlargement within the patient, that is, but it would from the cosmetic and career standpoint do him little over-all good and, as far as the patient was concerned, it would be quite a pulpous mess, not to say a final one. Quicker and quicker on the boulevards, then, the metastases being carried like an awful little secret which the patient himself may never know; a high, penetrating hum over all of this which might only be one's nervous reaction. Although I believe differently. I believe it to be the song of the metastases, overtaking itself and making a carol of release. To the exit point (which I similarly dare not reveal) and into the light.

Perch on a table top.

Sing with the metastases.

One waits then. Sometimes one has exited too fast and there are terrible moments for this peculiar elf as he sits with legs dangling, wondering if this is the time that the Roof Falls In and then at last—

Ah, at last! There is a feeling of unfolding, flowering, heightening, and elevation as the reconstitution at last begins. To come right to the point, it feels *sexual*, not an erection merely of that quivering, useless organ, but of the axillae, the papillae, the deltoids, the jugular and so on, blood filling all the cavities as they rise to terrible authority, snapping like a slide rule, and finally, full height restored (it takes only seven or eight seconds but how long is an orgasm?), one stands glinting from angry, mature eyes, toward the form lying on the bed of life.

For all that this form knows or cares it might as well be on the moon; it is beyond analysis, as insensate of what has been done to it as if it were roaming the blasted surfaces with power pack and nightmare, and one sighs, one packs up his equipment. It is all too much. Buttoning the little cancer securely into a flap, the figure trundles wearily through the hall to turn it in for analysis.

In the hall they look at you. They know. They always know when it has happened and what you have done and there is a rim of terror underneath the inquiry and the smile. For the way they look at you, you might as well have been fornicating with a sheep or committing self-abuse in a sterile washbasin, and yet I want to say to them, How can you look at me in this way? It is only a Messenger, a faithful Messenger, dedicated servant of man and enemy of cancer, moving wearily through these outer corridors; can you not understand that? Can you not understand that it is merely a process, a process more difficult than most but devoid of irony? Why do they look at us in this way?

I think I know the answer.

They see it, you understand, they see it and so do I, so say it and be damned, let it come then and no way around it. Knock down the door and kill me, take my notes and burn them, hang me before the Institute as warning to all who pass below, do that and more, and yet it must be said and in its purity and finality cannot be escaped.

Say it once and for all time, gentlemen: this intimation

buried like the ant at the heart of the blooded rose, forty years age, deep in the gnarled gardens of Hulm's darkness. Say it, see it:

I LOVED MY WORK.

AVON ◆ MEANS THE BEST
IN FANTASY AND SCIENCE FICTION

JAMES BLISH

Cities in Flight	09258	1.25
And All the Stars a Stage	19216	.95

THOMAS DISCH

Camp Concentration	03392	.75

J. T. McINTOSH

Flight from Rebirth	03970	.75
The Suiciders	17889	.75
Transmigration	03640	.75

ROGER ZELAZNY

Creatures of Light and Darkness	19869	.95
Lord of Light	05652	.95
Nine Princes in Amber	19851	.95
The Doors of His Face, The Lamps of His Mouth	18846	1.25

THE SCIENCE FICTION HALL OF FAME

The Greatest Science Fiction Novellas of All Time

Edited by Ben Bova—
Chosen by the Science Fiction Writers of America

Volume II A
(19489/$1.75)

CALL ME JOE Poul Anderson • **WHO GOES THERE?** John W. Campbell, Jr. (as *Don A. Stewart*) • **NERVES** Lester del Rey • **UNIVERSE** Robert A. Heinlein • **THE MARCHING MORONS** C. M. Kornbluth • **VINTAGE SEASON** Henry Kuttner and C. L. Moore (as *Lawrence O'Donnell*) • ... **AND THEN THERE WERE NONE** Eric Frank Russell • **THE BALLAD OF LOST C'MELL** Cordwainer Smith • **BABY IS THREE** Theodore Sturgeon • **THE TIME MACHINE** H. G. Wells • **WITH FOLDED HANDS** Jack Williamson

Volume II B
(19729/$1.75)

THE MARTIAN WAY Isaac Asimov • **EARTHMAN, COME HOME** James Blish • **ROGUE MOON** Algis Budrys • **THE SPECTRE GENERAL** Theodore Cogswell • **THE MACHINE STOPS** E. M. Forster • **THE MIDAS PLAGUE** Frederik Pohl • **THE WITCHES OF KARRES** James H. Schmitz • **E FOR EFFORT** T. L. Sherred • **IN HIDING** Wilmar H. Shiras • **THE BIG FRONT YARD** Clifford D. Simak • **THE MOON MOTH** Jack Vance

Where better paperbacks are sold, or direct from the publisher. Order by title and number. Enclose 25¢ per copy for mailing; allow three weeks for delivery. Avon Books, Mail Order Dept., 250 West 55th Street, New York, N. Y. 10019

FLARE/AVON/18093/$2.95
IN CANADA/18101/$3.45

THE TABOO-
BREAKING FICTION
COLLECTION
FROM THE BRITISH
AVANT-GARDE

EDITED BY
MICHAEL
MOORCOCK
AND
CHARLES PLATT

NEW WORLDS #5